Once Upon a Knight's Time: Seeker of the Sword

D to the Fourth Books & Scripts, LLC

Cover Design by: Neha R

ISBN: 979-8-9907023-3-2

D to the Fourth Books & Scripts, LLC

Stanley, NC

United States of America

To my granddaughter, Jordan Rosalez, who kindly read the two books in this series.

Pronunciation of Names

The following guide to pronunciation of names or titles is meant to serve as an aid when reading. This is not an official pronunciation style.

Alejandra Maldonado	Ah lay hahn druh Mal duh nod o
Alvarado	Al vuh rahd o
Aramis	Air uh mus
Ati	Ah tee
Athos	Ath os
Blanchemal	Blanch mul
Bonaparte	Bone a part
Brokkr	Brok er
Buenaventura	Bwayne ah ven tura
Capistrano	Kap ih strahn o
Cartagena	Kar tuh hay nah
Castizo	Kahs tee zo
Citlali	Seet lah lee
D'Artagnan	Dar tan yun
Dagda	Dag duh
Diega	Dee a guh

Excalibur	X cal uh bur
Fitzooth	Fit sue th
Fontainbleau	Fahn tain blow
Friar Felipe	Fry er Fay lee pay
Galahad	Gal uh had
Gawain	Gah win
Gersemi	Gair sim e
Gingalain	Gene guh lain
Guillermo	Gee (hard g) air mo
Halcón	Al kohn
Hnoss	Noss
Jean Lafitte	Jawn Lah feet
Joaquin de Arrillaga	Wah keen day Ah ree lah gah
Lancelot	Lan sa lot
Leprechaun	Lep ruh kahn
Lohengrin	Low un green
Mazarin	Mah zah rehn
Mestizo	Meh stee zo
Miguel	Mee gale
Odr	Oh der
Peon	Pay ohn

Porthos	Por thos
Pueblo	Pweh blow
Pulido	Puh lee doh
Rafael Ximeno y Planes	Rah fah el Hee may no e Plah nez
Ragnelle	Rag nel
Reina	Ray nahF
Richelieu	Ri shuh loo
Sæmingr	Say ming er
Sesasi	Say sah see
Sindri	Sin dree
Thoth	Tho th
Versailles	Vair si
Xalapa	Sha lahp ah

TABLE OF CONTENTS

Once Upon a Knight's Time: Seeker of the Sword

by Dewey Dellinger

2025 AD

Diega slept lightly but snugly; she always had been a morning person. *One of those*, was the phrase she often received, along with a roll of the eyes, from people who were not. She turned off the buzzing alarm that unknowingly was trying to badger her awake. Diega's warm feet hit the floor, leaving temporary footprints on the wood flooring. She brushed her teeth while in the shower, something her mother constantly reminded her was unladylike. But she had been in the U.S Marine Corps, and it had taught her to ready herself quickly. She dressed in a light, comfy sweater and sweatpants and tied her hair in a ponytail. She would let her hair dry on the way. Grabbing the bag she had packed the night before, she left her apartment in Jacksonville, Florida.

The traffic had been unusually heavy for that time of the morning, but she still arrived early. She changed into her fencing clothes and went out to meet Monsieur Blanchet, her fencing and French instructor, for their weekly fencing lesson followed by a French lesson. Monsieur Blanchet was a no-nonsense instructor, who was a former Olympic medalist in sabre fencing.

Diega and Monsieur Blanchet faced each other with their sabres ready. Monsieur Blanchet called "en garde" from underneath his protective face gear. His first move was a feint to try to lure Diega out of position. That didn't work; so, he immediately lunged, which Diega successfully parried and riposted. No points or touches yet. As Monsieur Blanchet set up for another lunge, Diega performed a running flèche, striking Monsieur Blanchet in the torso with her sabre. "Stop," he said in a frustrating tone. "How many times do I have to tell you that a flèche is illegal in sabre? You know it is illegal for the back foot to pass in front of the front foot."

"Yes, but if this were a real fight, why would I follow the rules? As my dad often says, *dead right don't mean a damn.*"

"We're training for a sanctioned fencing match. You're not auditioning for a swashbuckling movie starring Errol Flynn!"

"What does Bug Bunny have to do with this? Oh, that was Elmer Fudd. I'm not sure I know who Errol Flynn is," deadpanned Diega.

"I don't understand how Americans think everything they say has to be funny, when nothing they say ever is. If you're not going to take these lessons seriously, then you need to stop wasting my time. There are plenty of other people who would love my coaching to prepare for the Olympics."

"I don't want to go to the Olympics. I just want to learn more."

"That's another reason I should stop teaching you. You have no aspirations for international fencing competition. You are already a very talented fencer, but I don't know what your goal is in taking these lessons."

No aspirations. There the phrase was again. How many times had she heard it from her parents? They were fine with her joining the Marines for four years, and she had done quite well. She achieved the rank of sergeant and earned a black belt in Marine Corps Mixed Martial Arts. She had already earned black belts in Taekwondo and Krav Maga prior to joining the Marines. She thought about trying to become a Marine Raider in the Marine Special Forces training but instead left the Marine Corps after four years. Her parents begged her to go to college instead of wasting her time on fencing lessons and French lessons. She couldn't tell her parents, but she had Sir Gawain to thank, or curse, for her interest in fencing and French. She had time-traveled to 920 AD and had met Sir Gawain of King Author's Knights of the Round Table aboard a Viking ship. Sir Gawain had the unique ability to understand and speak all languages. He was the only one who could communicate with her in her language in this time period. Sir Gawain had taught her a lot about sword fighting, more than Monsieur Blanchet had, and he piqued her interest with his tales of the Three Musketeers, which was why she wanted to learn more French. She didn't know if her time travel was a one-time fluke or if she would travel again through time. If she did travel again into the past, she wanted to be better prepared. She studied a lot about Sir Gawain when she arrived in her own time. What she read was supposedly myths and made-up stories about the legendary knight. Some stories painted him in a good light while other stories did not. She couldn't bring herself to believe that the kind and caring man she had met could have done some of the things she read about. Deep down, she almost hoped to meet him again. She had lots more questions she wanted to ask. The only thing that Sir Gawain couldn't pique an interest for her was in history. She hated it and couldn't bring herself to study much.

"Ms. Scott. Ms. Scott!" repeated Monsieur Blanchet.

The tone reminded Diega of her alarm clock buzzing. "I'm sorry," she replied.

"Daydreaming again. I'm afraid we need to terminate our sabre lessons. Your stubbornness is something I can no longer tolerate."

"What about our French lessons."

"I was only doing that as a bonus. We can have another lesson since we are both here, and I don't have anything else scheduled, but I'm afraid I will need to terminate those as well."

Diega knew some French prior to her lessons, but the lessons with Monsieur Blanchet had helped her grasp the language much better. She still considered herself only passable with her speaking ability, but it was much better than it had been.

Diega finished her French lesson, changed her clothes and headed back to her apartment. What to tell her parents now. Her parents helped supplement her apartment rent with the amount she paid from her savings, but she was afraid that would end soon unless she succumbed to their demands to start college. The term *aspirations* entered her mind again. What was wrong with her? Why did she not have something to which to aspire? On the way back to her apartment, she had the feeling she was being followed, but she didn't see anyone following her. When she reached her apartment, she found her boyfriend, Spencer Atwater, waiting outside her door. She had met Spencer six months ago, a couple of months after she arrived back in her time from her travel to 920

AD. She was not sure if the relationship had a future, but he was a likable person. She had not dared tell him or anyone else about her time traveling experience.

"Hi, Diega," called Spencer as he was leaning against her door. "When are you going to give me a key?"

"When I feel there is a reason to give you a key," she replied half-kiddingly and half seriously.

"How did your lessons go?"

"Monsieur Blanchet fired me!"

"Shouldn't that be the other way around?"

"Let's just say he thought I was wasting his time. Now my parents will definitely be on to me to start college."

"That wouldn't be a bad thing. Surely there is something that interests you. Perhaps you could go to a community college to take something practical, or you could always move in with me."

"I'm not there yet on either."

"Do you want to grab an early lunch?"

"I don't really feel like it. Would you be terribly upset if we met up tomorrow? I just want to lock myself up in my apartment and feel sorry for myself today."

"That's fine. I brought you your favorite bottle of wine. I thought we could share it later, but you look like you could use it now."

"You brought me a bottle of Tempest merlot? You're the best."

"Just don't make a habit of drinking by yourself."

"I promise," Diega said with a smile.

Diega uncorked the wine as soon as she was inside her apartment. She poured herself a large glassful and pulled out her phone. She saw that she had a missed call from her mother. She sighed, wondering whether to call her mother now or later. The latter won out, and she decided she needed the wine to give her the courage to call. The light was bright in the room, not the mood she was looking for; so, she walked over to turn the blinds. She looked out and saw a man standing outside. The feeling of being followed returned, and she wondered if this was the person she sensed had been following her. Maybe it was her imagination, and she turned the blinds to block the incoming light. She kicked off her shoes and felt the floor against her bare feet. She downed the glass of wine and felt bad for not savoring it. Although she had been a beer drinker while she was in the marines, she had learned to acquire a taste for wine. Blame that on Sir Gawain, or D'Artagnan, too for those stories of the Three Musketeers, she thought. Reluctantly, she phoned her mom, fortified by the wine and now ready to face that inquisition. "Hi, mom. Sorry I missed your call."

"How did your lessons go?"

She told her mom about the events that transpired that morning with Monsieur Blanchet.

"That sounds like a sign that you need to start college."

"Don't start, mom."

"Diega Scott." Her mom only called her that when she was irritated with her. Usually, she either called her Diega or honey or some other term of endearment that one would expect to hear from a waitress at the Waffle House. "You can't go on taking self-interest courses or learning from YouTube. Why don't you move back home, and we can talk about your future?"

Diega listened to her mother's plans for her future for thirty minutes before she made an excuse to hang up. Her parents meant well, but Diega thought starting college now would be a waste. She just didn't know what she wanted to do. And move back in with her parents? That was a hell of its own. She loved her parents immensely. They just didn't understand her, or her reluctance to start college now. Her parents, James and Sofia Scott, lived in New Bern, North Carolina. Her father was serving his final years at the Marine Base at Cherry Point before he planned to retire in two years. After that, he wanted to work in a sheriff's office for a few years before retiring completely. Her father had been a lifelong Marine, and she had traveled from base to base while growing up. She was their only child, and her father saw her as a son as much or more than a daughter. He was an American of various European descents, and her mother was born and raised in

Puerto Rico before meeting her father and marrying him. She learned English from her father and from school, and she learned Spanish from her mother. The result was that she spoke both English and Spanish fluently.

Perhaps all the moving while she was growing up contributed to her inability to want to settle down to one thing. She didn't want to think about anything at the moment; so, she poured herself another glass of wine and plopped on the sofa. A picture frame caught her eye and she rose from the sofa and walked over toward it. It was a picture of a runestone she had taken in a museum, the same runestone she had seen with Sir Gawain in England or Scotland or wherever they were stranded when Eric Bloodaxe dropped them off the Viking ship. She remembered Gawain's unique language abilities that allowed him to translate the stone that most experts believed was a forgery. *The trickster rids the land of magic, but himself becomes entrapped. After many centuries, the progeny of the wielder of the sword shall free the imprisoned, but not without much peril.* What was that supposed to mean? She wondered if she were the progeny. Why else was she transported to that time, in that place, where a person who could translate the runestone happened to be?

Diega pulled out her phone and called Spencer.

"Hey babe. Miss me already?" he asked.

"I called to see if you wanted to go out to eat tonight. Does that answer your question?"

"Maybe not directly, but I'll take it. Where do you want to go?"

"Restaurant Orsay?"

"Expensive tastes today, have we?"

"It's been one of those days. Besides, I can pay my own way."

"I know you can. But between my job as a Junior VP and my inheritance, you can let me treat you occasionally. What time should I pick you up?"

"How about six o'clock?"

"Great. See you then. Oh, and I knew you would change your mind about waiting until tomorrow to go out after talking with your parents."

"Yes, I changed my mind about waiting until tomorrow. I'm a woman; it's my prerogative."

Diega sipped her wine as she finished her dessert that night at the restaurant. The meal was good. She finally decided that time was running out for her to tell Spencer what she had meant to tell him. "I'm going to see my parents," she blurted.

"When?" quizzed a surprised Spencer.

"Soon. I don't know how long I'll stay. Sorry to spring this on you, but my mom has pretty much demanded that I visit."

"If it's about money, you can always move in with me."

"I appreciate the offer, but I'm not going to be dependent on anyone." She realized what she had just said; so, she added with a sigh and slight smile, "other than my parents."

"I may be out of town myself for a few days," added Spencer. What do you say we go to the whisky and cigar bar for one more drink just in case I don't see you before you leave?"

At the whisky and cigar bar, Diega drank a Weller bourbon on the rocks and smoked a Dominican Cohiba as rhythm and blues played in the background. She thought about what Gawain had mentioned about all the times he drank with the three musketeers. It had sounded fun, but surely it wasn't better than this. Spencer's voice brought her back to the present. "What?" Diega asked.

"I said be careful, if you think someone has been following you."

"I will. Don't forget. I'm a fourth-degree black belt, a former Marine, and I have a concealed carry permit for a Springfield Hellcat."

500 AD

King Lot's castle appeared on the horizon. Sir Gawain could hardly believe he was there. He didn't remember crossing the ocean, or anything of his journey for that matter. The entire journey had been a blur. To him, he had just left Camelot, left Blanchemal, who was the only person other than his son, Lovell, to whom he had any connection. The entire trip, he dwelt on all those he had lost in his life, Lancelot, Constance, Freya, Ragnelle, and Marian. He would probably never see Blanchemal again either. Lancelot, Mordred, and Morgan le Fay, especially Morgan le Fay, had taken, or was the cause of, so much he had lost. He couldn't blame the loss of Ragnelle on Morgan. But wait, had Ragnelle's death been due to Morgan as well? What little anger he could muster in his exhausted and ravaged body rose within him at the thought. He knew he could have stayed with Blanchemal, and he didn't know what had stopped him. He couldn't love Blanchemal the way he loved Ragnelle or Marian. Perhaps that was the reason. Or perhaps it was the overwhelming emotions he had when he left Camelot, feelings of despair, guilt, and unworthiness. He wasn't experiencing any of these emotions now; he was completely numb in body, spirit, and mind. Blanchemal's magical healing of him had seemed to have worn off; yet, if she hadn't helped heal him, he would have died before he could have left Camelot.

Gawain willed himself to walk the remaining miles to his father's castle and the embrace of his father. Stumbling into the castle like a drunkard, he expected to see the warm smile of his father, but what awaited him was the cold sight of his father's body lying in state. Everyone in the castle stared at Gawain. Finally, someone came to his aid and helped him to where his father's body lay. There were about fifty people gathered, and someone called out, "Hail to the new king." There were a few murmurs before someone else said, "Why should he be the next king?" Voices escalated, and swords were drawn. If this were a coup, Gawain had neither the strength nor the ability to prevent bloodshed.

Before anyone could act, a familiar being appeared out of thin air. Gawain's heart skipped a beat when he saw the arrestingly beautiful woman with long flowing red copper hair, fiery-colored bracelets and torc against a white cloak, and gladiator-style sandals laced up her calves. "Drop your swords and pay homage to your new king," she commanded. Swords dropped, and people knelt in obedience to their goddess. Freya smiled at Gawain, and he fainted.

Gawain awoke in what had been his father's bedroom. The beautiful, glowing face of Freya smiled. "I've waited nearly two millennia to see you again," she beamed. "I thought it would be a while, but I didn't know I was that much older than you! And what did you do but make we wait another three days."

"Was I really out for three days?"

"Yes, and I didn't expect you to be half-dead when I saw you."

"Half-dead was a whole lot better than what I was a couple of weeks ago."

"I can't imagine that you were much worse than three days ago. If I hadn't arrived when I did, you would have been in the grave before your father." Freya saw the wince on Gawain's face and changed the subject. "It looked as though someone had used magic to heal you, but it took a lot more of my healing powers to get you to this point."

"God, it's so good to see you."

"Let's get you cleaned and dressed properly, and I may say the same to you."

Freya lovingly bathed Gawain in a tub of warm water and shaved him. She had new clothes laid out for him, and he was able to dress himself.

"Much better," she exclaimed. "You look like yourself again, only a little older."

"Mortals age, but it appears you haven't aged at all."

Freya repeated the words he had said earlier. "God, it's so good to see you."

Gawain smiled.

"I'm sorry about your father. He died three days before you arrived."

"I so wanted to see him. There was so much I wanted to tell him and so much comforting I hoped he could give."

"Tell me."

Gawain told her all that had happened to him since he had left from their first meeting.

"I'm sorry for all the hurt you've been through. What are you going to do about your son?"

"I don't know. I feel so much guilt for abandoning him, and I fear taking him from the only person he remembers may do more harm than good. Lancelot grew to an adult during the time he spent with the Lady of the Lake, while only a few years passed in the mortal realm. If the same happens with Lovell, he may already be an adult by now."

"I don't want to add to your disappointment, but I must tell you something. I loved you when we first met, but time moves on, and I'm married now. If you could have stayed, things would be different now. Even though I still love you, I love my husband more."

"I wanted to stay, but the sword made the decision for me."

"I know," she said comfortingly. "The sword has tremendous power, almost as if it were a living god itself. Even my power was of no avail against it."

Gawain wondered if Freya had indeed tried to use her powers as a goddess to keep in Norway all those years ago. But, there was no point thinking about what couldn't be undone in the past. The future was another matter. "You are a seer. What's to become of me?"

"You will be a well-loved king to your people, reigning for forty years in a time of peace in your kingdom. I can see there is still some adventure ahead for you and love as well. You will have a good life."

"Do you know that it was the thought of seeing you again that kept me going when I left Camelot?"

"I'm glad, and I've thought of you for almost two millennia."

"I'm sorry."

"Don't be. We've lived the lives we were supposed to live, and you left a great gift with me."

"Oh," said Gawain somewhat perplexed. "What was that?"

"A daughter."

"We have a daughter?"

"Yes. Her name is Gersemi. My husband raised her as his own. She doesn't know that he is not her father. I have another daughter by him. Her name is Hnoss."

"What is your husband's name, and is he a god?"

"Odr, and yes, he is a god. He has been away a long time on adventures, but my heart is still with him."

"I hope he is not the jealous type," quipped Gawain.

"You don't have to worry."

"Then let me say, 'God, you're so beautiful'."

Freya laughed. "You're still very good looking yourself, even if you do look older." Freya's countenance turned serious. "I know this is not fair to you, but I can't let Gersemi know about you."

"I think my fate is not to be able to see my children, but I'm not going to feel sorry for myself. I understand why you can't let me see her. Will I see you again?"

"I wish that, but I don't know."

"Aren't you a seer?"

"Yes, but I don't really see what happens with me or my family personally. I did want to tell you about our daughter. The night we spent together and the love I feel for you have been among the greatest joys of my life. If I never see you again, know that I have loved you all of these years. Carry that with you as I have carried that with me. Now, let your people see their new king." With those words, Freya disappeared, and Gawain walked out and into the great hall.

Back in the bedroom, Freya reappeared. A tear ran down her cheek. The door opened and Freya startled. The person who walked into the room was a stunning woman with blonde hair, blue eyes, and alabaster skin. Her shoulder-length hair hung loosely. Her low-cut cloak showed off a gold torsade necklace. She wore matching gold torsade bracelets and a gold torsade belt. Gladiator-style sandals encircled shapely calves. "I heard everything, mother. I was outside the door the entire time you two were talking."

"Gersemi," startled Freya. "How are you here?"

"A goddess doesn't appear every day to mortals. When the rumors spread that you were here, I had to come and see why. Is that man really my true father? I perhaps could understand why you kept it from me, but were you really not going to tell me now?"

"He's a mortal, and he wouldn't take immortality if I offered it to him. I thought it best not to tell you. He's only going to live forty more years, and then you would never see him again."

"That should be my choice to make not yours, and how long has it been since I've seen the man I've thought was my father? It's been centuries. How did you two even happen?"

"He can travel through time, something even the gods cannot do. I met him when he was on a quest. I won't go into the details of it."

"I'm going to meet him!"

"Gersemi, don't. You'll just get your heart broken."

"You mean like you? I'm willing to risk it. What I don't understand it why you don't. It's been centuries since Odr left. The person you first loved is here. Why not be with him?"

"Because more of my heart belongs to Odr, just like more of your father's heart belongs to someone else."

"Don't try to stop me."

"I won't. You got stubbornness from both of us, but please think before you act. Make sure this is something you can live with."

The Great Hall was filled with people. Gawain asked a squire why all of the people were gathered here. "The goddess Freya commanded everyone to be here. You are to be coronated. No one would dare disobey Freya." A bishop was waiting near the throne. Two knights led Sir Gawain down an elaborate twelve-foot carpet, and two knights followed. Upon reaching the priest, Gawain knelt before him.

"Do you, Gawain, son of Lot, accept the responsibility of serving as Monarch of Norway, Orkney, and Lothian and promise to uphold the laws of the kingdom with justice and compassion?"

"I do."

The bishop dipped his fingers in oil and made the sign of the cross on Gawain's forehead. "Do you, Gawain, son of Lot, promise to God and to our kingdom to be a faithful king, ruling your kingdom with honor and concern for the welfare of all those over whom you are king and to lead them in good times and bad times?"

"I do."

The bishop again dipped his fingers in oil and made the sign of the cross on Gawain's forehead. "Do you, Gawain, son of Lot, promise to humbly serve the triune God and be his representative on earth?"

"I do."

For a third time, the bishop dipped his fingers in oil and made the sign of the cross on Gawain's forehead. "In the name of the Father, the Son, and the Holy Spirit, I crown you King of Norway, Orkney, and Lothian. Rise and seat yourself upon the throne."

Gawain rose, walked to the throne that had been his father's and sat. The bishop walked to a spot directly in front of the throne, knelt, and bowed his head. He rose and motioned for a group to approach him from the left side facing the throne. A village boy carried a pillow supporting the crown. The bishop took the crown and held it up toward Heaven and spoke some words in Latin. He then placed the crown on Gawain's head. The boy departed, and then a woman from the kingdom approached with a pillow supporting a scepter. The bishop repeated the process and presented the scepter to the new king. Finally, a Knight of the Highest Order approached the bishop. The knight took off his belt and removed a sword and scabbard. He held the sword in its scabbard parallel to the floor, and the bishop took it. The bishop presented the sword and scabbard to the king and laid it in his lap. "Tell us, Sire, the royal name you wish your people to call you and any words you wish to say to them."

Without hesitation, Gawain exclaimed, "I am to be known henceforth as King Lot II. You have heard my oaths to you and to God. I do not take such oaths lightly. I will rule to the best of my ability as a servant to God and as a leader to you. May it be said truthfully that my reign was just and compassionate."

The bishop spoke in a loud voice, "All hail King Lot II."

The crowd gathered echoed, "Hail, King Lot II."

"We have had a time of mourning for our former king. Let us now celebrate our new king."

Food and drink were immediately brought into the Great Hall, and the Hall was filled with the sounds of music and conversation while everyone feasted. The king ate, drank, and conversed. He thought that Freya must have healed him completely. He was hungry, and he was able to hold down solid food. He knew many of the people from when he was here with Lancelot to kill Grendel. Many people remembered him as well. Several people called him Sir Bearwolf before they remembered he was their new king. He didn't mind though. He had been a knight for a lot longer than he had been a king. He preferred being a knight; he didn't know if that feeling would ever change. After several hours, he felt confined being amongst so many people, and he walked over to a corner near a hallway where no one was gathered. "Psst." He thought he heard a noise. "Psst." He heard it again.

"Is someone here?" he called. He heard the noise again in the dark hallway and decided to investigate. He grabbed an unlit torch from the wall and lit it. He heard footsteps scamper as the torchlight gave chase. A door closed to a room, and the king pushed hard against the heavy wooden door. The sight of the mesmerizing woman stopped him as if he had run into a rock wall. "My God. You look so much like Freya. Are you Gersemi?"

The woman smiled coyly at first, much like a two-year old who meets a new person. Then her smile broadened. "Father." She ran to him and hugged him, and he felt as if he were being squeezed by Hercules or Thor. I was listening outside the door as you and mother were talking. I can't believe she wasn't going to tell me about you."

King Lot II was speechless for several seconds. He put his hands on her shoulders and stood at arm's length to get a good look at her. "My heart is about to burst. So many bad things have happened recently, but seeing you gives me so much joy. I can't believe I have a daughter."

"Mother said she could offer you immortality. Will you accept it?"

"Eternal life only comes from God. I cannot accept the offer. Long lifespans may be the norm for some beings, but for humans that is not meant to be."

"May I stay with you?"

"As long as you wish, as long as Freya is alright with it."

"She said that was my choice to make."

"I've lost so much time with you; I don't want to lose a minute more. Come. Will you let me introduce you as my daughter?"

"Of course, but won't that be awkward?"

"Never."

King Lot II led Gersemi out of the room and into the Great Hall. She strode beside him, her hand in his. The crowd was in such a celebratory mood that no one recognized at first the scene before them. Slowly, a few people noticed and then more. Eventually a hush came over the entire group gathered in the Great Hall. Everyone seemed to know that they were looking upon a goddess, especially with her resemblance to Freya. King Lot II stood beside his throne and his happy eyes looked over the crowd. "I have had several great gifts today. First, was seeing a long-lost friend. Second, was the crown. Third, was the acceptance that you all have given me. Now, I share with you the news that I have a daughter. Please welcome Princess Gersemi!"

1650 AD

Fear ran through Diega's body, and she could feel the adrenaline. Her head was pounding. She was disoriented and nauseated. She had felt this before, and without opening her eyes, she knew that she had traveled through time again. She slowly opened her eyes, which provided her verification, as if she needed any. At least she was alone, no bloodthirsty Vikings, yet. Of course, when and where she was could be worse, she thought. She put her hand inside her purse and felt the Springfield Hellcat. The gun was fully loaded with eleven rounds of 9 mm ammunition. Two extended magazines held an additional thirteen rounds each. She had a total of thirty-seven rounds. Although that wouldn't hold off a horde of whoever was out there, she felt safer that the gun was with her. No smartphone, she had left it charging on the nightstand. Of course, what good would it do her here anyway? Would she show someone a photo? Hey, wanna see a picture of me at South Beach? Or, was she going to show her parents when she got home? Wanna see a selfie of me with King Henry VIII? At least she still had a sense of humor.

She remembered coming home and sitting down. She must have fallen asleep with her jacket on and her purse around her shoulder. At least she wasn't in pajamas. That would be really awkward. She rifled through her purse looking to see if she had anything of value. Nothing. Lipstick, credit card, and paper money. She might be able to sell them as a novelty. Gold or a diamond ring would be good about now, but she had neither.

Diega examined her surroundings and noted the position and height of the sun. The time was around 10:00 am. She was in a wooded area, but she could see some sort of road just beyond the tree line. She walked to the road and carefully looked to see if anyone was coming from either direction. She saw no one, but she did see a city to her right about three miles away. She was almost one hundred percent certain that she was in the past.

She thought better of taking her gun with her. Although it gave her a sense of safety, getting captured with it wasn't an appealing thought. Sure, let a person who is unfamiliar with a gun start waving it around and pulling the trigger. She made note of some distinctive landmarks and buried her purse, with the handgun in it, on the north side of a red oak. She smoothed the dirt and covered it with leaves. Hopefully, the only person who would come here would be a drunk pedestrian needing to relieve himself behind a tree.

Now what to do about her clothes? She remembered Sir Gawain saying that he stole some clothes from a clothesline. She supposed that she would have to do the same. She began walking toward the city, careful to stay along the tree line. She darted into the woods a few times when she saw pedestrians or horses. She was definitely in the past. The tree line ended near a house. In was rectangular in shape and made of timbers with a thatched roof. Stealthily, she made her way to the house and hurriedly listened for noises inside the house while keeping her eyes peeled on the road and surroundings. She checked the door; it was unlocked. This wasn't anything like her neighborhood back home. She quietly opened the door and snuck inside. As she gently closed the door behind her, she listened intently for any signs that someone may be inside. Wondering where people of this social status in this area may be during this part of the day, she looked around for where clothes might be kept. She found a niche in the wall and an armoire. Some feminine-looking clothes were in the niche. She gathered what she thought would be an ensemble. The thought of stealing someone else's clothes repulsed her, but she didn't know what else to do. The family apparently didn't have much, but there was nothing of value to leave in their place. The sound of a door opening startled her, but there were few places to hide. She hid in the niche in time to hear the door close. Footsteps led toward the other end of the house. Silently, Diega crept out from the niche with the clothes in her hands. Peering at the end of the house, Diega saw a woman with her back facing Diega. Quickly, Diega made her way to the door, turned the knob without making any noise and opened the door. Approaching her was a girl, probably nine or ten years of age, looking down. Diega's heart pounded as if it wanted to burst through her chest. Pulling the door partially closed, she made her way to the right to try to avoid the oncoming girl. The plan was of no use; the girl looked up and saw Diega sneaking away with her mother's clothes. The girl screamed and Diega ran as fast as she could around the back of the house and into a wooded area. Thankfully she still had on her tennis shoes, which aided in her escape. From the woods, she could see the woman and her daughter at the back of the house. Fortunately, the woods were thick enough to prevent her from being seen. Keeping inside the woods, Diega walked parallel to the road. When she thought she was far enough away, she decided that changing clothes would probably be safe now. The old-style clothes were puzzling to Diega, and she didn't know if she had grabbed the correct clothes. There was something she supposed was an undergarment and a dress. The woman she saw was shorter than she was. After struggling for almost half an hour, breathless and heart still pounding, she was dressed as good as she was going to be. Looking down, her heart skipped a beat. She had not gotten any shoes of the period. Also, the length of the dress for her height looked laughable. There was nothing else to do though. Rather than leave her original clothes in the woods, selling them as a novelty might not be a bad idea after all.

Diega angled her way out of the woods and back onto the road. Soon she was in the city where she heard people speaking French. Although this city could be in another French-speaking country, she was probably in France. Even though she had taken many French lessons upon arriving back from her previous time traveling journey, fully understanding the spoken language was difficult. Damn Sir Gawain and his magical language abilities. What she wouldn't give for that for herself right now. People were staring at her, and she assumed it had to be because of her dress. She walked up to the nearest person, a man standing on a corner, and spoke in hopefully passable French. "Excuse me, but I've been walking for a while. Could you tell me what city I'm in?"

The man looked at her with what she thought was half amusement and half horror before answering. "You're in Paris, of course."

"Really? I don't see the Eiffel Tour or the Arc de Triomphe." As soon as the words left her mouth, she knew how stupid she sounded. These probably hadn't been erected yet in Paris. Damn history, she thought to herself. Why hadn't she paid more attention to it when she was in school?

"What are you talking about?" asked the man. "Are you crazy?"

Diega thought to herself, *yes*. I am. She hurriedly walked away. More stares and some distance later, she saw a man selling what appeared to be newspapers. *La Gazette* was what she thought he said. She went and grabbed one and then handed it back pretending to have forgotten her money. She quickly observed the date before handing it back. 1650 was the date printed on the newspaper. Loneliness suffused throughout her being, and she felt as alone as she had when she was captured by Eric Bloodaxe. Tears welled within her eyes, and she fought them back. Through the blurriness, she saw an elegant church.

The call of the church alleviated her feelings of loneliness, and she went inside. The church was ornate with beautiful stained-glass windows and elaborate carvings. Diega lit a votive candle and knelt by the side-alter. She offered gratitude for her safety, asked forgiveness for her theft, and sought help for the journey that lay ahead of her. She genuflected and rose, feeling much better than a few moments before. When she turned to leave, a priest stood in front of her.

"Is something troubling you child?" he asked in an assuring voice.

Although she couldn't tell the entire truth, she decided that a sin of omission was better than a sin of commission. "I'm not from here, but I came here in search of something. I just feel out of place. I don't even have the proper clothes to wear, and everyone stares at me. I came in to regather courage."

"You came to the right place. I don't know that I can help you materially with much, but I believe I can help you with clothes. Wait here." The priest walked away and was gone for a couple of minutes before returning with an armful of clothes. "These should fit you."

"They are so elegant looking."

"They are. In fact, they are formal enough that you could appear before Queen Anne, Regent of King Louis XIV and not feel out of place!"

"But I don't have money to offer you."

"Your prayers were your payment. Go in peace, child. But first go and change into your new clothes."

The priest led Diega to a room where she changed in private. She thought he must have sensed her confusion, for he identified the pieces of clothing and the order in which they were to be put on as he handed her each piece. Having privacy and more time to change under ordinary circumstances was much easier this time, but it was still somewhat of a challenge. Diega put on the bodice, which fortunately laced in the front, followed by a salmon-colored gown with white sleeve linings fastened back. The gown had dropped shoulders, but she wore a scarf around her shoulders that knotted almost like a low-cut collar. The shoes were made of silk, but the high heels and pointed toes were nowhere near as comfortable as her tennis shoes. The shoes fastened with a belt and gold buckle. She kept her bundled up twenty-first century clothes but left the stolen clothes in the room. She wanted to return them but knew that that would probably not end well. Maybe there was some other way she could pay the family back. She thanked the priest again and left the church feeling much more confident.

She found a shop and presented the proprietor with her twenty-first century clothes, the plastic credit cards, the assortment of American paper money along with a few coins all totaling to eighty-five dollars and some odd cents, and her tennis shoes, which she hesitantly parted with. The proprietor seemed puzzled by the odd assortment, but Diega asked him what she could get for these novelty items. He gave her two livres. She didn't question the amount and had no idea what it was worth.

As Diega made her way back onto the streets of Paris, she was approached by a man identifying himself as a constable. "What is your business in Paris?" he asked.

"My business is none of yours."

"It is unless you want me to take you in for further questioning."

Diega wondered quickly what to say. She obviously wouldn't pass for French, and she wondered if her lack of knowledge of history would betray her again. What were the relations between

Spain or England with France at this time? She opted to go with Spain knowing that she was going to be in trouble either way as soon as she answered. "I'm an ambassador from Spain," she said with insouciance.

The constable appeared utterly shocked. "You need to come with me." She thought about fighting and running away, but where could she go? Another constable was approaching, and Diega decided that fighting and escaping was probably not the right answer at this point; so, she went with them. She was placed in a holding area with two guards outside the door. Again, she could easily escape, but to what avail? She waited for over an hour before two gentlemen entered the room.

"I'm the Lieutenant General of Police," blustered one of the men, "and this is His Eminence, Cardinal Mazarin."

Diega remembered Sir Gawain, as D'Artagnan, speaking of Cardinal Richelieu. "Where is Cardinal Richelieu?" she asked.

"Cardinal Richelieu died eight years ago," answered Cardinal Mazarin, "and you would not have fared any better with him."

Diega humorously thought to herself, this is why I would not have made it in the Marine Special Forces.

Cardinal Mazarin continued. "You are either the worst spy I've ever seen or the most brilliant. I'm leaning toward the former, but I can't rule out the latter just yet. You claim to be an ambassador from Spain, a country we are at war with, and you're a woman."

Shit, thought Diega. *If I ever make it back, I really need to study history.*

The cardinal abruptly switched to speaking English and asked her name. Without thinking, Diega answered in English, "Diega Scott."

"You speak English as well, though not with an accent of which I'm familiar. So, perhaps you are an English spy rather than a Spanish spy. Your name appears to be a combination of both Spanish and English. Tell us why you are really in Paris."

Before Diega could answer, someone knocked on the door and entered. The man whispered into the cardinal's ear, and the cardinal's face betrayed shock. "You're going to accompany us to the palace."

"I've never been to Versailles," blurted Diega.

"The palace is not at Versailles," said the cardinal.

Diega wished she could have kicked herself. She wondered why she was so chatty when she was nervous and why she couldn't keep her mouth shut.

They arrived at the palace and were asked to wait while the squire went into another room. Shortly, he returned and led them into a much larger room. A woman stood in the room. The woman had an air of authority about her. She looked to be in her late forties with an oval-shaped face. Her hair was lightly curled and was a reddish blonde that was beginning to fade with age. The dress the woman wore was truly exquisite, but it lacked a lot of color. It was off the shoulders with white lace at the front and white feather-like plumes extending from the shoulders around the back. The sleeves were turned back at the wrists with white lace and smaller feathered plumes that matched the top. The dress itself was mostly black but was covered with embroidered gold-colored shapes that were perhaps fleurs-de-lis. As for jewelry, she had a pearl necklace, a gold broach, and gold bracelets.

The squire's voice broke Diega's trance. "Her Majesty, the Queen Regent." The cardinal and the lieutenant general of police bowed, and Diega quickly curtsied.

"Inform me of the young woman in your custody," commanded the queen regent.

Cardinal Mazarin addressed the queen regent. "She says that her name is Diega Scott and that she is an Ambassador from Spain."

The queen regent showed shock on her face. "Are you accusing me of something?"

"Definitely not Your Majesty," replied the lieutenant general awkwardly. "We know that although you were Spanish born, your loyalty is with France and King Louis XIV."

"As I told the young woman, she is either the worst spy I have ever seen or the most brilliant," interceded the cardinal.

"Or perhaps neither," posited the queen regent coolly.

"She doesn't seem to know that we are at war with Spain."

The queen regent looked directly at Diega. If the Spanish government wanted to talk with our government, they wouldn't send a lone woman ambassador to wander around the streets of Paris. An entourage would be sent directly to the palace. If you are a spy, you are rather an inept one. There is also some speculation that you may be English, but it is not for me to ascertain such things. I have trusted officials, such as Cardinal Mazarin or the lieutenant general, for such purposes. I have asked you here for another purpose. Something turned up recently in the palace that seems more than coincidence with your arrival. His Majesty, the late King Louis XIII, had a relic that disappeared from the palace around twenty-five years ago. Yet, it magically reappeared a few days ago."

"Perhaps it was misplaced the whole time," interrupted Diega.

"Don't play coy with me," erupted the queen regent. She turned to the squire and said, "Bring it out."

The squire bowed and immediately left the room to retrieve the relic. When he came back, he carried a sword on a pillow. Diega immediately recognized it as Excalibur. "That sword is why I'm here," said Diega. She grabbed it from the pillow and started to run to the door through which they had entered the great room. Unfortunately, she was at the other end of the great room and had some distance to travel. The door opened, and four soldiers brandishing swords ran into the room. One soldier ran ahead of the others. Diega charged, not slowing down. As the lead soldier thrust his rapier, Diega spun to the right around him three hundred sixty degrees so that she was facing the same direction.

She was almost back-to-back with the soldier. Before the soldier could turn around, Diega thrust Excalibur backwards plunging the fabled sword into his back and out through his chest. She jerked the sword out of him as he fell to the floor, and she faced the three remaining soldiers. With a flick of her wrist, she disarmed the soldier to her left and his sword flew up in the air. Quickly, she tossed Excalibur from her right hand to her left, piercing his heart with Excalibur. She withdrew Excalibur from his chest and pointed it at the other two soldiers. While their eyes were trained on Excalibur, Diega caught the falling rapier in her right hand, swung it across her body, and slashed the throats of the other two soldiers. Blood spurted forth from their throats, and Diega heard the queen regent scream.

With no one else standing in her way she ran out the door to the exit of the palace. As she ran out of the palace, she came up against a group of about twenty musketeers with flintlock muskets, all aimed directly at her. Diega knew she had no chance of escaping this situation. She dropped Excalibur and the rapier and held her hands up in the air. A breathless Cardinal Mazarin, followed by the lieutenant general, ran up behind her.

"Take her to the Bastille," ordered the cardinal. "Give her the mask," he said turning to the lieutenant general.

Diega was forcefully taken to the Bastille with her hands bound. Upon arriving at the Bastille, she was taken inside. The clothes she wore were cut from her, and she was searched. Upon finding nothing on her, she was provided a ragged-looking plain dress.

"Make sure she gets the mask," commanded the lieutenant general.

A jailor kicked Diega's legs from under and she fell, her chin hitting the hard, stone floor almost knocking her unconscious. The jailor pulled out a knife. "If you want to fight like a man, you should look like one," he said while cutting her hair. The knife wasn't the sharpest, and the jailor pulled her long hair as he roughly cut. Each cut pulled her head, and she felt as if her hair were being pulled out by the roots rather than being cut. When the jailor finished, her hair hung unevenly just below her ears. She tried not to cry, not wanting to give him satisfaction. "This is the mask," exclaimed the jailor as he pulled out a black leather hood and put it over her head. The hood hung to her collar bone, and the jailor tied it around her throat with a rough rope. He took his knife and cut out two eye holes and a hole for her mouth.

"You're not to speak unless spoken to by an official," spat the jailor. "If you do, or if you are unruly, you'll be wearing this instead of the mask." He pointed to an iron helmet consisting of two pieces with screws to lock and tighten it. Diega couldn't help but shiver.

Two men led her, with her hands still bound, through the dark building that was to be her prison. They reached a thick wooden door. They cut the rope binding her hands and shoved her into the small room. The door was pushed hard behind her, and she heard a lock snap closed. She could have taken off the leather hood, but fear of being found not wearing it prevented her from removing it. The room was dark and dank, and it took a while before her eyes could adjust to her new surroundings. Even through the mask, she smelled the staleness of the air. The gap between the door and the floor, presumably for sliding food under, was the only view she had to the outside of the room. A large bucket was in a corner. Diega thought that this must be for use as a chamber pot to use the bathroom. A rat scurried across the floor and through a small hole in the other back corner. Despair permeated Diega, and she sat with her knees to her face. Her chin ached, and she fell asleep from despair and exhaustion.

Athos arrived at the palace at the request of the queen regent. He had not been told why she wanted to see him. He was escorted to a waiting room when he saw Porthos and Aramis. The three former musketeers had not seen each other in years.

"It's good to see you," smiled Athos. I can't recall how long it's been, but you two have gotten older and fatter."

"You must have not looked in a mirror lately either," jabbed Porthos.

The three hugged each other.

"What are you doing here?" asked Aramis.

"Probably for the same reason you two are. I was summoned by the queen regent," replied Athos, "but I don't know for what reason. Do either of you know?"

"No," replied Porthos and Aramis in unison.

The ornate double doors opened, and an attendant walked out. "Her Majesty, the Queen Regent will see you now."

As the three walked in, they could see the queen regent standing in the middle of the room. They bowed and stood waiting for her to speak. "I suppose you are wondering why I asked you here," she finally stated.

"To be honest, yes, Your Majesty," answered Athos.

"I wasn't sure who else to turn to. I recall that you three along with the late D'Artagnan were present when the Duke of Buckingham and Constance ...." The queen regent choked up as she brought up Constance's name. "I'm sorry. I still think often of Constance, and I'm always saddened at the tragic loss of her life." The three former musketeers remained silent out of respect for the queen regent's feelings. She composed herself and continued, "when the Count de Rochefort stopped the coach. I'm sure you know that he wanted to steal a sword that I had given him from the treasure room of King Louis XIII. When I gave the duke the sword, that was the last I had seen of it until a little over a week ago." The queen regent paused as surprise slowly suffused the faces of the three men.

"I'm not sure I follow," said Athos. "Are you saying that the relic sword is back?"

"That is what I'm saying."

"But how?" interceded Porthos. "Who brought it back? Are you positive that it is the same sword?"

"I'm certain the sword is the same one that was here twenty-five years ago. I don't know the answer to the question of who brought it here, but it arrived at almost exactly the same time as a woman, named Diega Scott arrived. The woman spoke erratic French. Her native language was either Spanish or English. She claimed to be a Spanish Ambassador to France."

"What?" interjected Aramis. "She actually said that while the two nations are belligerents? Was she of sound mind?"

"I think she was," said the queen regent. "I thought that the arrival of both her and the sword was not coincidence. I had the sword brought out to question her about it. When the woman saw the sword, she became possessed as if by a demon. She said the sword was why she was here. She grabbed it and ran. Four of my best soldiers came in to stop her. All four had rapiers and were fine swordsmen." The queen regent paused as if looking for what to say next. "I've never seen anyone use a sword the way she did. That is why I said she seemed demon possessed. She was very acrobatic, and she killed the four soldiers so easily that it was almost if they were unarmed. I've never seen anything like it."

"I only know of a few people who were that good with a sword," said Athos. "One of them was D'Artagnan, and he may not have been as good as what you just described."

"What happened to the woman?" asked Aramis.

I had twenty musketeers stationed with muskets outside the palace. That was the only thing that stopped her. I had her taken to the Bastille as a prisoner."

"Pardon me, Your Majesty," said Athos, "but why have you called us?"

"One reason is that you were among the last to have been near the sword when the Duke of Buckingham had it."

"Are you suggesting that we took the sword from the duke?" questioned Porthos.

"Of course not."

"What is the other reason you wanted to see us?" asked Aramis.

"I want you to talk with this woman to try to determine her true story. As I said, you three were among the last to have seen the sword."

"I don't see the connection," replied Porthos.

"I have no other ideas, except to keep her in the Bastille, if we can't determine her true intentions. You might have more persuasion that the cardinal, the lieutenant general, or the jailers."

"We haven't served as musketeers in twenty-five years, and even then, we were soldiers, not interrogators," stated Athos.

"I'm aware of that. Athos, you returned to your life of nobility and now have a son, Raoul, who is fourteen. Your wife died in childbirth. Porthos, you married a widow, have a nice sum of money, and are still married. Aramis, you joined the priesthood."

"I see that Cardinal Mazarin has informed you quite well," said Athos.

"And I see that you three are still as impertinent as you were as musketeers," retorted the queen regent.

"Cardinal Mazarin didn't have to tell her that," said Porthos.

"Enough of this juvenile behavior. If you want to know why I'm asking you to talk with this woman, the reason is that your insolence matches her own."

"I have signed a writ allowing you to speak with her. It is in effect until rescinded by me." The queen regent handed the writ to Athos. "Keep me informed of your findings."

"Not meaning to be impertinent, may I ask why the interest? She's just one person. How much trouble can she cause?" questioned Athos.

"I'm curious as to why the sword has shown up now, after all these years. Is it meant to be a warning? Could it be a threat on the king's life? Or is she truly innocent and in the wrong place at the wrong time? I have no desire to keep someone prisoner if they don't belong there."

"All right. We'll find out what we can," replied Athos.

Diega had been in the Bastille for three days. No one had come to see her. Once a day, food and a cup of water had been slid under the door for her. The chamber pot had yet to be emptied. She had killed two rats and had shoved them under the door to try to keep the room from smelling of decay. The despair she felt had worsened.

For the entire day, she had heard scratching noises coming from the corner where the rats had darted out and in. Must be more rats. The noise had become increasingly louder throughout the day. Out of the corner of her eye, she thought she saw one of the floor stones jiggle. My mind must be playing tricks on me. As she walked over to investigate, however, she definitely saw it wobble. Surely that can't be a rat, or I've got big problems. The stone popped out of place and was raised slightly on one end. Diega grabbed the stone and began to pull to see what was causing it to move. The pulling from her end and the pushing from the other was enough to dislodge the stone. She moved it to the side, hoping the noise was not enough to cause a guard to come to investigate. A hand suddenly appeared out of the hole that the stone had covered. However, the hole wasn't big enough for a person to get through. Because one stone had been moved out of place, moving the adjacent stone didn't require as much work. Once two stones had been moved, a person began to crawl out. Whoever this prisoner was, he or she was wearing a black leather mask like the one she wore. The person crawled out and was breathing heavily through the mask.

"Do you speak French?" came a male voice from under the mask.

"Not fluently, but enough to understand and enough to be understood."

"What language do you speak?"

Diega didn't know if this was an elaborate trap to gather more information, but it was a lot of trouble and scheming if that were the case. She decided to trust the situation as what it appeared to be, another prisoner from the adjacent cell perhaps trying to escape. If he were trying to escape, the effort had been for naught because he merely arrived in another cell. Finally, she said, "English or Spanish."

"Let's go with English. How long have you been in here?"

"Three days. What about you?"

"A week. Whoever had been in the cell before me had dug a tunnel, probably hoping to escape. I discovered it two days ago. The tunnel is clear for the most part. I don't know how the person removed the dirt, but they must have had some help in removing it. Perhaps they were connected enough to pay a guard. Whoever dug it apparently didn't have a good sense of direction or they would have dug it to exit this place rather than to enter an adjacent cell."

"We can't leave it like this. What if a guard were to come in?" asked Diega.

"We'll have to put the stone back into place, but so far, the guards have only come into my cell once. I imagine they physically check inside these cells once a week."

"I'm not willing to bet on a hunch."

"I won't stay long then. Just give me a couple of minutes to catch my breath before returning."

"What's your story for being here."

"It's hard to explain."

"You'd better try if you want me to trust you."

"Let's take turns. I'll tell a little; then, you can tell a little. I was caught near the palace. I gave a name that they apparently didn't like. I also didn't have a good explanation as to why I was near the palace; so, they put me in here. Now, you're turn."

"I said I was the Spanish Ambassador, not knowing that France and Spain were at war. I was taken to the palace and killed some soldiers when I tried to flee. In hindsight, I've thought, Diega, how could you have been so stupid."

"Diega! I thought your first sounded familiar. It's me, Gawain!"

"Gawain! Oh, thank heavens you're here," she said hugging him tightly. Diega paused, realizing what she had said. "I'm sorry you're in here. I was just excited that someone is here I know. You were trying to get Excalibur, weren't you? I actually had it. The queen regent questioned me about it, and I grabbed it and ran. I killed four soldiers, but when I got outside of the palace, I came face to face with about twenty armed musketeers."

"I thought Excalibur must be here, which is why I was outside of the palace. But King Arthur was already dead in my time, and I moved to Norway, where I'm king. With King Arthur being dead, I had thought my quests involving Excalibur had ended."

"What name did you give them that they didn't like?"

"D'Artagnan, of course. I didn't know that they thought he was dead. I suppose me turning up after all this time didn't look good."

"Do you think there is a way out of here?"

"I don't know. I think we will have to be patient and look for an opening. I don't think forcing anything will work to our advantage."

"I don't know how long I can be patient, but knowing you are here has lifted my spirits tremendously."

"I'm glad to see you as well. I just wish it were under better circumstances. I'll head back to my cell. Maybe you can leave the corner stone slightly ajar so that we can move it easier next time."

"I wish there were some way to camouflage it. I dare not move the chamber pot over here. The guards would certainly notice the stone ajar when they come to empty it. One of my sergeants in the Marines said that the best way to hide something sometimes was to leave it in plain view. If I can keep the guards away from this side, they may not notice, especially if it is only slightly ajar. The stones are uneven in here anyway."

"That sounds plausible. I'll try to check on you if we can establish for certain that they have a weekly schedule. Remember, be patient. We'll get out of this mess somehow." With this last statement, he made his way back through the tunnel.

Diega moved the stones back over the hole, leaving the corner stone slightly ajar. "Goodbye, Gawain, or D'Artagnan, or whatever you're calling yourself." She knew he didn't hear what she said. "Be patient," was what he had said. I can certainly be more patient now that I know there are two of us on the same side.

Two weeks had passed since Diega was imprisoned in the Bastille. She had seen Gawain, or D'Artagnan as he had been known, two times. Guards had also come into her cell once a week to empty her chamber bucket. Faint voices outside of the cell door drifted into her cell. Then came the sound of a key turning the lock. The door was shoved open, and three men walked inside. They weren't wearing uniforms of any kind, but they were carrying swords. The guard closed the door behind them. Diega was frightened as to what the men might do. In her mind, she was thinking how to disarm one and kill them. Even if she did that, her rational mind told her that that wouldn't help her situation; she still couldn't escape. One of the men must have read her mind.

"If I were you, I would be thinking how I could disarm one of us and use the sword to kill all three," said Porthos. "We've heard how good you are with a sword. The three of us used to be musketeers, and while you've killed four soldiers at one time, we are not average musketeers. Well, we were good swordsmen at one time anyway."

Aramis interjected, "stop talking so much. We didn't come here to scare the woman." He turned his attention to Diega. "We're here to talk with you."

"So, why did they let you in here with swords?" asked Diega.

"We didn't give them a choice," said Athos, "and before you ask why we're not wearing musketeer uniforms, we haven't been musketeers in a while." Athos paused as if looking for what to say next. "I don't want to alarm you. I like to see to whom I'm talking. I'm going to walk over and take off your mask. That's all I'm going to do, then I will back away. You could try to grab my sword, but I would advise against it. Even if you killed all of us, there are plenty of people you would still have to go through to get out. Nod, if we have a deal."

Diega nodded affirmatively, and Athos walked over, untied the rope, pulled her mask off, and stepped back to his starting position. Diega felt such a relief to have the mask off.

"Let's start with introductions. I'm Athos, and my companions are Porthos and Aramis," he said pointing to the others as he mentioned each name.

"I know you!" exclaimed Diega excitedly. "I mean I don't know you, but I've heard of you."

"I seriously doubt that," replied Athos. "What is your name?"

"My name is Diega." She raised a hand to brush the hair off her face, something she sometimes did when she was nervous, before realizing that her hair was too short to be in her face. She saw that Athos had a strange look on his face, which quickly switched to anger. He stormed over and grabbed her right arm forcefully.

"Where did you get that?" he said in a rage.

"Where did I get what?"

"I asked where you got that?" Diega's face showed puzzlement. "Where did you get the ring? That is my ring?"

Diega replied much calmer than she expected. "Take your hand off my arm, and I will tell you. Leave it there, and I'll break it." Athos huffed and released her arm.

"Alright, I've let go. Now tell me."

Diega searched for something to say, and she would have to come up with it quickly. She hoped they couldn't tell she was lying. At least she could tell some truth. "I got the ring from D'Artagnan."

"You mean you stole it from him, or you got it from someone else who had stollen it from him," yelled Athos.

"I got it from my father, D'Artagnan."

"D'Artagnan is dead. He has been for twenty-five years," said Aramis.

"No. He is very much alive."

"That can't be," said Porthos.

"Well, maybe if I tell you the story, you will believe me," replied Diega. She tried to remember what Gawain had told her, and then she would add in a fake ending. "Milady stuck Constance with a poisoned needle, and Athos was seriously injured from a musket shot. Aramis, you gave D'Artagnan Athos' ring, because all of you had become so close, before he went to England to warn the Duke of Buckingham that Milady and the Count de Rochefort were coming to kill him. D'Artagnan arrived before Milady and the duke but not by much. The count and Milady killed the duke's sentries and arrived to find D'Artagnan talking with the duke. The duke had given D'Artagnan the relic sword to take back to the queen. The Count de Rochefort challenged D'Artagnan to a duel; if D'Artagnan survived, he could have his freedom. From what D'Artagnan described, it was a sword fight of the ages, but D'Artagnan eventually disarmed the count. Milady fired a musket, which backfired and disfigured her. D'Artagnan shot her to put her out of her misery, and the Duke of Buckingham took the Count de Rochefort prisoner." Diega took a deep breath and paused. That much was true; now, she would have to improvise to make up a fake ending to try to explain why D'Artagnan did not come back to France. She obviously couldn't tell them that D'Artagnan was really Sir Gawain who time traveled back to the time of King Arthur. She hoped she could make the story convincing. "Cardinal Richelieu sent a messenger to the duke, who arrived before D'Artagnan left England. This messenger told the duke that D'Artagnan was a double agent, spying on both the English and the French. He urged the Duke of Buckingham to imprison D'Artagnan. He didn't want D'Artagnan back in France because the queen had taken a liking to him because of Constance. The messenger told the duke that if he cared for the queen, he would save her from embarrassment and suspicion by keeping D'Artagnan a prisoner in England. The cardinal's messenger then went to D'Artagnan and told him that if he ever went back to England, then the three of you would be assassinated. The duke imprisoned D'Artagnan for a few years but then began to question the cardinal's motives; so, he released D'Artagnan. Fearing for your safety, he decided to remain in England. He met my mother who was from Spain and married her. I was born shortly afterwards and learned to speak both English and Spanish. He taught me some French, but I'm nowhere near as good with French as I am the other two languages. My mother died a few years ago, and my father yearned to come back to France. He did and took the sword with him to give back to the queen, but he was going to sneak it into the palace since she believed him to be dead. I didn't leave with him, but I felt troubled and decided to leave about a week after he left." Diega finished the story and took a deep breath.

Aramis was the first to speak. "I've been a priest for a long time now, and I know when someone is lying. You are lying."

"If you don't believe me, then ask D'Artagnan yourself," replied Diega curtly.

"That's a rather convenient story you want us to verify when D'Artagnan is nowhere around," snipped Athos.

"Oh no," said Diega smugly. "He's in the next cell over."

"What? How would you know that?" asked Porthos.

"Because I've spoken with him twice since I've been here."

"The guards said you have not had any visitors," said Porthos.

"Do you see the stone in the corner that's ajar? It covers a tunnel leading to the next cell, and D'Artagnan has crawled through it to get to my cell."

"Stay here," Athos told her.

Where else can I go, thought Diega.

Athos banged on the cell door until a guard unlocked the door. "I want to see the prisoner in the next cell. Bring him in here."

The guard sounded puzzled. "I can't do that. Your writ from the queen regent only specifies that you are allowed to talk with this prisoner."

Athos drew his rapier and pointed it at the guard's throat. "Will this writ satisfy you?"

"Alright. Alright. I'll bring him over," said the guard nervously.

The guard muttered as he left. Diega could hear him walk to the next cell and unlock the door. He cursed at the prisoner and told him to come out carefully without attempting anything. The guard led the hooded prisoner to the door of Diega's cell and shoved him in. The guard had bound the prisoner's hands behind his back with rope. Then, the guard closed the door.

All five people in the cell stood still momentarily, as if wondering what to do next. Finally, Athos broke the stalemate and used his rapier to cut the rope binding the prisoner's hands. He untied the rope around the prisoner's neck holding the hood in place and slowly pulled off the hood. Athos and D'Artagnan stared at each other for a long moment. Tears welled in both men's eyes, and they hugged each other with the ferocity of two bears. Porthos and Aramis rushed over, and they all hugged each other and sobbed.

Diega wondered if they would ever break the group hug, but then she heard the famous words. D'Artagnan said, "All for one." Then all four joined in saying, "and one for all."

"How can this be?" asked Athos.

Diega quickly told the fake ending of her story so that D'Artagnan could affirm what she had said.

"I don't care if it did risk our lives. You should have come back."

"Cardinal Richelieu had too much influence, connections, and power," replied D'Artagnan. I had lost Constance. I couldn't risk losing you all as well, even if it meant I had to live an expatriated life in England."

"Well, if it's any consolation," said Porthos, "you were posthumously awarded France's highest honor and received the rank of Captain of the Musketeers. And from what I've heard, you passed along your skill with the sword to your daughter."

"I guess it's the least the cardinal could have done for all the harm he caused. As for Diega, I taught her a few things, but she's quite a natural when it comes to the sword."

"It's her heredity. I just hope she didn't inherit your ability with using a musket," joked Aramis.

"At the end, I actually became quite good. Tell me what happened in the aftermath of me going to England."

Athos told what had happened after D'Artagnan had left for England. "I recovered from the musket shot, and we were called before the king. We feared the worst and told him that we were resigning as musketeers. The king was livid over what happened without his knowledge. He almost accused us of being traitors, but then Cardinal Richelieu did something quite uncharacteristic. He came up with this story of how we had foiled Gaston, the king's brother, of a coup. He said that you and the Count de Rochefort had died gallantly defending the king. That's when the cardinal asked that we receive France's highest honor and that you be posthumously awarded the rank of Captain of the Musketeers. That same day we stopped being musketeers."

"I'm so sorry for that," said D'Artagnan. "I feel it's my fault that you had to stop doing what you loved."

"We didn't love it," replied Athos. "You taught us what it was to truly live. Each of us had been using the musketeers as an escape. We owed it to you and ourselves to go and live the lives we wanted."

"And what was that?" questioned D'Artagnan.

"I've been in the priesthood," said Aramis.

"And I married a rich widow," answered Porthos.

"I returned to my life in the nobility," said Athos. "I, like you, married and had a child. His name is Raoul."

"Then you should have this ring back," said Diega taking the ring off.

"No, said Aramis, "You keep it. The ring was given to D'Artagnan."

"And he gave it to me; so, now I want to give it back to you to give to your son. Please accept it."

"Alright. I'll take it and give it to him. Thank you so much, Diega."

"This has been a great reunion," said Aramis, "but how are we going to get D'Artagnan and Diega out of here?"

"We can just go to the queen regent and tell her that D'Artagnan is alive and that Diega is his daughter," replied Porthos.

"Freeing D'Artagnan and Diega won't be that easy," said Athos. "Freeing D'Artagnan might be easy. The queen regent liked D'Artagnan; she would probably free him because of his connection to Constance, but Diega killed four French soldiers. I'm actually surprised that she hasn't been executed yet."

A shiver went through Diega at the mention of execution. D'Artagnan noticed it and said, "I want let that happen, Diega."

"I'm sorry, Diega, but your story just doesn't add up," said Athos. "Why masquerade as a Spanish Ambassador? I mean, why didn't you just tell the queen regent that you were D'Artagnan's daughter? And why take the sword if D'Artagnan put it back. Even if you can explain all of that, she is not going to excuse the fact that you killed four soldiers."

Diega wasn't sure what to say. She certainly couldn't tell them she time traveled. The only thing to do was to expound on her lie. "I had never been out of England. I didn't know that D'Artagnan was imprisoned here until I was here myself. I was scared and nervous; so, I made up a story. I wasn't thinking about a war between France and Spain. With my father's stories about the scheming and sinister Cardinal Richelieu, I thought he might have been killed when he arrived. You have to admit that something is going on, or he wouldn't be imprisoned here. Especially when I saw the sword, I thought that something awful had happened; so, I grabbed it and ran. If the soldiers hadn't come after me with raised swords, I wouldn't have fought them."

"I have to agree with Athos," said Aramis. "Even if all you say is true, they're not going to just let you go. Even if the queen regent were inclined to do so, Cardinal Mazarin has a lot of power and would not let that happen."

"We could tell the queen regent that Diega was a made-up name and that her name is really Constance, named after D'Artagnan's first love. The loss she felt over Constance might cause her emotions to override her rational side."

"I think the easiest thing is to convince the queen regent to release D'Artagnan first. Then we can work on freeing Diega," reasoned Athos.

"I can't just leave Diega in here while I'm free, even if we do try to work on getting her released," said D'Artagnan.

"No one is getting released until we talk with the queen regent," said Athos. "Try not to worry, old friend. We still mean what we told you years ago, *All for one and one for all.* We'll forcefully free both or either of you, if it comes to that."

Diega motioned to D'Artagnan that she wanted to tell him something. D'Artagnan went to her, and she whispered in his ear. D'Artagnan turned to the ex-musketeers. "Diega has a powerful weapon that she hid when she arrived. It's small, but like I said, it's powerful. She can tell you where it's buried. Would you get it in case we need it?"

"Of course," replied Athos.

Diega told them where she buried it and that it was concealed in a bag.

"We'll go there first, before we go to the queen regent," said Athos. "Put your masks back on, and we'll tie the ropes." Hesitantly, they did as Athos had asked. Athos banged on the door, and the guard came and unlocked the door. He grabbed D'Artagnan, closed Diega's door, and took D'Artagnan back to his cell. The ex-musketeers hurriedly left the Bastille.

Athos, Porthos, and Aramis rode out to the location given by Diega, following her directions. They found the tree that she described and dug along the indicated side until they found her purse. "What on earth and under heaven is this?" exclaimed Porthos at seeing the purse. "I've never seen anything like this in my life."

"It is very unusual looking," said Aramis. "Look inside and get the weapon."

Porthos dug around in her purse, pausing at odd-looking objects. Finally, he pulled out the Springfield Hellcat and the extra magazines of ammunition. "This looks like a miniature hand-held musket. This has to be the weapon they were talking about. It's so small. How can this toy musket be as powerful as Diega said?"

"It's strange indeed," answered Aramis, "but they said it would be small. I wonder what these other metallic-looking things are? They must be some type of projectiles. I'm not sure how this will propel them though. We'll have to trust that it's as powerful as they said."

"Here's a bottle containing some liquid," said Porthos pulling it out of the purse. "I wonder if this is needed as well. The words written on this look like English. Can you make it out, Aramis?"

Aramis studied the words and read, "Pepper Spray. At least I think that's what it says, but it doesn't make sense. Let's take it along though."

Athos hid the items. The three mounted their horses and rode into Paris and went directly to the palace. When they arrived, they found the squire attending the queen regent.

"Is Her Majesty, the Queen Regent expecting you?"

"She told us to report to her as soon as we learned something," said Athos.

The squire disappeared and returned a few minutes later. "Her Majesty can see you briefly. Follow me."

The three followed the squire into a room in the palace where they found the queen regent. They bowed and straightened when she began speaking. "Good day, gentlemen," she said. "Have you discovered anything?"

The ex-musketeers had decided to let Athos start with the news and tell as much as he thought the queen regent could handle or believe. "Yes, Your Majesty. We bring good news. D'Artagnan is alive!"

The queen regent staggered, but quickly straightened herself. "What? How can that be? We were told he was dead."

"That was a lie by Cardinal Richelieu. D'Artagnan went to England to warn the Duke of Buckingham of a plot to kill him. D'Artagnan successfully fought the threat and saved the duke's life, but the cardinal sent a messenger with a falsehood that led to D'Artagnan being imprisoned in England. The cardinal made up the other story and claimed that D'Artagnan had been killed, but we actually saw D'Artagnan in the Bastille. We can all three vouch that it is really him."

"That's such wonderful news that he's alive. Constance would have been so happy that he lived. We must free him at once. Cardinal Richelieu's schemes never fail to amaze me, even after his death. But how does all of this connect with the other matter that I assigned you to investigate?"

"D'Artagnan was released from prison after a few years but remained in England due to a death threat against us by Cardinal Richelieu if he returned to France. He finally decided to come back, and since the Duke of Buckingham was dead, D'Artagnan decided to bring back the sword that you had given the duke. He snuck it into the palace but was arrested and taken to the Bastille."

"But why did he do so in such a covert manner? He could have brought it to me personally."

"Think about all that he had gone through. Twenty-five years later, he didn't want to announce that he was alive after all the time that had passed. The woman, Diega, is D'Artagnan's daughter. She was frightened and didn't know what had happened to her father. Her charade was certainly stupid, but in her mind, she feared for his life. When she was brought here, she was even more afraid and grabbed the sword to protect herself. When she faced four armed men ready to kill her, she did what she had to do to protect herself."

"I'm going to write an order for the immediate release of D'Artagnan." As the queen regent was writing the order, Cardinal Mazarin walked in and bowed to the queen regent. She quickly recited what Athos had told her. "Cardinal Mazarin, I expect you to reinstate D'Artagnan as a Captain of the Musketeers, if he so chooses. I want your oath that you will personally patronize D'Artagnan's career as a musketeer, even after King Louis XIV takes full control."

"You have my word, Your Majesty," said the cardinal.

"What about Diega?" asked Athos.

"I'm afraid we can't help her," answered the cardinal.

"I have to agree," added the queen regent. "I'm truly sorry."

"I've already sent a squadron of musketeers to execute her," said the cardinal. "You may present the order to release D'Artagnan, but you are not to interfere in any way with the musketeers as they carry out the order of execution. She has probably already been executed, but I will go there personally to make sure she is."

Athos tried to remain as calm as he could. "The situation is regrettable, but we understand, Your Majesty." He bowed. Porthos and Aramis imitated, and they left the palace.

Once outside the palace, Porthos and Aramis exclaimed in unison. "You don't mean to let this happen, do you?"

"Of course not, but I couldn't give them the impression that I meant to stop it. We must hurry before it is too late." The three hurried to the Bastille and presented the jailor with the order from the queen regent to free D'Artagnan. Although the ex-musketeers were allowed to take their weapons with them on their first visit, they were required to leave them in the front room on this visit.

The jailor led them to D'Artagnan's cell where he unlocked the door and released D'Artagnan. As the jailor started to lead them out, a group of ten musketeers exited Diega's cell. Diega was bound with her hands tied behind her back. Athos, hoping what he was about to do would serve as a shock factor rather than a warning, shouted, "All for one and one for all." This startled several of the musketeers. D'Artagnan shoved the jailor hard against the stone wall, knocking him unconscious. The quarters were too tight for the musketeers to use their muskets, but they drew their swords. Athos, Porthos, Aramis, and D'Artagnan immediately tried to take swords away from four musketeers. Athos was almost immediately run through in his shoulder with a rapier. Diega headbutted one of the musketeers from behind. She dropped, her hands still bound behind her, and used her legs to knock down two musketeers. D'Artagnan grabbed both of their rapiers while they were down. He threw one to Aramis. Porthos had already wrested a rapier from another musketeer. D'Artagnan quickly cut the rope binding Diega's hand. Athos called for her and indicated for her to reach into his cloak. She did so, pulling out the Springfield Hellcat, extra magazines, and pepper spray.

One of the musketeers reached for her, and she sprayed him directly in the eyes with the pepper spray. He fell to the floor, writhing in pain. She took his rapier and crushed his windpipe with her foot. Now, Diega, D'Artagnan, Porthos, and Aramis had rapiers. In less than a minute, all the musketeers who were sent to execute her had been killed. The guard who had unlocked the door ran away from them down the hall.

"How are you, Athos?" asked Porthos.

"I'll live, but I'm not going to be much of a help if we have to fight our way out." Porthos handed Athos a rapier, and Athos took it with his uninjured arm. "At least you can try fighting with your good arm until we can get you to a doctor."

D'Artagnan, Porthos, and Aramis each picked up a flintlock musket. Aramis quickly explained the difference between firing a flintlock and firing a matchlock to D'Artagnan. No sooner had he finished the explanation than they heard footsteps and shouts coming between them and their freedom.

"If that small toy has any use, you'd better use it now," shouted Porthos to Diega. Diega readied her Hellcat. She had thirty rounds between the two magazines. The sound of the footsteps stopped. Diega looked up to see twenty or more musketeers stopped ahead of them. D'Artagnan, Porthos, and Athos already had muskets trained on the musketeers in front of them. From the back of the group of musketeers, Cardinal Mazarin called out. "I told you not to try anything. You're outnumbered and will never make it out alive. Drop your weapons now!"

Diega bravely walked in front of her comrades and held up the Springfield Hellcat so that all could see. "Actually, you're outnumbered. I can fire off thirty shots in thirty seconds. That's more than enough to take care of all of you. The musketeers broke into laughter at the sight of Diega's small and strange-looking weapon.

The lead musketeer called, "Ready." Before they could raise their muskets, Diega's Marine training took over. She was an expert with firearms. She shot the lead musketeer, who was still smiling, between the eyes before he could say, "Aim." She quickly emptied the magazine, each bullet killing its intended target. She ejected the extended magazine and snapped the other extended magazine into place and fired off additional shots. In less than thirty seconds, with an extended magazine still remaining, twenty-four musketeers lay dead on the bloodied stone floor. Cardinal Mazarin had fled before she could shoot him. Her four comrades were mesmerized; they hadn't fired a shot.

"What in the devil is that?" asked Aramis. "You didn't have to load a musket ball or powder; it just kept firing."

"This is the firearm of the future," she said coolly.

"D'Artagnan didn't teach you to do that." Diega thought that Aramis had tried to say that jokingly, but the statement was one of shock and awe.

"I don't want to disappoint anyone, but we're not out of this yet," asserted Athos. "How many more times can that thing fire?"

Diega ejected the spent magazine and inserted the remaining magazine. "I have thirteen rounds left."

"Rounds?" questioned Porthos.

"Shots," she replied.

"Who knows what lies ahead," restated Athos. "I've never met a cardinal yet I trusted." Athos' and Aramis' eyes met. "You're not a cardinal, and don't ever be one."

"Let's not sit here; let's get out," said Porthos. "We need to be careful though. D'Artagnan, you help Athos. Aramis and I will scout a little ahead, but we'll stay close."

D'Artagnan supported Athos on his uninjured side with one arm as he carried his musket in the other. The gunfire in the closed-in quarters had temporarily impaired Diega's hearing. The others had to be experiencing the same thing, which was not ideal in their situation. Other of her senses were heightened. The passageway was dark, and the stones were uneven. She could feel the out-of-step footsteps of Porthos and Aramis up ahead and could see Athos' labored breathing with her peripheral vision. The smell of gunpowder mingled with blood still lingered in the air. Light was beginning to appear ahead; they would have to be extra careful. Suddenly, a musket shot interrupted the inconsequential sounds that Diega could hear.

Porthos ran back to them, "A musket ball got Aramis. He's dead."

"Look out," cried Diega, but her warning was too late. A grenade landed a few feet behind Porthos and exploded. The small blast indicated that the gunpowder was old, but it was potent enough and close enough to Porthos to kill him. He lay on the stone-cold floor with his eyes open. Without knowing it, he had acted as a shield and probably saved their lives.

Athos and D'Artagnan were knocked to the floor but otherwise uninjured. D'Artagnan rose from the floor, helped Athos to his feet, and leaned him against the wall. D'Artagnan readied his musket in preparation for a charge. As the smoke began to clear, a musketeer stepped through the dispersing cloud with his musket ready to fire. The musketeer spotted Athos against the wall and took aim. As he was about to fire, smoke erupted from D'Artagnan's musket, and the musketeer dropped. "Damn, you really have improved with the musket. That's twice you saved my ...." A shot rang out from the musket of another musketeer, halting Athos in mid-sentence. Diega fired her handgun, killing the musketeer.

Athos lay on the floor. D'Artagnan bent down and held up Athos' head. Diega kept an eye on their exit in case any other musketeers were to come through. Blood issued from Athos' mouth. He pulled off his ring, the ring that Diega had just recently given him. With labored breath he spoke sporadically and softly. "Give ... this... to my son, ... Raoul. Meeting you ... again ..., old friend ... has ... meant more... than you ... know. You ... were my first son ... always. All for one."

"And one for all," finished D'Artagnan. He closed Athos' eyes with his hand. I promise you. I'll get this ring to Raoul. I'm sorry our reunion was cut short. I would have given almost anything to have seen you all again, but I would not have done so if it meant costing you your lives. Athos, Porthos, and Aramis, farewell till we meet again."

"I'm so sorry," said Diega, "but we have to get out of here before reinforcements come."

"You're right." D'Artagnan rose and picked up his musket. He quickly loaded it. Diega slid forward hugging one wall, and D'Artagnan did likewise along the opposite wall. Diega motioned with her hand for them to look peek diagonally into the entry room as they approached. Debris from the explosion partially blocked the doorway into the entrance room. Seeing no one remaining in the entrance room they entered. The double door leading to the outside was standing open. "They could have a marksman waiting for us to exit."

Diega performed a quick visual search of the room. Finding a shattered mirror, she picked up a piece. She walked to the door, and remaining inside, stuck her arm out the doorway with the mirror in her hand. She used the mirror to sight what she could; then she moved to the other side and did likewise. "From what I could see, there is one sharpshooter on top of the adjacent building to the east."

"He picked a poor position with the sun in the west. Can a musket shot travel that far?"

"If the right amount of powder is packed, it should."

"You're a better shot. Let me have the mirror, and I'll try to use it to reflect sunlight into his eyes to distract him. When I say go, step out and take your shot. Are you sure you just saw one shooter?"

"Well, I wouldn't bet my life on it; on second thought, I guess I am betting my life on it."

"If we don't take a chance, our lives will be forfeited anyway. I hate to ask you to step outside first, but you're the better shot. If you are shot, I won't be far behind you." D'Artagnan took the mirror, stuck his arm outside and began experimentally angling the mirror to get the desired effect. "Now," he said suddenly.

Diega quickly stepped out, raised the musket while making mental calculations of the distance and wind. A memory of her father and her watching an old John Wayne movie entered her mind along with the words spoken by the character played by John Wayne, *windage and elevation*. She chuckled to herself, remembered her mission, and quickly dismissed the thought. This is the best estimate I can make, she thought. The sharpshooter had his musket raised, and the reflected sunlight suddenly left his face. A shot rang out and smoke filled the air. Diega coughed. "I should have dismissed the thought sooner." The dead body of the musketeer fell from the building.

"Should have dismissed what thought sooner?"

"A thought entered my mind from an old movie telling me *windage and elevation*. I almost waited too long."

"I'd say you were being looked after. For this task, that was an appropriate thought. Perhaps the three musketeers are looking out for us."

"Well, if they have movies in the afterlife, I'm glad they saw that one first rather than one of the myriad of movies about them!"

D'Artagnan and Diega moved along the wall, looking all around them. After reaching the corner and looking around, they raced the short distance across the street, and zigzagged from building to building until they were certain they were safe.

Upon reaching the Musketeer headquarters, Cardinal Mazarin was breathless.

"What happened?" asked the captain.

"Every one of the musketeers you sent are dead."

"That's impossible. That can't be."

"It can be, and it is. There is a hell of a mess at the Bastille. Get a group of men you can trust who won't say anything. There are thirty to forty bodies to dispose of, and an explosion has wrecked the room where the jailor was stationed. That will need to be repaired as soon as possible."

"I don't care who you are, I don't have to take those orders from you," snapped the captain.

"Apparently, you don't know enough about me. One word from me and you will be executed before sundown. If you think the queen regent or the king rules this country, I'll show you otherwise right now."

The captain backed down immediately. "I'm sorry Your Eminence. I'll see that it gets handled discreetly and immediately.

"How old are you, Captain?"

"Forty-five."

"Are you married?"

"No, Your Eminence."

"Then you'll do. From now on, you are Captain D'Artagnan. I made a vow to the queen regent. Do as I say, and you will advance quickly, perhaps even becoming Marshall of France. I'll see that you get a hefty sum as well. You'll be a wealthy man."

"Yes, Your Eminence!"

The cardinal walked outside and mumbled to himself. "Now, I just need to think of an excuse to keep him from seeing the queen regent. The man reasonably resembles the real D'Artagnan, and so many years have passed since the queen regent laid eyes on D'Artagnan. Still, I can't be too careful, and keeping him away from the queen regent will be my safest course of action. I'll need to explain the deaths of Athos, Porthos, and Aramis to the queen regent. I think I'll tell her that the woman, Diega, tried to escape and the three ex-musketeers were killed before Diega was finally executed. The fake D'Artagnan will be too disturbed to face the queen regent, but he vows to serve king and country as a loyal musketeer. What a mess."

D'Artagnan inquired and found a friend of Athos. He told him that Athos had been killed while in service of the queen regent. He asked him to give Athos' ring to Raoul. The man promised to take the ring immediately to Raoul.

"I would like to have taken the ring to Raoul personally, but I don't want to wake up tomorrow with the ring in Norway."

"We don't have Excalibur. Do you really think we'll wake up tomorrow back in our own times?

"I've always retrieved Excalibur before traveling back to my time," stated D'Artagnan, "but somehow this time feels different. I can't really explain the feeling. I think my time traveling adventures may have come to an end, and the mantle has now been passed to you. If this is our last night here, what do you want to do?"

"This may sound utterly crazy, but there is something I would really love to do."

"Name it, and we'll try."

The old tavern that D'Artagnan used to visit almost every night with Athos, Porthos, and Aramis had changed very little over the course of twenty-five years. The old table where they used to sit was vacant; so, they went to it and sat. D'Artagnan saw the bartender eyeing them suspiciously, and the bartender started to make his way inconspicuously to the door. "Excuse me, I'll go see if we can get something to drink." D'Artagnan caught the bartender halfway to the door, and he put his hand on the bartender's arm, grasping firmly. With the other hand, he grasped the hilt of his rapier. "I don't know if you know who I am. I suspect you do, and if you do, you know what I can do. You have a choice to make. You can walk out the door and tell whomever you plan on talking to, perhaps end up getting yourself killed, and guarantee that his tavern will be demolished. Or, you can serve us, and you'll never see us after this night." D'Artagnan released the bartender's arm and took his hand off the hilt of his rapier. "What's your choice?" The bartender skulked back to the bar. "Oh, there was a nice bottle of red wine that Porthos used to order frequently. Do you know it?" The bartender nodded. "We'll have a bottle."

Back at the table, the bartender brought a bottle of red wine, opened it, and poured some into two glasses he had brought. He left the bottle and returned to the bar. "I'll keep an eye on you, if you know what I mean, in case we need some more," said D'Artagnan.

"Tomorrow, I will deeply mourn the loss of my three friends, my family, but tonight, they would want us to celebrate, and that's what we'll do." He held up his glass, tipped Diega's, and said, "Cheers."

Diega grew saddened. "They're dead because of me."

"They died fighting for a cause they believed in, and they would have preferred that to dying of old age. We can blame ourselves for any misfortune in life, or we can accept that what happened, happened, and go forward living our lives in service to others. Besides, I could say that I'm to blame for their deaths. If I had not been connected to the sword, the queen regent would have never summoned them. Let's celebrate. We might not have tomorrow. If we do, we can grieve then. Deal?"

"Deal."

"What's happened with you since I saw you all of those years ago?"

"Not much time has passed for me. Not much at all. I took French lessons. It's a good thing I did, but my French is still not that great. I envy you and hate you at the same time for your ability to speak any language perfectly. I don't really hate you. That's just a figure of speech."

"I know."

"Of course, you know. Also, I took fencing lessons from an Olympic medalist, but he stopped teaching me because I wouldn't follow the rules."

D'Artagnan let out a hearty laugh. "Athos, Porthos, and Aramis would have been proud of you. In a fight where no one follows rules, I'd say that you were right. I heard about your skills in the palace and briefly saw them in the short sword fight we had in the Bastille. I'd say you're one of the best ever, better than D'Artagnan and maybe even your fabled Lancelot."

"What about you, what has happened with you? When I got back to my time, I read every story I could find about you. There were quite a few. Some of them seemed contrary to the person I know you to be."

"For one, I finally faced that Green Knight that everyone kept referring to. That was a harrowing experience. Lancelot and I used fake names and killed a creature called Grendel."

"Did you say Grendel?

"Yes. Why?"

"In high school, I read a story called *Beowulf* who killed a monster named Grendel. Were you Beowulf?"

"Lancelot called himself Bear, and I called myself Wolf. My father knighted us as Sir Bearwolf. I guess over the years, the name evolved to Beowulf."

"Wow! You seem to be in every legendary story I've ever read. So, what else happened?"

"I married a woman named Ragnelle, but she died. We had a child named Lovell, whom I haven't seen in years. I wronged him terribly. I left him with the Lady of the Lake to raise. I was in a really bad place when Ragnelle died, and after so many years I felt too guilty to go back for him. I'm sorry, but I still can't talk about it very much."

"I'm sorry."

"I went to the future, at least the future for me, and took the name Robin Fitzooth, but people started calling me Robin Hood."

"You were Robin Hood too. I can't believe it. He's even more famous than D'Artagnan. I'm going to have to go back and read more about him now. I wonder who else famous you may have been? Did you have merry men with you, and was there really a Maid Marian?"

"I don't know that I would call them merry. I started out with a group of women, and the leader was called Marian. She was known as the Green Knight of the Hood, and her followers were known as the Order of the Green Hood. That's how I ended up getting called Robin Hood." D'Artagnan told Diega about his time as Robin Hood and how they made gunpowder from his memory about Aramis describing how it was produced.

"That's not at all how the stories described it. Marian wasn't portrayed that way at all."

"You can't believe everything you read in books."

"I've missed hearing you say that," smiled Diega. "Were you really that good of an archer?"

"That, you can believe from the books and movies. I grew to enjoy using a bow as much as I did using a sword."

"Was the part about splitting the arrow true?"

"It is, but I had a little help on that one with a magical arrow. They called the shot a *Robin Hood.*"

"They still do. Tell me more about Marian."

"She was a fiercely independent woman and a true warrior, one of the best I've ever seen, along with you. The leadership and organization she showed in forming an army of women was truly remarkable, and she led men, who said they would never be led by a woman. She was remarkable. She was my greatest love. I married Marian, and the next day I traveled back in time. I still miss her tremendously to this day."

Diega noticed the sadness on his face at the mention of having to leave Marian, and she changed the subject. "What are you doing now?"

"Currently, I'm the King of Norway, Orkney and Lothian. I'm King Lot II. Oh, I have a daughter named Gersemi. Her mother is named Freya."

"Isn't she a goddess!"

"Yes."

"You have the most interesting life of anyone I've ever heard of."

"My life has come with its share of heartbreaks too." He told her about the treachery and deception of Morgan Le Fay, Mordred, his fight with Lancelot, and how he faked his death by using his last wish. "The masquerading of Mordred, as me, ruined my reputation. I'm sure that's why you've read conflicting stories about me."

"I can't imagine how hurtful that must have been. You deserve so much better. I hope that you can find peace, love, and joy in your life once you return home." Diega had pulled out the black hood that she had been forced to wear in the Bastille and was fumbling with it.

"Why are you still carrying that with you? I would have thought that you would have rid yourself of it."

"I'm going to keep it. I don't know why, in case you were going to ask. I just want to keep it as a remembrance of the hopelessness I felt in the Bastille and how I still got past all of that. It's somehow therapeutic."

D'Artagnan reached out and put his hand on hers. "I also wish you peace, love, and joy when you return to your time."

"I'm going to miss you terribly. I don't want to think of not seeing you again."

"My love will always be with you."

"Do you think that I'm a descendant of yours? I could take a sample of your blood back and get it DNA tested to see if we are related."

"I can't help but think we are related, perhaps through Lovell or Gersemi."

"Or another child you may have that you don't know about," smiled Diega.

"You're making me out to be promiscuous." D'Artagnan smiled to show Diega that he had not taken offense.

"Do you really think this is the end of your time traveling? I wonder if I will have more adventures ahead?"

D'Artagnan motioned for the bartender to bring another bottle of wine and thought for a moment. "As I said, I have a feeling that I won't time travel any more, and I do think that Excalibur has more adventures in store for you."

Diega swallowed the last of the wine in her glass, enjoying the taste of the wine as the bartender brought another bottle and poured some more into her glass. Diega sniffed the wine inside her glass. The fruity aroma was intoxicating. She swirled the wine in her glass, took a sip, and held it in her mouth, experiencing it to the fullest. "This is probably the best wine, I've ever had."

"Keep drinking, and it **will** be the best wine you've ever had, at least, until tomorrow when you wake up with a headache."

"I don't care. It's worth it to be here with you. I went out with my boyfriend to a bar shortly before I traveled to this time. While I was there, I couldn't help but dream about sitting here with you drinking and talking in this tavern. Do you think they have bourbon and cigars here? That would be the ultimate!"

"I don't think so."

"Well, you can't have it all, I suppose. Back to Excalibur, you talk about it as if it were sentient. Do you think it is?"

"Rationally, it doesn't make sense for a sword to be sentient. I can't help wondering though if the sword is a reflection of someone just as the brilliance of the sword in daylight is a reflection of the sun. I don't know how else to explain all of the coincidences and connections otherwise. Just think about how we met the first time, and me just happening to be in the cell next to yours this time, and there just happening to be a tunnel already dug from my cell to yours."

"Who could be behind it all though? God?"

"I don't know, and I don't know for what purpose. It seems to have gone beyond just being a sword destined for King Arthur."

Several hours and several bottles of wine passed as the two kept talking.

"This was one of the worst days of my life and one of the best nights of my life," said an inebriated Diega.

"Likewise."

"What happened in the books and movies about the Three Musketeers?" asked D'Artagnan.

"It's complicated, and it depends on the movie. The book has Athos and Porthos dying and Aramis left alive at the end. D'Artagnan becomes Marshal of France just before he is killed in a battle. There is also a part of the book devoted to the Man in the Iron Mask. I feel like it had to be based off what we just went through. I was even told I would have to wear an iron mask if I was disobedient."

"What do you plan to do when you get back?"

"You mean until I'm swept away again on some time traveling adventure? I think I'm going to study history, as much as I hate the subject. I do have to admit that experiencing it makes one more appreciative though. I don't want to get caught unaware like I was this time. I can't believe I said I was from Spain when there was a war going on between France and Spain. Completely stupid! I think I will also make it a point to keep my Springfield Hellcat with me at all times. I'm afraid if I sleep with it, I may accidentally shoot myself! Carrying something valuable is also a must, but I remember you saying that something can't exist in two different places at the same time and that it was easier going into the future with something valuable than it is going into the past."

"That gun of yours is something that's still hard for me to believe. Everyone was shocked when it kept firing without you having to reload after each shot."

"There's so much in the future that would be inconceivable for people of an earlier time." Diega finished another glass of wine. Their current bottle was close to empty. "I think I'm definitely drunk. I can now say with certainty that this is the best wine I've ever had."

"I told you." D'Artagnan brushed a hand through his hair, and a strand fell loose.

Diega collected it without D'Artagnan seeing it. I am going to have this DNA tested, she thought to herself. "It's getting late; I dread this night ending."

"Let's keep talking while we can. Tell me about your boyfriend."

I haven't known Spencer long, but we hit it off well. We have fun together, but I don't know how serious our relationship is. I don't know what to tell him when I get back or how much time will have passed. Explaining my new haircut will be challenging. I know I'm telling you more than you asked. My parents think I'm wasting my life. They want me to go to college, but I don't have a desire to yet. I still don't know what I want to do with my life."

"Take it from me. What you want to do is ever changing. I don't know what's in store for me either or how much of my time will have passed. I could go back, and someone may have usurped my throne." D'Artagnan picked up the bottle to pour some more wine into his glass, but the bottle was empty. Besides them and the bartender, one other person remained in the bar, and he was passed out in his chair. "It looks like it's time for us to go, unfortunately."

"Have you thought about Constance?" burst Diega suddenly.

"I have. I've known greater loves since then, but I have thought of her, especially since being back here. I have no clue where she is buried or how to find out."

"Perhaps, if we're still here tomorrow, we can try to find out."

"I truly believe we will back in our own times tomorrow."

"I still can't believe we're going to leave Excalibur here. Shouldn't we try to retrieve it somehow? Maybe if you went to the Queen Regent, she would give it back to you."

"Perhaps, for both things you mentioned. If we're not here though, I'm sure Excalibur will find a way to bring you to it somehow, somewhere, in some time. Let's try to find a place to spend the night."

"Where?"

"I don't know, but it won't be safe around here."

"We could go back to where I arrived in this time. It's only a few miles outside of town. We'd have to spend the night in the woods though."

"I've done it many times. It might not be safe getting there though at this time of night."

"Who would mess with D'Artagnan, Beowulf, Robin Hood, the father of a goddess, and Sir Gawain?"

565 AD

Sir Perceforest walked into the room where Sir Galahad was lying on his bed. "We received word that Emperor Justinian has died."

"I'm not far behind," moaned Sir Galahad. Raised voices made their way into the room occupied by Sir Galahad. "What's going on in the other room?"

"Some of the knights are arguing whether you or your father, Sir Lancelot, was the greatest knight.

"Ask them all to come in."

"Are you sure you are up for it?"

"It's either now or never. I have some last words and instructions for them."

Sir Perceforest stepped to the door and motioned for the knights to come in.

"Gather close," wheezed Sir Galahad. "My voice is weak." The twelve knights gathered close to Galahad. "So, you were arguing which was the greater knight, Sir Lancelot or me. Don't you remember the disciples of our Lord and Savior, Jesus Christ, were arguing who was the greatest? Jesus answered by saying whoever among you who is the least, is the greatest. My father, Sir Lancelot, died many years ago, and he would be the first to tell you he made many mistakes. I may have found the Holy Grail and many other artifacts, but any who find the Master is greater. Stop arguing amongst yourselves. I have instructions that I want you to carry out. Believe me when I say that within one hundred years, the control of Jerusalem will change hands. There are many treasures that need your protection. The twelve of you will be among the first to guard the religious artifacts that we have recovered. Sir Lohengrin?"

"I am here," he stepped forward and knelt by the bed of Sir Galahad.

"You were with me when I buried my father and took Excalibur from him. Please lay Excalibur on my chest."

Sir Lohengrin walked to the corner of the room where Excalibur, in its scabbard, leaned against the wall. He picked it up, carried it to the bed where Sir Galahad lay, and placed the sword on his torso. He picked up Sir Galahad's hands and laid them on the hilt.

Sir Galahad coughed, and a small amount of blood dribbled from his lower lip. Sir Lohengrin took a cloth and wiped the blood off Sir Galahad's mouth. Sir Galahad spoke softly. "Thank you, old friend. This sword belonged to King Arthur. Bury it with me; it can't fall into the wrong hands. Bury me here in Jerusalem."

"I will."

"I love you all. We have been on many adventures together. Please leave me for a moment. I want to pray before I pass from this world. Until we meet again."

The knights exited Sir Galahad's room. In the main room, each one knelt and prayed for Sir Galahad. After an hour, they opened the door to Sir Galahad's room where he lay dead. His hands were in the position that Sir Lohengrin placed them. He looked at peace. A great knight had passed, and the great sword, Excalibur, was gone.

2025 AD

"Where have you been?" questioned Spencer, half angrily and half worried out of his mind. "You've been gone for weeks! You were supposed to go to your parents. When you never showed, they were worried sick. You didn't even give them my phone number! They came down here looking for you and basically camped outside of your door. Luckily, they had only been here a day when I came by to water your plants. When I told them that you thought someone had been following you, they were really scared. We went to the police and filled out a missing person report. And what did you do to your hair? It looks hideous. You need to tell me what's going on."

Diega's mind raced in an effort to find the perfect lie, one that would calm everyone down without everyone thinking she was crazy. The race for the lie wasn't going well. The car was circling the track, but the finish line was nowhere in sight. Damn, she thought. I'm going to have to make this up as I go, and it will be a car wreck, no, a train wreck, for sure. She finally just blurted out, "I couldn't go. You know how I dreaded facing them and getting the inquisition."

"You could have told someone, them, me. We thought something had happened to you. You don't let anyone know anything, and you come back weeks later looking like hell. Are you seeing someone else? Have you gotten mixed up in something?"

"Gee, I care about you too," she said sarcastically.

"That's the point. You don't care, or you would have said something. We thought the person following you had kidnapped you. And don't try to avoid the subject!"

"You know I can take care of myself."

"Stop right there. You always make yourself out to be some superhero, who can't be stopped, but there's always someone out there who's better, no matter who you are. Besides, they could have gotten the drop you on you."

"I'm sorry. I didn't know it was going to cause all of this trouble."

"Trouble's not the half of it. If you think I'm tough on you, just wait until you see your parents."

"I'll go to North Carolina tomorrow, and you can drive me there if it makes you feel better."

"Oh, we don't have to drive anywhere. They're still here. They've been staying in a hotel for weeks. They've been worried sick about you, but once your father finds out that you're ok, he is going to be really pissed for being gone so long from his job."

Diega was sick, herself. She still felt hungover from all the wine she had drunk. Wine and time travel do not mix well. Nor had she recuperated yet from her time in the Bastille, mentally or physically; the shock of the past few weeks had started to settle in now that she was back and safe. Add to all that the ordeal she was facing with Spencer and the upcoming knockdown drag out shitfest with her parents. She almost felt she would have been better off to have remained in France in 1650 ... almost. Absorbed in her own thoughts, she had not realized that Spencer was on the phone with her parents.

"They said for you not to move a muscle; they're on their way now. I don't envy you. Afterwards, we'll have to talk with the police." The anger and worry were suddenly sloughed off, and Spencer hugged her tightly.

Diega felt as though she would pop from its pressure.

"I'm sorry to be talking to you this way," he said. "I've been so worried about you. I was so distraught thinking that something bad had happened."

"I'm sorry too. I had to get away for a while; I didn't mean to cause this much angst."

Diega and Spencer went into her apartment, and within five minutes her parents were barging through the door. Her mother and father immediately ran to her and hugged her even tighter than Spencer had. Diega didn't need to be a psychologist to know the sequence of stages that were about to unfold. First, relief, followed by confusion, followed by anger. There would be other stages, but these first ones would be the hardest. What was she thinking? Hell, they would all be hard.

"We were so worried about you," said her mother with tears and sobs. They continued holding her for what seemed like minutes.

Finally, her father asked, "What happened? Were you abducted?"

"No. I just wanted some time alone to gather my thoughts. I knew I needed to decide what I really wanted to do with my life before I came to talk with you."

"Well, you could have told us so that we weren't worried to death that you were hurt or worse," exclaimed her father.

Before her father could say anything else, the veil covering her mother's eyes lifted. "What's happened to you? Your hair! You look like you've been beaten, and you must have lost fifteen pounds!

Both mother and father immediately turned to Spencer with angry looks. Spencer looked like a wild animal that had been caught in a hunter's trap.

Diega quickly intervened before the accusations started flying. "Spencer was in the dark as much as you. I haven't seen him this entire time. He wouldn't do anything to hurt me."

Relief showed on her parents faces but not for long.

"Then what has happened to you and where have you been?" asked her father. "Are you into drugs?"

"Lord no. You know I would never do that. I've been different places."

"There's been no activity on your credit cards. How did you pay for anything while you were gone?"

"I took cash," Diega said quickly. I was camping part of the time. I decided to get a new hair style, but I had no idea that the stylist would do what she did. She must have been one of those artsy, modern types. Believe me, I've cried for days over it."

"I can smell a lie a mile away," interjected her father. I don't believe one word of what you're saying. There's a whole lot of something you're not telling us. Do you know what strings I had to pull to be away this long?"

Relief to confusion had passed. Now they were in the full stages of anger.

Her mother started rattling off Spanish so quickly that Diega could barely keep up. Spanish was always the language she resorted to when she was this upset.

"You're coming back with us immediately, whether you like it or not," bellowed her father. We've had enough of this, you finding yourself. You're going to come back and live like a normal, responsible woman."

Now, it was Diega's turn for anger. "I'm supposed to live like a normal responsible woman of my age but under the roof and dictates of my parents!"

"I don't take back talking from anybody. We're going to get your life in order for you, like it or not."

Diega was ready to explode, but a spark of rationality entered her mind. She closed her eyes, breathed the way she had been taught as part of meditation in martial arts, and counted slowly to three. "Mom and dad, can we talk rationally about this for a moment?"

Diega's father started to say something, but Diega's mother gave him a *be open and patient* look. He stopped and let Diega's mother take over. Diega's mother nodded affirmatively.

"I'll go back with you to North Carolina, and we can discuss plans. I know you have my best interests at heart."

Spencer interrupted before she could continue. "With my job, I can probably move to North Carolina."

"What is your job, exactly?" asked Diega's father in a deliberate and agitated manner.

"Oh, he doesn't even know himself what his job is," stated Diega.

"How is that ...," began her father, but he was quickly interrupted. Spencer's face had already paled as the blood drained from it.

"I was kidding!" exclaimed Diega. "He just has one of those high paying, difficult to explain jobs. And I don't know if I want to relocate to North Carolina. That's something we can talk about, but I'm happy here in Jacksonville."

Diega tried to convince her parents that she would be ok to spend the night at her apartment by herself, and she promised that she would not go anywhere. Her convincing skills did not win out though. Her dad said that they had already spent enough at the hotel. Diega thought that was just an excuse to cover their fear that she would leave again. Of course, she had not planned on time traveling in the first place, and if she did again, her parents being in the spare room couldn't stop her. What a FUBAR mess!

Only now that she had time to really absorb the fact that she was back safely did she experience a breakdown. With her parents in the next room, she could not cry, rant, or rave; she had to suffer in silence. The fact that she killed several people in 1650 France bore heavy on her, as well as the fact that she had not grieved the deaths of the three musketeers. They had saved her life at the cost of their own. So much death and destruction were on her hands. It was all her fault, and the only thing she was doing now was arguing nonsense with her parents. She so wished she could go back and undo all that she had done. But, she remembered Sir Gawain's explanation of time existing all at once and that a person could not go back in time and change the past. Still, she felt she had robbed those men she killed of having descendants to carry on their lineage. She had never killed anyone before, and she felt as though she were going to be sick. If only she hadn't killed the first four soldiers who tried to stop her, things would have been different. Saving them would have spared the lives of the others she had killed. Her mind drifted back to the 1650 French tavern and her conversation with Sir Gawain.

"How do you deal with killing someone?" she asked. "You seem to be a very religious person. How do you reconcile killing with serving God?"

"All life is precious," answered Sir Gawain. "But that also includes your own. I'm not a priest, but Aramis explained it one time that makes a lot of sense. He said that murder is not the same as killing. Murder is taking a life in vengeance or for selfish motives. Self-defense is protecting your own life, which is also precious. Killing on the battlefield is self-defense for your country and its citizens. I don't know if that is the way God sees it or not, but what he said made a lot of sense to me. I'm sure there is a fine line in there somewhere, but you should not purposely try to cross it. Any time, I've had to kill, I still ask God's forgiveness, whether I thought I was in the right or not."

Diega's thoughts returned to the present, and what Gawain had said calmed her immensely. She immediately prayed to God, asking for forgiveness. With her mind more or less at ease, she drifted off into a deep and peaceful sleep that let her forget that day as well as the past few weeks.

Diega had been in North Carolina for a week. Her father went immediately back to work, but she spent a lot of time with her mother. They went to the coast several days that week, including Atlantic Beach, Fort Macon, Beaufort, and the Cape Lookout Lighthouse. The day trips rejuvenated Diega and brought her much needed serenity. Diega's mother did not push her during those outings, but back at home, she probed Diega to see what her daughter might want to do. "I wish I felt a true calling, a purpose," said Diega, "but nothing seems to resonate with me."

Diega rarely had time by herself. She thought that her mother and father were keeping a close watch on her in case she tried to leave. She wished she could confide in them about her ability to travel through time, but they would never believe her. She couldn't blame them; she wouldn't believe it herself if she were in their shoes. On one occasion when she was by herself, she inquired about having the hair from Sir Gawain DNA tested to see if he was an ancestor. The cost was more than she could afford. Besides, she was told that no tests were sophisticated enough to determine from a hair follicle the information she wanted.

Spencer remained in Jacksonville, and for the most part, left her alone. He called her one night and shared some research he had done into colleges. "I found a university that is accredited by an accrediting body recognized by the Department of Education that you might find very interesting. The university is relatively new. It's called the American Modern University. They allow a lot of experiential and military credit, and there is a program that you can tailor to your own needs. The classes are mostly online, and you can probably earn your bachelor's degree in a relatively short time."

Diega explored the university's website and found it very interesting. The program that Spencer mentioned would allow Diega to continue to explore a lot of personal interest courses. She completed an application, and they did a credit evaluation. She had taken several dual-enrollment courses in high school that would count as credit. Her military background gave her additional credit hours, and her fencing and martial arts background led to more credits. She also took and passed credit by exams in two levels of Spanish and one level of French. Combined, the credit awarded totaled about fifty semester hours. She would need one hundred-twenty hours to graduate. If she took eighteen hours in the fall, eighteen hours in the spring, and six hours in the summer, she could potentially have around ninety hours of credit after one year. That would leave about thirty hours of credit remaining, which she could easily finish by the spring of the second year. Her parents weren't entirely thrilled at this option, but Diega thought that they at least saw this as forward movement. With their partial blessing, she returned to Jacksonville and enrolled in eighteen hours online. To even her surprise, she found herself enrolling in several history courses: History of Western Europe to the year 1000, History of Western Europe from 1000 to 1800, Survey of History of the Americas to 1000, and Survey of History of the Americas from 1000 to 1800. She also enrolled in World Mythologies and a Great books course. She was able to use GI Bill Benefits to cover the cost of the fall semester. Although these were courses she had sworn that she truly detested, if she were to time travel again, these could help prepare her for whatever time she found herself in. She swore that she wouldn't make a stupid mistake again, if she could help it, like she did in France. Of course, if time travel took her to China, she would be screwed. In her spare time, she planned to take equestrian lessons, which she could also count as experiential credit. Depending on where she landed, if she did time travel again, being able to ride a horse could come in handy. By the end of summer of 2026, Diega had accumulated an unbelievable 102 hours of credit. Between her schedule and Spencer's work, they found little time to see each other, but the relationship still managed to survive. She only needed 18 more hours to graduate, which could be done in one semester. Unfortunately, the last semester would have to wait; Excalibur had other plans for her.

541 AD

King Lot II had ruled for forty years. He had been a good King, and his realm had enjoyed peace. At this moment, the trespasser to King Lot II's tomb had no interest in any of that, only in the Book of Thoth that lay enfolded in the king's arms with the king's hands resting one on top of the other. The top hand donned the magical ring made by the dwarves, Brokkr and Sindri. The trespasser removed the ring and vaporized it, leaving no trace of matter present. Since Gersemi wouldn't succeed her father, a new king now ruled, Sæmingr, the son of Odin. The ring would do him no good since it only worked for King Lot and King Lot II, but the Book of Thoth could be used by the new king to create a lot of trouble. The Book of Thoth definitely did not need to be discovered by King Sæmingr. "Gods need no more power than they already have," spoke the intruder aloud. "Taking this book will be in everyone's best interests, and surely, I can resist the sweet and deadly temptations issuing from the book."

1211 AD

Archer Fitzooth walked into the room where his mother sat by an open window. "Daydreaming again, mother?"

"Oh, you startled me, Archer. I was just thinking back about a time before you were born."

"Speaking of such, Will Scarlet and a woman are here to see you."

"Wonderful, send them in."

Archer beckoned them in, play-sparring with Will as he came in. "Still carrying that walking stick, I see."

"Yes," replied Will, "an old injury from back in the day that plagues me every now and then."

"I'll give you all some privacy," said Archer, as he left the room.

"Archer so loves to spend time with you, Will. You've been a good father-figure to him."

"Glad to help. Being the son of the legendary Robin Hood can't be easy."

"No. I'm certain it is not easy, but he's probably tired of me telling him about the old stories."

"The ones you don't tell, I do."

"Goodness, maybe you'd better tell me some of those stories yourself sometime. But I'm sure that's not the reason you're here. You know every time I see you, I'm amazed at how you haven't changed a bit while I just get older. Would you like to introduce your guest?"

"In a little while. The reason I'm here is actually an urgent matter."

Marian appeared shocked; she shifted in her chair uneasily.

"Oh, I don't think it's urgent for you," clarified Will, "but it is for us."

"You leave me quite curious."

"Let me cut to the chase. What I'm about to say may be very difficult for you to believe, but matters close at hand dictate that I be straightforward."

"I think you would be quite surprised that I take shocking news well."

"No doubt."

"So, tell me what is so urgent for you."

"When Robin disappeared, most people were quite upset and suspicious, suspecting foul play."

"I remember and prefer not to dwell on that."

"I understand, but what if I told you I was not shocked."

"I would have to ask why. You were close friends with Robin, I would think you would have been more upset than most."

"Oh, I was upset but not for reasons you may think."

"I believe you said you were getting to the point?" Marian was beginning to get unsettled.

"Very well. Robin Hood, or should I say Sir Gawain, was called back to his own time."

A shocked look came over Marian's face as the blood drained, leaving her pale. "What did you say?"

"Nothing that you don't already know."

"How do you know such a thing?"

"From my mother. Countess Marian, I would like to introduce you to my mother, Blanchemal."

"Why, she is no older than you! She can't be your mother."

"Blanchemal is a fairy."

"Such things do not exist."

"Most people would say the ability to travel through time does not exist. Long before, Sir Gawain, as Robin Hood, met you. Blanchemal conceived a son from Sir Gawain. That son is me. I had never met my father, and as many magical beings do not age, even those of mixed heritage, I longed for the chance to meet him when he traveled to this time. So, I took the name Will Scarlet and joined his group of merry men."

"This is true," confessed Blanchemal. "I loved Gawain. He saved my life, and I pledged to always help him. I helped him escape when he was imprisoned by King John. We only lay together once. I can tell you that when he returned to his own time, he was heartbroken over losing you. Even though I loved him, he didn't feel the same toward me. We were friends, but his heart belonged to you."

"What happened to Robin, I mean Sir Gawain, when he returned?"

"It is a long story, but due to treachery while he was here, his reputation was tarnished. King Arthur's kingdom fell apart, and Gawain was believed to have been killed by Sir Lancelot. He was not killed though, but he was badly injured, and I helped to save his life. He left shortly afterwards to go to Norway where his father was King. Everyone believed Sir Gawain to be dead. I hid my pregnancy from Gawain, and my son Gingalain was born after Gawain left for Norway. When Gawain arrived in this time as Robin, I didn't tell him about Gingalain, but I told Gingalain, who, against my wishes joined his father in your group."

"I'm stunned, exclaimed Marian. "And you never told him that he was your father?"

"No. I wanted to, but being by his side was enough, and I didn't want the news to distract him, which could have caused ill consequences."

"So, Archer is your half-brother. Why are you telling me this now, after all these years?"

"Magical beings have been disappearing for hundreds of years. Gingalain and I are some of the very few who are left. I believe that our luck has run out and that we will also disappear very soon."

"I thought magical creatures were just myths. Why did they disappear?"

"I don't know," replied Blanchemal, "but I suspect I will soon find out. We are being hunted by someone, and I sense they are close by. We've been able to hide for a long time, but this hunter now has our scent and won't relent until we too are gone."

"So, what do you want me to do? Are Archer or I in danger too?"

"We suspect not," answered Blanchemal, "but out of a sense of being extra cautious, we felt we must warn you."

When Blanchemal and Will Scarlet left, Archer went in to see his mother. "Who was that with Will?

"It's a long story, perhaps better for another time."

"That was awkward," replied Blanchemal, once they had left Marian's estate and were on the road leading through the woods.

"I know. Why did you wait so long to say anything to Marian?"

"Once you've been in love, you'll understand. Whoever said love is not jealous must have been talking about a completely different kind of love than what I've seen. Don't get me wrong. I always wanted Gawain to be happy, and if it weren't with me, then I wanted him to find it with someone. That doesn't mean it doesn't hurt though."

"So, what are we going to do?" worried Gingalain. "How do we hide more than we've been hiding? And how is this being who is hunting us able to know that we have magic or even how to find us?"

"I don't know the answers to any of those questions," contemplated Blanchemal.

"I'd be happy to answer them for you," came a voice from nowhere, startling them.

Blanchemal and Gingalain spun around but didn't see anyone. When they turned back around, the face of another person was inches from their own. Both Blanchemal and Gingalain jumped back.

"You're the one who is causing the disappearances, aren't you?" shuddered Blanchemal.

"Yes, indeed. I must commend you on being able to elude me all of these years. It's actually quite ironic when I come to think about it. Don't worry, you'll understand what I mean by that in about one minute from now. You and your son are among the last magical beings. I can count on one hand the magical beings who are still left. Now, I'll be happy to answer any questions you have. I assume they are the big three: Who am I? Why am I doing this? How did I find you? Am I right?"

"You're really gloating right now, aren't you?" Blanchemal stated, matter-of-factly.

"Wow! That really took me by surprise! I have to give you credit on that one. Good for you. That's a question I've never been asked before. But the answer is ... Yes! I'm taking great pleasure in this. Now, I assume the rest of your questions are what I call the big three; so, I'll just randomly pick one and answer it. Let's start with, *how did I find you?* This object right here ... hold on ... I have it here somewhere ... Ah here it is. I pulled in right out of thin air as if by magic." He held it up to them. "This is like a magnet that directs me to any person or creature who has magic."

"What is that?" quavered Gingalain.

"This is called the Book of Thoth. I bet your mother knows what it is, don't you Blanchey?"

"Yes. I do. How did you get it? Sir Gawain had it."

"And I let him keep it. But once he died, I assumed he would have no further use of it. And there was no point in letting it lie there with him."

Tears filled Blanchemal's eyes.

"I didn't mean to make you sad, dearie. Everyone does eventually die. Well, that is everyone but me. I've heard it said that there is always someone who can beat a person, no matter how strong that person is. I suppose the same would have to hold true for death. You see the logic in that don't you? By the way, there is the irony I was alluding to, earlier. Was that a minute? It's hard to get a feel for time when you have an eternity of it. You get the irony, right? You loved Sir Gawain, who had the book, and you're one of the last magical people I find. Think of all the time you've had as a gift from me to honor Sir Gawain."

"Stop being so flippant and just do what you came to do," fumed Gingalain.

"Careful. I can make this as painless or as painful as I wish. Besides, I haven't answered all of the questions yet. Let's see. Let's go with, *why am I doing this?* This book will give one the knowledge of all magic in the world. But, it's full of traps. Morgan le Fay had the book and avoided many of them, but she still fell into one of them. She had the right idea about Excalibur though. That sword has magic that will cut through all of the trappings. Once I get the sword, I'll cut through all of the trappings, finish reading the book, and have all the magic there is. In the meantime, the book grows stronger with each magical being it ensnares, which gives me more power even without reading it all the way through. I've captured gods, fairies, leprechauns, elves, dwarves, genies, sorcerers, you name it."

Blanchemal and Gingalain huddled against each other and clung tightly to one another.

"And now for the last answer to the last question, *who am I?* And pause for effect! Some people call me the trickster god, but I go by the name Loki!

The book began to glow in Loki's hands. He opened it, and Blanchemal felt herself being sucked in through a vortex. She used all the magic she had, to disappear, to push herself back, to vaporize the book, but nothing worked. Loki just stood smiling as Blanchemal and Gingalain struggled to keep from being sucked in.

Even as they struggled, Loki continued to deride them. "Hurry up, will you? I've got just a couple more people to find."

Blanchemal could hold on no longer. She was pulled into the book and disappeared. Gingalain was being pulled even more strongly now that his mother was in the book. The vortex was too strong, and Gingalain was finally pulled in. Loki began to shut the book, but it wouldn't close. He pushed hard against it, but it wouldn't budge. He looked down and saw the hooked end of Gingalain's walking stick jamming the book, preventing it from closing. The Book of Thoth shook violently and fell from Loki's clutching hands. Slowly, the book began to open wider. Gingalain was propping open the portal with the stick. Appearing next to Gingalain was a host of other magical prisoners.

"This can't be," sputtered Loki.

Suddenly, beams of light exploded from the book. The thoughts from a myriad of languages were being inscribed in midair, a few words from one language, followed by words from different languages, all juxtaposed against one another as if the thoughts of hundreds or thousands of beings were vying for primacy over the other.

Panicked, Loki did the only thing that came into his mind, which was to wrestle away the stick from Gingalain. Loki grabbed the hooked end, and all was quiet. Nature was going about its usual business, oblivious to the magical cataclysm that had unfurled. Birds were singing. Small mammals scurried over leaves. The breeze was blowing gently. Gingalain was standing shakily, propping himself up with the Club of Dagda, and holding the Book of Thoth.

From the trees, Archer ran up and grabbed him. "Will, what just happened."

"Help me back to your estate. I need to sit down."

Peering from behind a tree was a figure who was unnoticed by the two.

With the Club of Dagda on one side and Archer on the other, Gingalain was able to make it back to the estate. Archer took him into the sitting room where Marian was still looking out the window.

"Will," shrieked Marian. "What happened? You're as pale as a ghost!"

"I think it's time that we be truthful with Archer."

"If you think it best," replied Marian.

"Truthful about what?" challenged Archer. He glanced back and forth between Will and Marian. Beads of sweat popped out on his face, and the hair on his arms stood erect.

"Although you know me as Will Scarlet, my real name is Gingalain." Gingalain repeated the story to Archer that Blanchemal and he had told Marian not more than an hour before.

"I can't get beyond the fact that we're half-brothers," marveled Archer. "As a matter of fact, I still can't get beyond what I witnessed in the forest. You were using the walking stick. Is it more than an ordinary walking stick?"

"It's called the Club of Dagda. Sir Gawain, or Robin Hood, procured it on one of his quests. Blanchemal, my mother, told me that it allows people to step through time and could supposedly bring back people from the dead. I never really believed any of that, but it brought me back from whatever realm I was in. When Gawain left for Norway, he gave the Club of Dagda to Blanchemal. He didn't want the Club of Dagda, the Book of Thoth, and Excalibur all together because someone might use them for evil intentions, which is exactly what happened."

"How does this Club of Dagda work?" wondered Archer.

"I don't really know. Whatever happened that allowed me to escape was by accident rather than intent."

"I wish there was someone here who knew," chimed in Marian.

Gingalain scratched his chin. "You may be on to something there."

"I don't know anyone around who would know. You said yourself that almost all magical beings are gone."

"Not really gone, just imprisoned in this book, which seemed to exist outside of time. But there is one person, who may not have been captured."

"Really? Who could that be?" questioned Archer.

"I remember tales of Merlin. He had supposedly been killed by the time I was born, but perhaps the Club of Dagda could reach back to a time he was alive in the past and bring him here."

"You can use the Club of Dagda to do that!" said Archer excitedly.

"I have no clue, but I can certainly try."

"How?"

"Maybe if I concentrate on Merlin hard enough, the Club of Dagda might bring him to me."

"Well, I don't think trying would cause any harm," speculated Marian.

Gingalain held out his arm parallel to the ground with the hooked end of the club away from him. He tried to clear his mind and enter a meditative state. He concentrated on his breathing and let his mind go completely empty. When he felt at peace, he began to concentrate on Merlin, thinking about what his mother had said of the man. Marian and Archer were afraid to move or make a sound for fear of breaking his concentration. What seemed like an hour passed with Gingalain in the same position as when he started. At first, Marian thought she felt a slight push against her. A few more minutes passed, and she felt a stronger push. Then, everyone in the room was knocked backwards. They shakily stood up, and standing before them was a man with long white hair and beard, dressed in a tunic of some sort. He was smiling at them.

"I take it you want to see me?"

"Merlin?" hesitated Gingalain.

"Yes."

"You speak English?" questioned Archer.

"I read the first page of the Book of Thoth," he said smiling. "Curiosity got the better of me."

"I don't understand," replied Archer.

"Your father," interjected Marian, "was able to speak our language because he read the first page in the Book of Thoth. He told me that reading the first page allows the person to speak any language fluently."

"That's correct," praised Merlin. "The trick is that once most people read the first page, they want to continue reading, which inevitably leads them into some trap that prevents them from reading further. Sir Gawain was one of those rare individuals who had the self-discipline to stop after reading the first page."

"Aren't you dead by now?" inquired Archer.

"Maybe. Maybe not. But I don't think you asked me here to discuss my state of being."

Gingalain frowned at Archer, "We don't want to be disrespectful, but we have lots of questions that we hope you can answer." Gingalain provided Merlin with a summary of the events that had transpired.

"I have the gift of foresight, and I foresaw this happening one day. So let me cut to the chase and give you some information without you having to ask questions one after another. Sir Gawain had four children, Archer by Marian, Gingalain by Blanchemal, Lovell by Ragnelle, and Gersemi by the goddess Freya. Ragnelle was a dear love. Blanchemal was a friend with whom he sought intimate solace on one occasion. Freya was out of duty, but also lust. Marian was his truest of loves, his soulmate." Merlin smiled at Marian. The last sentence had comforted her.

"Gingalain and Gersemi, due to their mothers having magic, remain youthful. Archer will age as a normal human. Lovell is an enigma. Since both of his parents were mortal, he should age just like Archer. However, Lovell, due to his rightful feeling of abandonment, has misjudgingly sought dark magic and power, which he found in Morgan le Fay's spellbook and magical objects, including an amulet that lets him take over the body of another person. He remains youthful due to magic. He is one you need to look out for should you ever cross his path. To have come from love, he has turned murderous and evil. He killed the Lady of the Lake, a fairy who raised him. Lovell seeks to do harm to anyone associated with Sir Gawain. Probably, Gawain's greatest mistake was abandoning his son, Lovell. Sir Gawain was not in a good frame of mind at the time to raise Lovell, but that is no excuse. He had an opportunity to make things right. But, no one is perfect. Sir Gawain is closer to perfection than anyone I know, but close still misses the mark."

Merlin continued explaining to the assembled group before him. "In the forest, when Gingalain held open the portal of the Book of Thoth, you said that beams of light inscribed a message in midair. This message is a prophecy that the progeny of Sir Gawain will make things right, but she must endure many hardships along the way. I will transport the message to a monolith along the coast of England where she will one day see it, or should I say has already seen it, and Sir Gawain will translate the mixture of languages for her. The name of this woman is, or will be, Diega. She is a descendant of all of Sir Gawain's four children. The blood of Sir Gawain that has been dispersed amongst his four children will once again become as one at the appointed time. She will fulfill the prophecy and will make things right. You do not know what that will be. Only one of you will find out what that is. At this moment, the sword Excalibur is in the future. One day, Excalibur, the Club of Dagda, and the Book of Thoth will come together once more to fulfill a purpose."

Archer formulated his thought slowly. "If this person, Diega, will fulfill the prophecy in the future, then there is nothing for us to do, is there?"

Merlin laughed. "For one, you must have children! But don't link a prophecy with inaction on your part. For what is faith, but the fulfillment of belief based on action? In fact, young Archer, there is one thing I will ask you to do now. Marian, you still have Robin's bow and arrows."

"I do."

"That was a statement on my part, not a question," he smiled.

Marian left the room and returned momentarily with Robin Hood's bow and quiver of arrows.

"Let's all go outside," suggested Merlin. Once they were outside, Merlin instructed Marian to give the bow and arrows to her son. "Archer, you are appropriately named. I believe you have skill similar to your father's skill in archery."

"He's very good!" affirmed Marian.

Merlin observed the arrows. "There is one arrow from three given to Sir Gawain by the goddess Athena that has not yet been fired. Two of the arrows were imbued with magic to hit the target that the archer desires. Once shot, they lose their power and become regular arrows. Sir Gawain fired *a calling arrow* shortly after receiving the arrows. He fired another as Robin Hood." Merlin picked out an arrow. "This is the last of the three arrows given by Athena that is still imbued with magic. Gingalain, I want you to stand at twenty-five paces and hold the Club of Dagda in front of you. Archer, I want you to concentrate on the Club of Dagda, aim, and shoot."

Archer did as Merlin had instructed. He fit the arrow in the bow, concentrated on the Club of Dagda, aimed, and fired. The arrow sped to the club held by Gingalain in front of him. Instead of striking the club though, the arrow disappeared. "Where did the arrow go?" puzzled Archer.

"The arrow is in the Club of Dagda, waiting to be released," answered Merlin.

"How and when is the arrow released?" asked Gingalain.

"You will know when the time is right and what to do. You will go to the future, to Diega, using the Club of Dagda to get there. She will need your help."

"How? I don't know in what year she will be, where she will be, or even who she is?"

"Just like you brought me here, you will concentrate. This time you will concentrate on the progeny of Sir Gawain who is the descendant of all four of his children. The Club of Dagda will do the work and transport you there."

"Can the Club of Dagda be used to transport someone else through time?" asked Marian abruptly.

"You wish to go to Sir Gawain?" posited Merlin.

"I do. Archer, I love you and don't want to leave you. But I also wish to be with Sir Gawain. If there is a way for me to get there, I want to go."

"It's a huge risk!" cautioned Gingalain. "I don't know if I can do it. What if I send you hundreds of years before or after the time of Sir Gawain?"

"As Merlin said, have faith and take action. I have faith in you. Are you alright with my decision, Archer?"

"Of course, mother. I wish I could go with you, but I know that I am needed here. I will miss you. Please tell my father that I wish I could have met him, and that I'm proud to be his son."

"Of course, I will. When I leave, you will be the Earl of Huntingdon and Locksley." Marian and Archer hugged each other, and Marian kissed her son on his forehead with tears in her eyes. She turned to Merlin and Gingalain. "I'm ready."

"Can I take Marian there to make sure she is in the right time, and then come back?" inquired Gingalain.

"Unfortunately, no. You were already living then, and you can't go back and exist as two people at the same time." Merlin turned to Marian. "Get something warm to wear before you go. You will need it. Sir Gawain was known as King Lot II, and he lived in Norway."

Marian hurried inside and returned with several articles of clothing. Anxiously, she stood before Gingalain. "I will tell him about you too, Gingalain."

Gingalain smiled and nodded. He held out his arm parallel to the ground with the hooked end of the club away from him, went into a meditative state, and after several minutes, Marian disappeared. Both Gingalain and Archer were quiet for several minutes. Breaking the silence, Gingalain asked, "Do I take the Book of Thoth with me?"

"No," replied Merlin. "The book is filled with so much magic, and with magical creatures who can't concentrate with you, that you will not be able to transport the Book of Thoth through time with you."

"Then, how do we keep it safe until then?"

"I'll help with that," exclaimed Archer. "I will establish a group of knights, whose sole purpose will be to guard the Book of Thoth and keep it safe."

"That is wise," announced Merlin, "but this group will not always be able to guard it personally. There will come a time when they must hide it for safe keeping."

"Will Diega be able to find it?" asked Archer.

"Let me show you both something from the past," responded Merlin. "Hand the Club of Dagda to me." Gingalain presented the Club of Dagda to Merlin. "This Club can act as a mirror into time. I'm going to think about an event, and you will see back into time."

Gingalain and Archer focused on the Club of Dagda, not sure of what exactly would happen. As Merlin concentrated, a scene played out before their eyes.

475 AD

"I ask you to do one thing for me," said the genie.

"If I can," replied Gawain.

"Take the book with you. I trust your character to keep the book safe, especially since you avoided the temptation to keep reading further after you read the first page."

"Why don't you just destroy the book?

"The Book of Thoth cannot be destroyed, at least not without more powerful magic than even I have. It is to be a permanent reminder to me of my betrayal to my family. Will you do this for me?"

"I will."

"Do not doubt that your first wish will eventually come to pass, and use the remaining wishes wisely. Once they are gone, you will have no more."

The genie transformed into blue smoke that dissipated into nothingness.

The fifteen-year-old Sir Gawain turned and walked away. While Sir Gawain was walking away, blue smoke appeared and materialized into the genie. The genie pointed his finger towards Sir Gawain's back and spoke as though he were casting a magical spell on Sir Gawain or the Book of Thoth. Sir Gawain was far enough away that he apparently did not hear what the genie said. "A descendant of Sir Gawain will find the Book of Thoth and use it to fulfill a prophecy." Having spoken those words, the genie, once again, transformed into blue smoke and disappeared.

1211 AD

"So, Diega will be the descendant to find the Book of Thoth in the future," speculated Archer.

"That is correct," replied Merlin. "Walk with me into the forest." The three entered the forest and walked to the message that still hung in midair. Merlin put both hands on the message as if it were a physical object, and it disappeared. "I transported this to the coast of England where Sir Gawain and Diega saw it in the year 482 AD."

"I cannot fathom how time works," exclaimed Archer.

"Almost no one does," answered Merlin. "Now, Gingalain, are you ready to go to the future?"

"Before I go, please answer one more question. How did I escape from being held in the Book of Thoth?"

"The Club of Dagda can allow one to step through time. According to folklore, the Club of Dagda was fashioned from the very first tree on earth, but it would take more than that to allow one to travel through time. When Excalibur was created, an element from the beginning of time was placed into the cavity where the jewel was placed, along with blood from Sir Gawain. This is what linked Sir Gawain to Excalibur, and the element allowed Excalibur and Sir Gawain to travel through time. The element was created before the dimension of time was set and fixed. It was formed within the blink of an eye, before the most basic elements began to take shape that would go on to bind together to form the water, the sand, the air, and everything else you see. Only a few such elements exist that did not undergo the change to those that now exist. One of these same elements is in the Club of Dagda. That is what allows the Club to transport people through time. When Loki touched the Club, it allowed you to change places, so to speak, with Loki. You were freed, and Loki was imprisoned."

"I'm ready. Good-bye brother, and thank you, Merlin for all you've done and explained."

"Before you go, don't forget to send me back to where I was when you summoned me," smiled Merlin.

Gingalain entered a meditative state, and Merlin vanished. Keeping his eyes closed and remaining in the meditative state, Gingalain also vanished, leaving Archer alone, holding the Book of Thoth.

518 AD

"Always in a forest," Sir Gawain, or King Lot II as he was now known, muttered to himself. "Why can't I wake in a warm bed? I'm getting too old for this." The adjustment of his body to time travel never seemed to get any easier; nausea and confusion were always present with each travel. Perhaps it was appropriate that he was alone in the forest. He already missed Diega, and the loss of Athos, Porthos, and Aramis was especially bitter. King Lot II felt like Diega did. If he had not traveled back to 1650, the three musketeers would still have been alive. He didn't even have an opportunity to spend any quality time with his former friends and mentors.

The air was cold in the forest, but the trees at least blocked the wind. The previous night had been a celebration at seeing Diega again and for merely being alive. What he had told Diega was that today, if they were still alive, would be the day to mourn. King Lot II sat on a log and cried bitterly. Then he shouted to the top of his voice. Nothing eased his pain. All the loss, the betrayals, the sin of not taking responsibility for his children ... All of it was almost more than he could bear. He wished that Thor would come and smash him into the ground with Mjolnir.

After spending three hours alone in the forest, he felt spent and could neither mourn nor feel sorry for himself any longer. The exhaustion had also caught up with him. As he walked in the direction he thought the castle should be, he wondered how long he had been gone in this time. The time that had elapsed for him had been about a month. Had a month passed from him leaving to his return? As he got within sight of the castle tower, he saw a young, blonde-haired woman running to him. At least I have Gersemi.

"Father," shouted Gersemi. "I'm so glad to see you. One day, you were just gone! Did you travel through time again?"

"Yes."

"Where and to what time did you go?"

"I returned to France where I had been once before. The time was twenty-five years later. I witnessed the deaths of three of my closest friends. Deaths that were caused by them helping me. It was a very difficult time."

"I'm sorry, father. At least you are back here with me now. I'll take care of you."

King Lot II hugged Gersemi, and she bent down so that he could kiss the top of her head. "Thank you, Gersemi."

"Why do you think you traveled through time?"

"The sword Excalibur was there, but I think my travel had more to do with a person this time than with the sword."

"A person? Who?"

"Her name is Diega, and she can also travel through time. She may be a descendant of mine, and perhaps of you, but I don't know. I had met her once before. She reminds me a little of you, fiercely independent and ready to take on the world. That had gotten her into trouble though, but in the end, we both lived."

"In case you want to know," speculated Gersemi, "you've been gone for about a month. I told everyone that you were going on a mission of goodwill to another country and that you might go hunting afterwards; I have been ruling in your absence."

"You have, have you?"

"It's not something I ever want to do for long periods of time, but I'm happy to do it for you if you need me to."

"Well, thank you, Gersemi."

"Was there any trouble or excitement while I was gone?"

"Just a little. A woman arrived about a week ago. Some knights found her wandering in the forest and took her back to the castle. No one can understand her, and she can't understand us. We've not allowed her to leave the castle, but we've treated her kindly."

"Perhaps she's Diega," King Lot II said excitedly. "I would like for the two of you to meet."

"You've described Diega as young. This woman is almost as old as you."

"Perhaps she came back to his time after she has aged. By the way, I caught your reference to my age. You know that you're older than I am."

Gersemi giggled. "Come now father. How can a daughter be older than her father?"

"Let's go see who you've detained in the castle. Whoever it is, probably thinks we are not very hospitable." King Lot II walked to the castle with his arm around his daughter; she was the bright spot in his life. Once King Lot II arrived in the castle, he was greeted warmly by all who were in the castle. Several asked him how his ambassador mission had gone and where it was, and he gave vague answers. "Where is this person?" he whispered, leaning toward Gersemi.

Gersemi looked around. "There she is over there."

King Lot II was trying to look around people when a woman came charging toward him. The King's Guard blocked her before she could reach him. He still hadn't gotten a clear view of the woman. The guards let her go, and King Lot II's mouth dropped in astonishment. Tears streamed down the woman's face, and she ran and clung to him.

"Marian, how can it be? Is it really you?"

"Yes, Robin, or King Lot II. It's me."

King Lot II kissed her passionately and held onto her tightly, lest time snatch her away from him. He was oblivious to all else around him. A mere half an hour earlier he would have gladly given his life to Death. Now, he wanted an eternity to spend with Marian. Eventually, he noticed people staring at Marian and him, including Gersemi.

"I take it that this woman is not Diega," jested Gersemi.

"No. This is my wife, Marian."

"Your ... wife?" exclaimed Gersemi.

"Let's go to my Counsel Room." He repeated this in two languages so that both Marian and Gersemi could understand. Once the three were alone in the Counsel Room, he asked, "How did you get here?"

"I thought I hadn't," replied Marian. "I knew trying to reach you was a risk, and it was a risk I was greatly willing to take. Once I got here, and you were nowhere to be found, I thought I arrived in the wrong place or time. I couldn't communicate with anyone. I think I would have died if it were much longer before you came back."

"I was thinking about death myself an hour ago; now all I want is to live, to spend every moment with you."

They kissed and hugged again. Marian continued. "Then I saw this gorgeous woman who is in the room with us, and I thought that maybe as king, you had married a younger woman. She's not your wife, is she?"

King Lot II laughed. "She's my daughter."

"Oh, she's your and Freya's daughter."

"How do you know about Freya?"

"Merlin said ..."

"Merlin? Where did you see Merlin?"

"Father? Can you translate?" asked Gersemi.

"Yes. I'm sorry," he said as though he had forgotten all of his manners. He told Gersemi what had been discussed between Marian and him so far. Gersemi laughed heartily at the part where Marian thought Gersemi was his wife.

Marian continued. "I met your son."

"Lovell?"

"No. You have a son from Blanchemal, named Gingalain."

"That can't be," he started.

"Apparently, you had intimate relations once with Blanchemal, and Gingalain was born from that union. She didn't want to tell you because she wanted you to be happy and not feel forced to stay with her. You've actually met him!"

"I have?"

"Yes. We both knew him, but not that he was your son. Gingalain was Will Scarlet."

"Will Scarlet was my son, and I never knew? Why would Blanchemal keep that knowledge from me? Did he know that I was his father?"

"He did know that you were his father. He didn't want you to be distracted and put into danger by knowing that information."

"I wish I would have known. There is so much I would have told him." He thought for a moment. "Wait. Back up. Why was Merlin there? I assume he was in your own time."

"It's all very confusing. Someone was after Gingalain and Blanchemal. This person had been capturing magical beings, and they were only a few of those who remained."

"The last time I saw Blanchemal, she said that magical beings were disappearing, but I had no idea it was something so nefarious. I wish I would have taken more seriously what she was telling me. What happened?"

"Blanchemal was captured. Gingalain was as well, but somehow, he used the Club of Dagda and exchanged places. The being who had captured everyone ended up being captured in the Book of Thoth himself."

"But I have the Book of Thoth. Someone must take it at some point. Do you know who this person was who had captured magical beings?"

"I can't remember if his name was said or not. If I heard it, I have forgotten. I don't know who it was. Maybe you can destroy the book."

"I can't change the future. Besides the Book of Thoth can't be destroyed."

Marian continued. "When Gingalain was safe, he used the Club of Dagda to summon Merlin, and Merlin explained everything, as if he had known all along."

"That certainly sounds like Merlin."

"Gingalain was able to use the Club of Dagda to transport me here. I'm sure he would have done it sooner, but I don't think he really knew how to use the Club of Dagda."

"I'm just happy that you are here now!"

"By the way, you have another son!" smiled Marian proudly.

"Another?"

"Yes. Ours."

Tears came to King Lot II's eyes. "We have a son?"

"His name is Archer."

King Lot II laughed. "As much as I used a bow as Robin Hood, that is an appropriate name. Is he as good as I was as Robin Hood?"

"Almost. Now, I have to tell you what Merlin said. A descendant of each of your four children will somehow fulfill a prophecy and make things right."

"Did he tell the person's name?"

"Yes. What was it? I'm sorry. So much has happened that I'm having a hard time with names."

"Was it Diega?"

"Yes! He said you had already met her."

"Diega speculated she was a descendant of mine. I'm glad she is. She's a wonderful woman, brave, independent, and a warrior like you and Gersemi."

Marian started to tell him about what Merlin said about Lovell, but she decided that the information would only cause him grief. Although she regretted withholding information from him, she thought it would be best in this case.

King Lot II told Gersemi all that Marian had told him. "I'll have a child?" she exclaimed. "I don't know who the father could be. There's no one I like that much. I wonder if I will be captured too. We must think of something to do with the Book of Thoth."

"As I've told Marian, and as Merlin often told me, one cannot change the past or the future. Everything happens at once. The past, present, and future can interact with each other. According to Merlin, the past, present, and future are indistinguishable. It's all just an illusion because everything physical is governed by time."

"Should I tell mother that your wife is here?"

"I suppose she will have to find out sooner or later. Do you think she will be alright with it?

"She still pines for her husband. Besides, she would want you to be happy. Don't you remember? She told you that you would find love again. I thought she meant a new love, but what she said was literally what's happened. You found your love again!"

"Are you fine with Marian?"

"Of course, father. I'm just stunned that you have four children. I'm a little jealous now."

"You don't need to be. I'm ashamed that I didn't have the relationship I could have had with them, but I'm glad of the relationship I have with one of them, you."

"You can always count on me."

King Lot II turned to Marian. "I'll have to teach you the language so that you can communicate with people. I'm still so elated that you're here. I know it was a big change, tearing yourself away from Archer and from the life you had. I hope you won't regret choosing to be here with me."

"No. I don't and won't regret that," reassured Marian. I used to spend much of my days looking out my window, hoping to see you walking to the estate, hoping that you would come back to me. I'm sorry that eighteen years had to pass before we could see each other again, but whatever time we have left, I'm determined to live it to the fullest whether it be through adventures like we had in Sherwood Forest or whether it be mundane."

"Oh, it will never be mundane with you by my side!"

545 AD

Gersemi was in her seventh month of pregnancy.

"You look troubled, love," announced Loki. "That's probably not good for our child you're carrying."

"You've made me very happy these past couple of years," blushed Gersemi, "and I can hardly wait for our child to be born."

"Have you decided on a name yet?"

"No, not yet."

"So, what's troubling you?"

"I'm worried. Neither Odin nor Thor have been seen in months. Once I became pregnant, my mother saw me almost every day. It's been a month since I've seen her. I'm worried that something may have happened to them."

"What could happen to them? They can certainly take care of themselves. And you and your mother have gone much longer than a month without seeing each other. I think you're just overly sensitive now that you're pregnant."

"I guess you're right. Now that my father is gone, I would feel lost without you and my mother."

"Well, I'm not going anywhere, and you'll have a son or daughter before long to occupy you."

Gersemi laughed. "Every time I think about this, I can't help but laugh."

"Why's that?" smiled Loki.

"You are responsible for my birth with your request that Gawain do whatever Freya asked before you would return her torc. Now, you're responsible for the birth of our child."

"I'm glad it turned out as it did."

"I wonder what our child will be like?" pondered Gersemi. My mother is a seer and a warrior goddess, and you are a shapeshifter. I wonder if our child will have those qualities. He or she could be powerful indeed, maybe more powerful than either of us."

"Perhaps."

Gersemi thought that Loki appeared apprehensive at her comment. She wondered if that bothered him.

"I'm going out for a while," informed Loki.

"Be careful," cautioned Gersemi.

"Don't worry. I'll be back soon."

Gersemi did worry though. She felt uneasy about Odin, Thor, and now Freya seemingly missing. She didn't want to spy on Loki, but she wanted to make sure he was alright. She didn't want him to disappear as well. She debated about whether or not to follow him and finally decided in favor of just making sure he was not putting himself in danger. Pulling out a locket of his hair that he had given her, she used it to cast a tracking spell that would find him. Gersemi disappeared and followed the tracking spell to where Loki had gone.

Gersemi appeared in a desert, far from Norway. She wondered why he was here. Not wanting to be seen, she hid behind a sand dune. Loki was talking to a blue genie. She couldn't make out the conversation, but she could hear a sinister laugh coming from him, and the genie looked nervous. What came next nauseated and enraged her. Loki pulled out a book that resembled the Book of Thoth, and the genie was on his knees apparently begging. Gersemi focused, putting all her senses into hearing what was transpiring. The genie was saying that he had spent thousands of years imprisoned in a lamp and for Loki to have mercy and not condemn him to a similar fate. Loki seemingly disregarded the genie's plea. The genie looked to where Gersemi was trying to hide, but she was too enthralled by the scene before her to duck out of sight. She felt something, almost as if the genie transferred some of his power to her. It was an odd feeling that settled in her womb. The book began to glow, and Loki opened it. Although she could see no physical evidence of a vortex, the genie struggled, but his struggles were to no avail. Something pulled the genie into the book, and he was gone. Gersemi quickly disappeared and returned home.

Loki returned to Gersemi a short time later.

"What have you done?" she cried in rage. "I was worried that something might happen to you; so, I followed you and witnessed what happened. That was the Book of Thoth that you had. It was buried with my father. You desecrated his tomb and stole the book, didn't you? You are the one responsible for the disappearance of Odin, Thor, and my mother!"

"Let me explain," sputtered Loki.

But Gersemi didn't give him the chance. "You've been lying to me. I believed you when you said that you had changed because of your love for me, but you're still the same trickster! Are you planning on using the Book of Thoth to entrap me and our child?"

"I would never do that," he insisted.

"I don't believe you. Why would you ensnare my mother? You knew how worried I was about her."

"Let me explain," repeated Loki more urgently.

"I don't want to hear your explanation. You obviously don't love me, or you wouldn't have done this. Leave me. I don't ever want to see you again."

Loki appeared despondent and hung his head in shame, Gersemi thought.

"I would never hurt you or our child," he replied, voice trembling.

"Go, now!" Gersemi insisted angrily.

Loki disappeared, and Gersemi broke down in tears, her body heaving from anger, disappointment, and betrayal. She didn't know what to do, but she had to protect herself and her unborn child. A thought entered her mind, and she vanished.

Gersemi reappeared at the entrance to the subterranean caves leading to the home of the brother-dwarves Brokkr and Sindri. She was too upset to wander into the maze leading to their home; so, she called out their names. A short time later, the two dwarves scurried out of the hole leading to their home. Gersemi quickly summarized what Loki and done and warned them to be careful, lest they too become imprisoned in the book. "I'm worried that Loki may try to trap me and our unborn child in the book. Is there anything you can do to prevent him from finding me?"

"We'll help you," answered Brokkr. We always felt that we owed Sir Gawain more than we gave him for saving Sindri. The least we can do is help his daughter and grandchild. Brokkr and Sindri worked through the night. At dawn, they presented Gersemi with two rings. "One of these rings is for you; the other will be for your child. The ring is too big for a child, but you can put it on a necklace or bracelet until he or she has grown enough to wear it. As long as you, and your child once he or she is born, wear the rings, you will be undetectable to Loki."

"Thank you so much. I can never repay you for this."

"It's our pleasure," replied the brothers in unison.

"Please be careful," urged Gersemi. "Can you make such rings for yourselves?"

"We discussed that," answered Sindri, but we feel that with all of the tricks Loki has played on us, we need to face him. Now, please hurry, daughter of Gawain and Freya. Who knows what Loki will do if he is filled with wrath."

Gersemi thanked them again and disappeared. No sooner had she left than Loki appeared before the brothers, holding the Book of Thoth in his hands and smiling.

1807 AD

Marshal Duroc stepped into the Council Chamber of the Palace de Fontainbleau to find Emperor Napoleon I bent over a table scribbling notes on paper. Napoleon apparently heard Duroc enter, and he turned around with pen still in hand.

"You wanted to see me?" inquired Duroc.

"Yes. I want you to go to Spain and negotiate a secret treaty between me and King Charles IV of Spain. I have the notes here with your instructions. In order to invade Portugal, we will need to launch troops from Spain. The outline of the treaty will be to divide Portugal into three parts."

"Do you think King Charles IV will agree to this?

"Do I detect more to your question than what is on the surface, some underlying intent?"

"Yes, my Emperor," replied Duroc with some hesitancy.

"You are an insightful man. Yes. There is more to this treaty than its apparent intent. With troops in Spain, we will be positioned to take control of Spain, but you must assuage any concerns the Spanish may have. To them, the treaty is just to allow us the use of Spain to launch troops into Portugal."

"I will make certain that they see this as no more than a strategic plan for invading Portugal."

"Excellent. I would like for you to present this as a gift to King Charles IV as a goodwill gesture." Napoleon handed Duroc a sword and scabbard.

"May I?" asked Duroc.

Napoleon nodded his head. Duroc unsheathed the sword and examined it closely.

"This is a fine sword," commented Duroc. "What is its history?"

"To be honest, I have no clue. It was found at the Palace of Versailles among other objects of King Louis XVI. I have seen no record of this piece, and I don't know how or when it came into his possession. I have no attachment to it; so, it seems a small sacrifice to present it to the Spanish King. I have news from King Charles IV that he will have a representative to sign. I believe the man's name is Don Eugenio Isquierdo. You will give the sword and scabbard to him to present to His Majesty King Charles IV."

"It will be so." With those words Marshal Duroc left the Council Chamber and departed from the Palace de Fontainbleau.

1808 AD

The familiar feelings of nausea and dizziness told Diega that she was no longer in her own time. Damn, she thought. Where am I now? Anxiety flooded her body as she felt for the Springfield Hellcat, already knowing the answer. Another *Damn*. Diega tried to carry the handgun with her as much as possible for precisely this reason of traveling to another time. Unfortunately, there were times that she couldn't take it with her, and yesterday was one of those occasions. A slight chuckle escaped her mouth as she thought about *yesterday*. That day might be hundreds of years in the future or the past. Whatever the time reality, that day, she couldn't take it with her because she went to a university campus, which didn't allow guns on campus, to do a martial arts exhibition. She meant to put the gun and holster back on when she got back to her apartment. She always slept with it on her. It wasn't comfortable, but she had gotten used to it. It's a wonder that she hadn't accidentally shot herself in her sleep by now. She did have her fully charged iPhone. A lot of good that would do her. She also had a few objects for magic tricks as a way of possibly earning a small amount of money.

As Diega stood, she hoped that the nausea and dizziness would simply fall from her. They didn't, unfortunately. She could see rolling hills with trees and some grassy areas. In the distance, was what looked like a farm on relatively flat ground. She remembered her adventure in France when she tried to steal some clothes, which didn't turn out too well for her. She figured she didn't have much of a choice though. Rather than sneak into a house, she might try a more direct approach this time and actually talk with someone about getting some clothes and determining where she was. As she walked toward the farm, she saw a variety of plants and crops. She passed cacti, aloe vera, and what looked like coffee plants. As she got closer to the farm, she saw mangoes, avocados, corn, beans, sugar cane, and tobacco. The farm had a little bit of everything. This must be how the residents of the farm made a living. A girl, about ten years old, was picking corn from the stalks, and she startled, dropping some ears of corn, when she saw Diega.

"It's alright," said Diega in Spanish in a calm and soothing voice. "I'm not going to hurt you. Do you speak Spanish?"

"Yes," replied the girl.

"I know this will sound crazy, but where am I?"

The girl shook her head as if she didn't understand the question.

Diega heard a woman's voice and saw a woman appear around a row of corn. The woman walked up to the girl and suddenly saw Diega. The woman clutched the girl by the shoulders, pulled her in, and tightly wrapped her arms around her.

Diega repeated what she had said earlier. "It's alright. I'm not going to hurt anyone. I know this sounds crazy, but I'm from the future."

The woman startled and clutched the girl tighter.

"As I said, I'm not here to hurt anyone. I just want some basic information, and I'll leave. Alright?"

The woman nodded, her eyes narrowing and she suspiciously eyed Diega up and down.

The mother was passing her fear to her daughter, and Diega knew she needed to calm them quickly. In a calm, quiet, and soothing voice, she said, "My name is Diega. What are your names?

"My name is Ana, and this is my daughter, Maria."

"You see my clothes," said Diega. "I'm sure they are unlike anything you've seen before."

"You wear pants like a man!" commented Ana.

Diega pulled out her iPhone, and the woman started again. "It's not a weapon. Let me show you what it can do. She quickly took a photo of the woman and her daughter and showed it to them. The mother and daughter marveled over the picture, and both spoke excitedly. Diega found a tame song she had downloaded and played it for the two. That really excited them. They looked all around the phone. Diega assumed they were looking to see where the music came from. "As I said, I'm from the future. Can you tell me where I am and what year it is?"

"You are in New Spain, of course, and the year is 1808."

Well, this is closer to my own time than the other times I've been in, thought Diega, and New Spain is Mexico. "Is there a large city nearby?"

"The closest cities are Xalapa and the port city of Veracruz. Both are about fifty kilometers from here."

"Do you have some clothes I could have. I don't have any money, but I could give you the one's I'm wearing."

"That is unnecessary. We can find something for you to wear. Please stay and have dinner with us. You can stay the night, but let me talk with my husband first before he sees you."

Diega could only imagine how that conversation would play out, but she agreed. The woman walked away, taking her daughter. A few moments later, she could hear the raised voice of a man. Diega couldn't make out the words from this distance, but the conversation didn't sound like it was going well. Ana approached Diega several minutes later carrying some clothes. "You can have dinner with us," said Ana, "but my husband insists that you stay the night in the barn. I'm sorry, but that was the best I could do. And he wants to see the magic box you have."

"I understand. I would be cautious too."

Dinner was plain but good. Tortillas, beans, corn mixed with peppers, and mangos. Diega was nervous about drinking the water, but she was thirsty and drank it anyway.

"Pulque?" asked Ana's husband, who had never stated his name. He held a cup out for Diega.

"What is it?" asked Diega.

"Pulque is made from the sap of the maguey plant. It has been fermented."

"Oh, in that case, I'll try some." Diega was expecting something along the lines of Jose Cuervo, but this was white and thick. She didn't much care for it, but it was alcohol, and she would drink anything alcoholic at the moment, even if it was fermented shoe leather. She made a face after the first sip, and Ana's husband laughed. She was able to finish the drink though.

"Show me this magic box you have," ordered the husband.

Diega took out her iPhone. She showed him the picture she had taken of Ana and Maria, and she played a few seconds of the same song she had played for them before turning off the iPhone. She wanted to conserve as much of the battery as possible, although she didn't know why. The phone was pretty much useless in this time without data or the internet, except for a very few functions. The man was as much amazed as his wife and daughter.

"Does everyone have one of these where you come from?" he asked.

"Pretty much," said Diega. In my time, it can do much more. This won't do a lot now, but in my time, you can use it to talk with people across the ocean, or you can use it for directions to places."

The man just shook his head. "You must leave in the morning. My wife will show you to the barn."

The barn, as he called it, wasn't the barn she was expecting. It was a small adobe-looking structure with palm leaves for the roof. She shared the space with a few animals and some rudimentary farming equipment. Ana handed Diega a blanket, but as warm as it was, Diega didn't think she would need it. She took it just in case and thanked the woman. "How do I get to the port in Veracruz?" The woman pointed in the general direction of the city. "Good night." Ana gave a slight nod, turned, and walked away. Diega looked at the dress that Ana had given her. She thought this was what was called a huipil. She remembered a little about this from the history class on the Americas that she had taken. It was a loose-fitting rectangular tunic-like garment that was sleeveless. This one was off-white in color with a few red horizontal stripes near the bottom. Because Diega was taller than Ana, it reached to a little below her knees. She also had a reboza, which was like a shawl that she could wrap around her shoulders. For footwear, she had sandals made with some type of woven strips with thin soles. The distance of fifty kilometers, which she figured was about 30 miles, wasn't going to be an easy journey with this footwear.

The barn was hot at night with very little air stirring, and Diega slept off and on during the night. The next morning, she left as soon as the sun rose. She walked a couple of hours without seeing anyone. The route was rugged, and she wasn't going very fast. There was a creek to cross, but at its highest point only made it to her knees. Fortunately, she hadn't had to cross a river, yet. At this rate, getting to Veracruz would take two days. Perhaps she should have chosen to go to Xalapa instead, but something told her to head to the port city. After the first few hours, she began to encounter a few more people. With the clothes she was wearing, no one gave her much notice. She asked almost everyone she saw the direction to Veracruz, and after each time, she had to correct her heading. Whichever direction Veracruz lay, she was taking a zigzag path to get there, which would add more time and distance. She so wished that she could have used her maps app on the iPhone for directions. Occasionally, she would drink water from some small brooks and streams she came upon, and she did find some fruit along the way. The sun was getting low in the sky, and she estimated that she had walked at least ten hours, not counting the stops she had along the way. If she had been on level ground with no trees or obstacles, she would have been in Veracruz by now, assuming she was headed in the right direction.

She came to a farm where she saw a stone building with dirt all around it. She waited until she was certain the residents had gone to bed for the night, and she sat down with her back to the wall. It was still hot at night, but it wouldn't be as bad as another night in a barn or shed. After about an hour the breeze stirred a little, and Diega drifted off to sleep. The next thing she knew, she was being yelled at by the farmer. He started kicking at her and chased her off the property. Again, she encountered people who gave her slightly different headings than what she was traveling to get to Veracruz. Finally, someone told her of a road ahead that led to Veracruz. She eventually came to it and headed easterly along the road. The next person she saw verified that she was indeed on the road headed to Veracruz. In the late afternoon, she finally reached the port city.

Now what do I do, she thought? During this time period, no one would give a woman dressed in a huipil the time of day. She didn't like giving in to these societal norms, but she also had to be practical and realistic. The first order of business would be to somehow get some better clothes, and she had an idea as to how she might do that.

Mustering the best New York city swindler attitude that she could, she cried out, "Magic tricks for some spare change!" People looked at her strangely and kept walking. Not to be deterred, she kept it up. Finally, a seemingly well-to-do gentleman with his wife and daughter came along and stopped. She pulled out some playing cards and did a trick where she put her finger through a hole in a face card. She said some magic words and peeled a piece of black tape off the back of the card, revealing a now whole playing card. The family seemed amazed. She then did a trick where she appeared to stick her thumb through her earlobe. The little girl clapped enthusiastically, and her father threw a few coins into a quickly made makeshift money holder. As this family was leaving, an even wealthier looking gentleman and his girlfriend stopped. For them, she pulled out all the stops. "I can freeze you in time." She took out her iPhone, the battery life she was carefully guarding, and took a photo. She showed it to them, and their eyes almost popped out of their sockets at the sight of themselves on the iPhone. If she could have printed the photo, she would have made a small fortune. Even so, he generously rewarded her. She did some more card tricks as others stopped, and a few hand tricks such as biting her thumb and making it longer and making her little finger disappear and reappear. She took a hand fan and cut several gaps in it then fanned it making it whole again. More money was thrown into her money holder, and a large crowd had gathered. She continued with a few more tricks and received lots of applause and comments of amazement. She had quite a bit of money now and was reaching to get it before someone stole it when she heard a few loud voices. She looked up and two policemen or soldiers, she didn't know which, were making their way through the crowd and pushing people aside. She wasn't sure if what she was doing was legal or not; so, before she could find out, she used the same sleight of hand she had been employing with her magic tricks to blend into the crowd and escape.

Diega found a shop that sold clothing, and she bought something someone of a middle-class economic status would wear. Next, she found a place where she could eat and spend the night. She was hungry and felt people were looking at her as though she were eating like a field hand who had put in a hard day's work. The sun had still not set when she curled up in a bed. She fell asleep almost as soon as she hit the bed and slept the entire night without waking. The next morning, she awoke well-rested and reenergized. She ate a big breakfast, with people gawking at her again.

After leaving the inn, she thought about exchanging her coins for paper currency, but she did not see anyone using paper money. She went to the market and found a small bag that she could easily carry some of her belongings out of sight. No point in tempting a thief if she could help it. She found a shady spot and sat down to think what to do next. She chose Veracruz rather than Xalapa out of a feeling. They both were cities, but Veracruz was a port city, which meant ships. Perhaps she was supposed to sail somewhere. Although she didn't like relying totally on feelings, she didn't know what else to do; so, she arose and walked in the early morning heat to the docks.

Upon reaching the docks, Diega felt pulled to a ship that was named *Cartagena*, a three-masted ship. She didn't know what kind of ship it was: barkentine, schooner, brig, sloop, or whatever. Of course, none of that really mattered to her. A man with a piece of luggage passed Diega and walked toward the ship. Diega quickly caught up to him. "Does this ship take passengers?"

"I'm traveling on it if that answers your question."

The man continued walking, but Diega stopped at the sight of an official-looking man ready to disembark the ship down the gangplank. He wasn't wearing a uniform, but he had an air of importance about him. Someone, perhaps the captain of the ship, handed him what looked to be a coin purse that the official quickly stored in a pocket. Two soldiers were with him, and all three walked down the gangplank. Diega acted like a lady as best she could. When the official was almost face to face with her, she bumped into him, extracting the coin purse from his pocket. The official seemed irritated and chastised Diega for her carelessness. She apologized and kept going. Angst gripped Diega's insides. Why had she done this? She could have easily been caught. She didn't need the money enough to steal. Time travel seemed to bring out the worst in her. Not turning back to look at the official, she kept a steady pace up the gangplank. Once she reached the ship, Diega said, "I'm with him," nodding to the gentleman with the piece of luggage she had stopped earlier. The sailor let her pass without further word. First stealing and now lying, all within one minute.

Diega spotted some passengers of lower status and mixed immediately into the crowd. She knew the accommodations would not be good, but she didn't know what else to do, other than ask the man with the luggage outright if she could stay with him. After about an hour, the group was herded like cattle below deck, and the Cartagena prepared to set sail. Diega was right. The accommodations were not good. All of the passengers, about seventy in total, were in a common space with little to no privacy. Wooden beds were stacked two high. Although she had never experienced seasickness before, she had never been on the ocean in such conditions. A few people around her were already beginning to get sick within minutes of leaving Veracruz.

From conversations around her, Diega learned she was aboard a schooner headed for Havana, Cuba. Someone estimated the voyage to be at least four days. The passengers were not allowed to go above deck, except during certain periods of the day to go to the bathroom in shifts.

After two days of misery, a commotion arose both above and below deck. She heard cannons firing. One word started in a hushed tone at the opposite end of the quarters below deck. It was like a huge wave when it reached her, "Pirates!" Suddenly the whole ship shook violently, and there was a sound and feeling as if a large tree had fallen on the deck above. Allowed or not, Diega wasn't going to die below deck. As the others huddled together below, she made her way above deck.

When she reached the deck, Diega saw that what sounded like a tree falling was actually the ships' masts. Two of the three masts had been broken by cannon fire from the pirate ship, which was closing in fast. One of the broken masts was in the ocean. Part of the other lay across the deck. Those firing the cannons from the Cartagena were poor shots. Three cannon volleys fell well away from the pirate ship. The pirate ship fired again, and the cannon ball ripped through several crew members standing around a cannon and continued bouncing across the deck like a rampant bowling ball. The cannonball hit two more crewmembers and tore a large swath in the wooden deck. One more shot was fired from the pirate ship that followed almost identically the path of the previous cannonball. It tore through the deck and down into the hold where the passengers were. Th screams from the passengers below were barely audible over the booming cannon fire. Hardly any crew were left to fend off the pirate ship. Diega turned to look at the damage behind her, and she saw the captain lying dead on the deck. Within minutes, grappling hooks latched to the ship. Dicga ducked behind some of the debris on the deck when she saw the first pirates boarding. Soon, about twenty pirates were aboard. One of the Cartagena's crewmembers ran over to the pirates, but rather than being killed, one of the pirates hugged him.

Diega stood up without realizing it and was soon spotted by the lead pirate. She always had a particular image in her mind when she thought of a pirate, but this one did not fit that image. He was around six-feet tall, handsome, and muscular. His black hair was curly and came down to around the bottom of his neck in back. He had a black mustache, and his face was darkened with a five o'clock shadow of a beard. He wore what appeared to be something like an old calvary hat, and he reminded her of a picture of General Custer that she had seen. He smiled at her and mockingly bowed to her. "You speak Spanish, I presume?" he said, still smiling.

"Yes, or English, or a little French."

He looked astonished and spoke some French to her.

"I'm not part of your treasure yet," she exclaimed sternly.

He laughed. "So, you do speak French," he said in English.

"Enough to know what you said," Diega replied in English. "And with whom do I have the misfortune of speaking? Certainly, not Blackbeard since his time was about one hundred years ago."

"Nor the ghost of Blackbeard. My name is Jean Lafitte. Although I do run a smuggling operation, I'm not what you call an on-the-sea pirate. This is my first such outing, but it does have a certain excitement about it."

Diega had heard the name before. If he wasn't a full-fledged pirate yet, he would be in the near future. "Why did you attack this ship? It's merely carrying passengers."

"Ah, but you've been misinformed. According to my spy," he said nodding to the Cartagena crew member, "it is carrying quite a bit of gold to Havana, which was to be loaded on a ship bound for Spain to use against the French in the Peninsular War. I can't let that be used to fund fighting against Emperor Napoleon, and I have a much better use for it myself."

Gold, thought Diega. Perhaps Excalibur is aboard the ship as part of the treasure. "If there is a certain sword as part of the treasure, it is mine, and I can't let you take it. If it's part of the treasure, give it to me, and you can have the rest."

"I've come to take all of the treasure. I don't see how you can stop me, do you?"

"Actually, I do." The oddest thought entered Diega's mind. She picked up a nearby knife and cut the dress off at the knee; then she cut the sleeves off. She had purchased soft shoes to go with her dress, which was advantageous to her now. Sandals would have been awkward, and bare feet wouldn't do on the splintered wooden deck. She took off her bag, which she had strapped underneath the dress. During the entire ritual of preparing herself for battle, the pirates just stood watching as if in a stupor. Lastly, she pulled out her iPhone, which still had a good charge, turned up the volume all the way, and shuffled through the downloaded songs until she saw one that made her smile.

"Enough of this. Let's kill the wench!" shouted one of the pirates.

"I will not allow killing unless it can't be helped," interjected Lafitte.

"You may run a smuggling business in New Orleans, but you're not our real captain."

That statement was enough to convince the pirates that they didn't need to listen to Lafitte. Diega quickly pressed the play button, and from the iPhone came the song that made Diega smile, *Touch Too Much* by AC/DC. When the music blared from the iPhone, the pirates stopped in their tracks. Fear showed on their faces, but Diega knew that it wouldn't last long. Jean Lafitte had a look of curiosity mixed with humor. Diega knew the song well and at about what time certain things in the song occurred. Several pirates charged at the thirty second mark. Diega couldn't have timed it better. On the word *touch*, she caught the first pirate with a roundhouse kick to the head. She immediately landed a spin hook on the next pirate. Both hit the deck. A third pirate was right on her and grabbed her arms; so, she bent over and did a scorpion kick where she brought her leg up backwards over her shoulder to kick the pirate in the face. He immediately let go, and she used a front snap kick, hitting his nose with the ball of her foot. She immediately repeated the move striking his nose again with her heel. *Seems like a touch, a touch too much.* Blood gushed from his broken nose, and he fell to his knees covering his nose. Another pirate was running at her with a club. As he swung down, she sidestepped, grabbed the club on its downward motion and flipped the pirate onto his back. With the club in her hand, she pushed hard straight downward, striking him in the forehead with such force that his head thudded against the deck like a melon, bounced off the deck and smacked the deck again on the rebound. *She got a touch, a touch too much.* Pirates on each side grabbed her arms, and a third man charged her with a sword, bent over like a charging bull. Diega quickly grasped each man's arms with her hands and pulled the men slightly towards her. She placed her hands on their shoulders while they still held her arms. Diega used the men's shoulders as a brace and swung her body up, allowing the charging man to pass completely underneath her. *She had the face of an angel smiling with sin, the body of Venus with arms.* As her feet landed on the deck, the man with the sword turned quickly around. Diega grabbed one of the men and pushed him in front of her as a shield as the swordsman lunged forward. He plunged the sword through his mate's torso. Diega headbutted the other man in the nose. Then she rammed the impaled man into the man who stabbed him pushing him into the hole in the deck. Two more men ran toward her from each side, and she did a split kick, hitting the men just below their sternums. Three more pirates confronted her, and she jabbed with her fists to the beat of the chords in the song. Another pirate charged her with a knife. She backed up, grabbed the man's wrist bending it backwards with her right hand while pushing down on his elbow with her left hand. He dropped the knife and went to one knee. Diega rammed her knee into his teeth, upper lip, and nose. Two more men. She dropped and spun, knocking their legs out from under them. She immediately sprang up, ran towards a pirate and did a jump front kick, knocking him into the hole in the deck just as the swordsman was climbing back out. They collided, and both men fell to the lower deck. She used a fast kick, hitting a pirate below the sternum. Then she kneed him in the groin. While he was bent over, she performed an axe kick where her foot came down striking him in the top of the head. She used a swing hook kick to the jaw of a pirate who was unsure what to do. Ten more pirates came aboard the Cartagena from the pirate ship at the sound of all the commotion. At about the two-minute forty mark in the song, there was a strong beat. *Seems like a touch, touch too much. You know it's much too much, much too much.* Again, she kicked and jabbed to each hard beat of the music. *Cause you're much too much too much too much.* The guitar solo came in at the three-minute forty mark, and Diega went berserk with a barrage of kicks: butterfly, tornado, 540 spinning hook, aerial feilong, cartwheel, double roundhouse, turning side, and double front. Suddenly a shot rang out, and the music stopped. Jean Lafitte had shot the iPhone with a hand musket.

Diega was breathless. Satisfaction oozed from within her as she saw all of the men lying on the deck, some unconscious and others moaning. Her euphoria was short-lived, however. Four muskets were pointed at her from different angles. There was no way of stopping them, especially as out of breath as she was.

A few of the pirates who had recently come aboard quickly secured a plank. One man was an expert with ropes. To make sure the plank was doubly secure, a few pirates rolled a cannon on top of the end of the plank. One of the men with a musket pointed at Diega said, "Walk the plank." Another pirate held a sword to Diega. She stepped on the plank and walked to the end. She could feel the ocean spray hit her face. She tasted the salty water as some of it dribbled its way down into her mouth. Fortunately for her, they had not bothered to tie her hands, which was a mistake. At the end of the plank, she stepped off, turning as she dropped. She caught hold of the plank with both hands. Adrenaline pushed her breathless body to the limit. The pirate with the sword was on the plank. She swung her legs up to the plank, knocking the man off balance and he fell into the water. Diega had managed to get her body back onto the plank, but she was lying on her back. Another pirate rushed out with a sword to skewer her. As he ran and start to lunge down, Diega rolled up her knees and feet catching the man in the abdomen. She continued rolling her feet over her head and the man plunged into the water below. Diega was amazingly able to grab hold of the plank as her feet were going over her head, or she would have also ended up in the ocean. She swung herself back onto the plank again, crouched and sprang back onto the ship. Jean Lafitte was running to her with sword in hand. She pulled a sword from the scabbard of one of the pirates standing there. She raised her sword in time for it to clash with Lafitte's sword. She took a minute to study his style as she parried his thrusts. Lafitte was an excellent swordsman, but Diega was better. Once she got a feel for his style, she disarmed him within thirty seconds with the Lancelot maneuver that Gawain had taught her.

A man behind her held a musket to her head. "Enough of this. This ends now."

Lafitte spoke. "Whether you think I'm the captain or not. I order you to stand down. In my book, she has earned a shot at life. Put her into the jolly boat." Diega discovered that the jolly boat was a small ship-to-shore type boat that she would have called a dinghy. "Give her the bag she carried. You're an amazing woman," said Lafitte. I truly hope you make it."

As she was lowered into the ocean, she heard one of the pirates yell out. "The ship is taking on water. We have to hurry."

She heard Lafitte ask, "What about the passengers below?"

"We're here for the gold. You may not like to take lives unnecessarily but it's the gold or the passengers. We let you save the girl, but we're taking the gold."

Between Diega's rowing and the ocean current, she quickly drifted away from the Cartagena. She saw the pirates load the treasure onto their ship, retrieve the grappling hooks and sail away as the Cartagena began its journey to the bottom of the ocean. More death. Was this her fault as well? If she had not fought the pirates, would they have saved the passengers? They would have certainly had more time and more able-bodied pirates. The rational part of her mind tried telling herself that pirates wouldn't take all of the passengers onboard, but that only temporarily made her feel a little better. It seemed that for the past two time travels, death followed her like a shadow, killing anyone passing through that shadow. With all the martial arts training she had had, learning the most basic lesson still seemed to elude her. Instead of self-control, respect for others, and fighting as a last resort, she had let pride enter the equation. She wanted to show off her skills to the pirates. She wanted to inflict damage. What she wanted, really was a touch too much. The thought of her pride being the cause of the passengers' deaths clung to her as much as she was clinging to the lifeboat. Tears welled in her eyes, and she sobbed heavily. It seemed hours had passed before she was cried out.

When she finally stopped crying, she realized how hot it was on the open water. Fortunately, the pirates had put some drinking water into the jolly boat. Hopefully she would soon be picked up by a passing ship. Diega had always considered herself to be a brave and independent woman, but night brought a fear she had never experienced, even compared to the hell in the cell in the Bastille. There was complete darkness. The clouds covered the moon and stars. She could see nothing around her. If she had been ten feet from shore, she wouldn't have noticed it. She barely slept that night. The lifeboat bobbed up and down, and she would occasionally hear and feel bumps against the side of the boat. Was it just the waves, or was it a shark or whale? In the distance, she saw lightning pierce the dark sky. The flashes allowed her to see a little more, but that brought another fear, a storm. The lapping waves had already splashed water into the boat. How much more would stormy seas bring? She could sink or capsize before dawn. Fortunately, the storm remained in the distance. The night felt never ending. Thoughts of her parents and of Spencer came into her mind. How long would she be away this time? The last time travel had scared them badly. They were probably already worried, and what must they think of her? To them she would randomly disappear for weeks at a time. Should she tell them? They would only think she was crazy. Even if she brought back something from the past, that wouldn't convince them. Perhaps she could bury something and take them to it. But where could she bury something that would remain undisturbed for two hundred years? They still probably wouldn't believe her.

At some point, her thoughts ceased, and she fell asleep. She was awakened by a huge thud. She looked out and saw several sharks circling the boat. Her first thought was to try to undo an oar from the boat and use it to hit the shark, but she realized that even if she managed to hit a shark, it wouldn't faze it. She would just end up losing or breaking the oar, making it more difficult for herself. Eventually, the sharks left for an easier prize. The sun beat down strongly on her. She did have the rebozo. It was underneath her bag, and the pirates grabbed it along with bag when they put her into the boat. It covered her partially, and she moved it from one part of her body to another whenever part of her body was too hot. She wished now that she hadn't cut her dress. She finally removed what remained of the dress and used it, along with the rebozo, to cover herself from the sun. On one occasion, she dared to climb out of the boat and into the ocean to cool off, being careful to hold tightly to her floating salvation. The water was cool, but the thought of sharks kept her constantly looking around. She almost lost hold when a swell caused the boat to rise suddenly. Fear had almost paralyzed her, and she almost lost her hold again. Her mind's eye could see the boat floating away and the current preventing her from reaching it. She struggled to get back into the boat, but the sudden series of swells made it difficult. Her strength seemed to be sapped; she would pull herself up slightly but would be knocked down again. She was beginning to think all hope was lost. She tried to calm herself. She put the sharks out of her mind and concentrated on the task of getting back into the boat. She gave one final Herculean effort and managed to pull herself up enough to swing her leg up and catch the top of the boat. She tried to roll into the boat. Just as she was doing this, a swell gave her enough of a push to throw her into the boat. Her chest rose and fell as she took in rapid breaths. Realizing that her breathing was shallow, she switched to breathing with her diaphragm. She would not try that again! A gentle rain started to fall, cooling her down further. With what little energy she had, she cupped her hands and began trying to throw out some of the water that had accumulated in the bottom of the boat. After what seemed like an hour, most of the water still remained in the boat. She collapsed and fell asleep.

The drinking water saved her life. She was on the jolly boat for three days with only the water they had given her. She had no food. Realization came to her of what Lafitte meant about hoping she would make it. In her mind, she thought she would come to land or that a ship would come by and pick her up. The third day, she finally saw a ship come into view. When the ship was beside her, a grappling hook was dropped to prevent the boat from drifting away while a rope ladder was lowered, and a sailor came down to help her aboard. She was weak from lack of food, not enough water, and the heat of the sun. It took every bit of her strength, with the sailor's help, to get aboard the ship. The sailor gave her some water and told her to sip it and not drink too fast. She didn't listen and guzzled the water. Within seconds, she vomited over the side of the ship.

"I told you to sip," he said. He gave her some more and reiterated that she sip it this time. With water still in hand, she was led to the captain for questioning. She told him she was the sole survivor of the Cartagena. She said she fought the pirates, leaving out the part about how well she had fought them, and for her courage they gave her a chance to survive. She told the captain that there had been gold aboard and that one of the crew was a spy for the pirates. Diega noticed that the captain did not seem surprised when she told him about the gold.

"When the ship didn't arrive when expected, we set out to see if we could find it. We thought piracy had declined, but it has started to increase again. We've heard tell of a Haitian pirate named Henri Caesar. Do you know if it was him?"

"No. The lead pirate was Jean Lafitte, out of New Orleans."

"Thank you for the information. I'll let you stay in one of the on-deck cabins so that you can gather your strength. I think we can find a dress and shoes for you. We weren't sure what to expect; so, we brought along some clothes."

"Are we headed to Havana?"

"No. Veracruz."

Diega opened the door to her cabin but turned around. "By the way, what is the name of this ship?"

"The San Francisco de Asis, or I should say the San Francisco de Asis II since the first one was wrecked in the battle of Trafalgar three years ago."

When Diega was finally alone in the cabin, she looked inside the coin purse that she had stolen just prior to boarding the Cartagena. To her utter astonishment, it was filled with gold.

The only things that Diega did on the three-day journey back to Veracruz were eat, drink, sleep and use the bathroom. By the time the ship arrived in the port of Veracruz, Diega was back to full strength. As she left the ship, she thanked the captain for saving her life.

"I'm just sorry we couldn't have saved more," he said.

Diega wasn't sure if he was referring to people or the gold.

He continued. "I'm glad you were able to find something to wear. We found you in rags. The dress you have is one fit for the wife of a rich caballero. I suppose it is the least we can do for all that you went through."

Diega thanked him again and walked down the gangplank. Unsure of what to do next, she sat down in the shade of a small building along the entrance to the dock. She hadn't been there long when she heard the captain on the other side of the same building talking with someone.

"The gold meant to aid Spain in the Peninsular War, which is now needed to oust Napoleon's brother, Joseph, was taken by a French pirate living in the United States. You'll need to take a party to Acapulco and board a ship to Alta California to inform the specially appointed provisional governor that the gold was taken. He'll need to increase the gold shipments immediately in order to help Spain."

The destination that Diega was supposed to go to suddenly dawned on her. The ship she arrived on was the San Francisco de Asis. San Francisco was in California, which was where this party was to be sent to inform the Governor. She was beginning to think that Excalibur truly was sentient. She had been headed in the wrong direction when fate brought her back here and allowed her to overhear this conversation. When was the party leaving though? As if on cue, the answer was provided.

"We'll need two days to gather provisions and soldiers to make the journey. We'll leave at dawn the day after tomorrow."

Diega saw two soldiers walking, and she rose and tried to quietly leave the building without being seen. The captain and the person he was talking to had gone inside the building. As she was walking away, the two soldiers turned toward the building. Had they spotted her eavesdropping on the conversation? Diega kept walking, trying to act as nonchalantly as possible. When she was almost even with the soldiers, one of them eyed her with more than a mere passing glance, but she kept walking, as did they.

Diega found an inn to spend the night. She was downstairs having something to eat and trying to think of her next move when the soldier she saw earlier, the one who had looked at her, came into the inn. He walked directly to her table and sat down.

"I thought I might find you in here. You came off the ship, didn't you?"

Diega was unsure of the correct answer, but said, "yes."

"You're Señorita Diega Pulido, aren't you?"

Shock set in when Diega heard her first name. Not many women had that name. At first, she thought she was discovered, but then the last name didn't match her last name. Before Diega could tell him that he was mistaken, the soldier continued talking.

"I thought that was you when I saw you along the docks. You've been away in Madrid for several years, but I still recognize you. I'm sure you don't remember me. I'm Miguel. You don't have to answer that." Miguel paused a moment. "I suppose you want to get to your family's hacienda near Reina de Los Angeles."

Diega's heart leapt at this answer to her prayer. She was glad she had not interrupted this young man by telling the truth. "I do!" she said ecstatically.

"Where are your parents, Don Carlos and Doña Catalina?"

"They are still in Madrid, but they plan to come. They let me come ahead."

"The last I heard, your aunt, Doña Rosa was living in your family's hacienda and keeping it up. She must be in her late forties or early fifties now. I imagine it is getting to be too much on her." Miguel paused, as if in thought, which made Diega nervous. "Hey, how do you plan to get there?" Before Diega could answer, he posited an answer himself. "I suppose you plan on taking a ship out of Veracruz, sail around Cape Horn, and continue up the west coast all the way to Alta California."

"That's the plan." Diega thought that if she could keep quiet long enough, Miguel would give her all the information she needed.

"I have another idea! Wait right here. I'll be back shortly." Miguel stood up and practically ran to the door.

Diega was torn. She didn't know whether to leave or to stay. Miguel had been a great help, and perhaps he could be more help, but part of her still wanted to be overly cautious. Perhaps he was saying things that weren't true to see if she would agree. He could be going to someone now to bring them back to arrest her. She believed she had crossed from being overly cautious to being paranoid. The last few hours had given her greater clarity than she had had the rest of her time in New Spain. Perhaps waiting for Miguel to return was in her best interest.

Diega had waited thirty minutes. She was beginning to wonder if Miguel was going to come back. However, no sooner had she thought that than he came through the door smiling.

"You're in luck. I told you I had an idea. I'm leaving with a group the day after tomorrow to Alta California to deliver some information. Since you wish to go there as well, I spoke to my sergeant to see if you could come with us. At first, he said no, but when I told him who you were, he changed his mind. We're going to cut across land to Acapulco. From there, we'll catch a ship to Alta California. Now, I know you're thinking going by land will be tough going. It will be tough, but we'll be on a road. Plus, you'll have protection. Once we get to Alta California, I can take you directly to your hacienda."

"That sounds perfect to me. How much will it cost?"

Miguel's eyes widened. "Cost? Why, it won't cost you anything. It's a favor to your family. Of course, the sergeant hopes that when your parents arrive, you will put in a good word to your father."

"What can I do to help? I can help cook."

Miguel laughed. "A lady such as yourself cook for a group of soldiers? We wouldn't think of it. Besides we have a cook, not that it's the best food you've tasted, but I'm sure you didn't have great food on the ship from Spain either."

It was Diega's turn to laugh. "Hardly."

"You have tomorrow to get some rest and to get ready for the journey. The only request is that you bring only what is essential. We're packing as lightly as possible."

"Oh, you don't have to worry about that!"

Diega spent the next day buying a few more clothes. She didn't buy another formal dress; she expected she could buy one once she arrived in Alta California, and there was no point in lugging that with them. She did buy some practical traveling clothes. As much as she wanted to buy pants, she knew that wouldn't be a good idea. She did buy some practical footwear though as well as a larger bag to pack the clothes. Still, what she had was minimal.

Diega met Miguel and the other soldiers at dawn, the day they were to leave.

"I said to pack light, but I thought you would have more than that."

"No point in taking much on this journey."

"It will make traveling much easier," replied Miguel. "You can ride in the wagon, or you can ride a horse if you prefer."

"Let me start with a horse, but I may switch to the wagon if I get too sore." Diega was glad she had thought to take equestrian lessons. They would certainly pay off.

Although Diega knew she would be the only woman accompanying the soldiers, it was still a shock to experience it. She noticed several of the men's eyes trained on her. Apparently, the sergeant noticed as well, and he walked over to her. He was a heavy-set man, older than the solders he commanded.

"Señorita Pulido. I am Sergeant Gonzalez. I am pleased to make your acquaintance. Soldiers are not generally in the company of a lady, much less one as beautiful as yourself. You must let me know if any of my men act inappropriately, if you know what I mean."

"I do. I don't mind the staring or even rough language. Men will be men, you know, but I will certainly let you know if there is anything more than that."

"A lady such as yourself shouldn't have to accept even the staring or language, but I appreciate that you understand the nature of men."

"Women do. If only men understood women."

The sergeant let out a hearty laugh that shook is belly. "That will never happen. I have a feeling that we will get along well. Very few ladies have such a sense of humor."

Diega took a liking to the amiable sergeant, though not in a romantic sense. The first day, she found herself riding in the wagon more than on horseback. When they stopped for the night, she showed the sergeant some of her magic tricks. He was enthralled. He would just scratch his head and then ask how she did it. "A magician can't give away all of their secrets." Still, she showed him how to do a couple of them. He tried to replicate what she showed, but he only had moderate success. He tried showing one of the soldiers, but the tricks didn't quite work out. The soldiers would laugh, and the poor sergeant would get angry. As promised by Miguel, the food was not that great. Other nights, the sergeant would pull out a chess set. None of the other soldiers knew how to play; so, Diega played chess with the sergeant. She let him win on some occasions, and she won on others. The nights were pleasant; it was the days that were monotonous.

Towards the end of the land portion of the journey, she was able to ride her horse most of the day. The journey from Veracruz to Acapulco took about three weeks. They passed through mountains, dense wooded areas, and through or over rivers. They encountered a lot of people along the route, more than Diega expected. Some of the travelers they encountered warned them about bandits. Fortunately, they didn't encounter any bandits, probably because of the group of soldiers. Diega was relieved when they finally reached Acapulco and saw the Pacific Ocean. Diega thought that she could have probably arrived quicker by taking a ship around Cape Horn. Perhaps Miguel had taken a liking to her and suggested the route even if it may have been longer and more arduous. Perhaps there was a reason for her to have taken this route. She was getting to know the soldiers who would probably be stationed near where she was headed, and she had gotten more accustomed to riding a horse. The land route was certainly cheaper than the sea route would have been, and even though the journey was monotonous, the sea route would have been even more so. All-in-all, the land journey probably was more advantageous for her.

"How long will we be in Acapulco before we get a ship to Alta California?" asked Diega.

"We won't be," replied Sergeant Gonzales.

"Would do you mean?"

"We will board immediately. I sent someone ahead to have a ship ready as soon as we arrived. It's a Santa Ana class ship of the line."

Like that was supposed to mean something to Diega. The sergeant must have noticed the puzzled look on her face. "It's a Spanish naval ship," the sergeant said smiling. "It's a 112-gun three decker, fully rigged ship with three square-rigged masts." The sergeant poked her lightly and jovially in her side with his elbow. "You have your magic tricks, and I have my knowledge of the military."

"We can't all be good at everything," smiled Diega.

"We will celebrate our arrival in Acapulco," exclaimed the sergeant. He walked over to the wagon and pulled out two bottles. "I hid these, or they would have never made it here. You will celebrate with us Señorita Pulido." He grabbed a cup and poured some of the liquid contents of a bottle into a cup and handed it to Diega. "Mezcal!" he said. "The English Navy has their rum, but I prefer mezcal, if I can't get a fine Spanish wine. Salud!" The soldiers took a swig from the bottle and passed it around. Once that bottle was finished, they repeated with the second bottle. Diega took a sip. It certainly wasn't one of the finer tequilas she had had, but after the long journey, it hit the spot. She quickly drank the remainder.

The sergeant wasn't kidding. They went immediately to the ship. Diega was given a very nice cabin. She was told that the second part of the journey would take about ten days. After Diega's voyage on the Cartagena, she was anxious about pirates. Fortunately, the voyage was uneventful. They traveled up the coast, within sight of land the entire trip. Diega went out on the deck whenever she could, mindful to stay out of the way of the crew. The soldiers that had accompanied her, not being sailors, didn't have a lot to do. She spent a lot of time talking to Miguel, who did most of the talking. Diega was content to hear stories of his time as a boy in Capistrano, which provided Diega with some knowledge of the area where Diega Pulido had grown up. She became more convinced that Miguel fancied her. She also spent time with Sergeant Gonzalez, playing chess, talking, or drinking. Apparently, the ship was carrying a lot of wine, and the sergeant always seemed to be drinking. The wine was very good, but she tried not to get drunk, lest she say something that would give herself away. She thought about the tavern where she had drunk wine with D'Artagnan, or Sir Gawain. She wished she could see him again, but she didn't know if fate would allow a third meeting.

On one occasion, Sergeant Gonzales had a little too much to drink, which loosened his tongue, and he said more to Diega than he would if he were sober. Diega learned that Sergeant Gonzales was to report to Guillermo Alvarado, who was appointed by the Spanish Crown to be governor over an area from the Mission of San Juan Capistrano, which was south of Reina de Los Angeles, to the Mission of San Buenaventura, which was northwest of Reina de Los Angeles. The actual Governor of Alta California was José Joaquin de Arrillaga. Apparently, Alvarado presented papers from King Charles IV to Governor Arrillaga in Monterey that granted Alvarado governorship of a portion of Alta California. Shortly after King Charles IV signed the orders, he abdicated the throne to his son, King Ferdinand VII, who had a brief reign, before Napoleon installed Joseph Bonaparte.

"But neither King Charles IV nor King Ferdinand VII are still King of Spain," interjected Diega. "Napoleon forced the King to abdicate, and Napoleon installed his brother Joseph Bonaparte."

"Yes. Joseph the Intruder," replied the sergeant. "But Spain must rid itself of the French and put the real king back as sovereign." The mild outburst from Sergeant Gonzalez sobered his mind enough to drop the subject.

Diega wished she hadn't said anything and had let the sergeant keep talking. Why did the area need a special governor over part of the region, and if Joseph Bonaparte was now king, why did the real Governor Arrillaga continue to let Alvarado act as governor over part of the region? Something was up, she just didn't know what yet. Diega thought of asking the sergeant if she would get to meet Governor Alvarado, but she didn't want to rile him further.

On the tenth day of their sailing journey, their ship anchored offshore near Reina de Los Angeles. There was no real port there. Diega learned that there were ports in San Diego and San Francisco, but it was quicker to get word to Governor Alvarado this way than to dock in San Diego and make their way north by land. Diego had been to Los Angeles in her own time, and she could hardly imagine that this little spot would one day grow into the large city that she knew.

They had to use jolly boats to transport to the shore. Sergeant Gonzalez was on the first boat, which irritated Diega because she was hoping to find out what information was so urgent for the governor to hear. The jolly boat departed and returned several times, and Diega was on the final journey of the jolly boat to the shore. By this time, whatever information that needed to be passed to the governor had already occurred. As the boat neared the shore, Diega saw Sergeant Gonzalez standing with another gentleman. When the boat was near the shore, Miguel helped pull it the remaining distance to the shore and helped her out. Sergeant Gonzalez motioned for her to come over. As she neared the sergeant, she hesitated and almost stopped. She recognized the man with the sergeant. It was the man who had departed the Cartagena, the one from whom she had bumped into and robbed of the coin purse filled with gold. She hoped he wouldn't recognize her. He apparently didn't. He smiled as Diega approached and Sergeant Gonzalez made the introduction.

"Governor Alvarado, may I present Señorita Diega Pulido."

Unsure of what to do, Diega bowed, which made the governor laugh. "Why don't I receive such respect from you, sergeant?" laughed Alvarado. The governor took Diega's hand and kissed it gently. "I am honored to meet the daughter of such a respected caballero as Don Carlos Pulido. I've never met him, but I've heard tell of him. When will we expect to see Don Carlos and Doña Catalina?"

"I'm not sure," said Diega. "I hope soon, but I'm not sure when they will leave."

"Well, their journey should be more pleasant than yours. I expect they will sail directly from Spain around Cape Horn. Why did you not sail directly from Spain instead of going to Veracruz?"

Diega improvised quickly. "When my parents asked that I go ahead of them, the first ship was going to Veracruz. Had I known what I now know, I would have waited for a direct ship."

"Ah, the impetuousness of youth. I barely remember anymore what that was like. Welcome to Alta California and Reina de Los Angeles. I've given permission for your longtime friend, Corporal Miguel Navarro, to escort you to your parents' hacienda."

"Thank you very much. I'm sorry to burden Miguel and to take him away from his duties."

"Nonsense," replied Alvarado. "What greater duty can there be than to escort a beautiful señorita such as yourself, and the daughter of a caballero?" Governor Alvarado took Diega's hand and kissed it again. "I'm sure we will see each other again. I travel along El Camino Real quite frequently."

Diega knew that El Camino Real translated in English to "The King's Highway." She supposed it was a road linking the missions of Alta California. She thought about asking Miguel but knew that

Diega Pulido was supposed to know what it was. A sudden fear gripped her. She should have thought about it before, but the thought just now sank in. What would Diega Pulido's Aunt Rosa think of the sudden arrival of an imposter? She wanted to break away from Miguel and run, but it was too late for that now. She may have fooled Miguel, but she could hardly fool Rosa. She didn't even know Rosa's last name. Was it Pulido or something else? Diega didn't even know how long the real Diega Pulido had been away. Had she left when she was a girl? A teenager? She could try to bring up some of the questions to Miguel, but she didn't know a way to do that without causing suspicion.

Miguel was his characteristic chatty self as they traveled by horseback southeast along El Camino Real. They traveled at a very slow pace. Diega was certain that Miguel liked her and wanted the journey to last as long as possible.

"I'm glad you decided to come with us," blurted Miguel. "You made the journey much more interesting."

"I doubt that," laughed Diega.

"No. It's true. The life of a soldier can sometimes be boring. The governor says he plans to have some parties so that we'll have something to break up the monotony. Perhaps you wouldn't mind coming to one with me."

"That could be fun." Diega estimated that they had traveled about four miles when they turned off the road. After about a half a mile, they came to an adobe hacienda with a tile roof.

"Does it look the way you remembered it?" asked Miguel.

Diega wasn't sure how to answer. "Mostly." Diega's stomach was in knots as they walked to the door. "When was the last time you saw my aunt?"

"Oh, about a year ago." I should be stationed here for a while though; so, I'm sure we'll see each other frequently." Miguel knocked on the door, and Diega stood behind him. Approximately thirty seconds later, the door was opened by a woman in her late forties or early fifties. "Good day, Doña Rosa."

"Miguel, it has been a while since I've seen you last. What brings you here?" asked Rosa.

"I have a surprise for you. I've brought your niece, Diega. She sailed from Spain to Veracruz, which is where I happened to run into her. She accompanied the group of soldiers I was with rather than sail from Veracruz."

Diega, terrified, stepped out from behind Miguel. "Hello, Aunt Rosa!" she said, acting as excited as she could as she hugged the stranger in front of her.

"Diega!" exclaimed the woman, tears beginning to well in her eyes and run down her cheek. "Is that all you have with you?" she asked pointing to Diega's meager bag.

"Yes. With sailing from Spain and traveling over land with soldiers, I don't have very much."

"Well, we'll have to take care of that. Come in. Come in. Miguel, won't you come in and celebrate Diega's homecoming with a glass of wine?"

Diega could see a mixture of conflicting emotions in Miguel's face. He looked as though he wanted to accept Rosa's invitation.

"Thank you for the offer, but I really must get back. Governor Alvarado was kind enough to let me bring Diega here, but I mustn't take advantage of his graciousness." Miguel stood motionless for an instant. He turned to walk away but turned back around and kissed Diega's hand. "I'll see you soon." With that, he walked away, mounted his horse, and rode back toward the road to Reina de Los Angeles.

Diega gulped. Miguel's presence at meeting Rosa was comforting. Now, she would have to face Rosa on her own. She walked into the hacienda, and Rosa closed the door behind her.

"Now, let's get that wine," said Rosa, "but before we do, why don't you tell me who the hell you really are because you're not Diega Pulido."

"I was afraid, you would say that, but I'm glad you at least waited until Miguel left."

"It wouldn't have benefitted either of us for me to have denied you in the presence of one of the new governor's soldiers. Why don't you start by telling me your real name?"

"My first name really is Diega, but my last name is Scott. Since you know I'm not the real Diega Pulido, could you tell me how long she's been gone? I've wondered how Miguel could have mistaken me for her."

"I wonder that myself. To answer your question, Diega Pulido left here with her parents ten years ago. I think you are probably a little older than she is. Now you answer a question for me. Why are you here? Are you an angel?"

"Definitely not, but my story is just as unbelievable. Why do you ask if I'm an angel?"

"Because I've been praying to God for an angel, and then you show up at my doorstep."

"Why were you praying for an angel, if you don't mind my asking?"

"Because you are not the only one pretending to be someone else. Governor Alvarado is a devil behind that smile of his. In the short time he has been here, people have started disappearing, and taxes have been raised significantly. He has an army behind him; so, everyone is afraid to do anything. What is your unbelievable story?"

"It's not something I tell people. Only one other person knows, and he guessed it. I can't believe I'm going to tell you, but I really don't know what else to do at this point. As soon as I tell you though, you will kick me out of the house."

"Let me be the judge of that. Now, out with it!"

Diega closed her eyes, as if that would make what she was about to say easier. She silently counted to three and then blurted, "I'm from the future." She opened one eye and then the other, expecting to see the woman with a gun, forcing her out of the house. Yet, when she opened both eyes, Rosa was standing there nonplussed. "Did you hear what I said?"

"I heard you." Rosa paused, "Wherever you're from, I think you're still the answer to my prayer, not what I expected, but God always delivers the unexpected."

"How can you believe me? I mean people just don't travel from one time to another! My own parents wouldn't believe me."

"Have you told them?

"No. As I said, only one other person knows."

"And I suppose he knows because he traveled through time as well?"

"Yes. You're very perceptive."

"You know, you seem to think you know your parents' reaction, but they just might surprise you if you told them. Rosa went over to a stand and retrieved a bottle of wine. She brought two glasses to a table and motioned for Diega to have a seat. "I have a feeling that we might need this while each of us tells our stories." She poured the red liquid into two glasses, a hearty amount in each. "There's another bottle if we need it. So, first, let's talk about where you come from in the future."

"The year I came from was 2025."

"Blessed Mother! What were the other occasions you traveled through time and why do you think that happened?

Diega told Rosa about her travel to 920 AD where she faced the Viking Eric Bloodaxe and met Sir Gawain. Then she told about her second trip in time to 1650 AD where she met Sir Gawain again, as D'Artagnan. Finally, she told of her journey to this time and the events she had encountered. She didn't tell her about the magical beings that Sir Gawain had encountered. The woman could probably only handle but so much, and stories about fairies and gods might put her beyond the limit of what she could accept.

Rosa mostly remained quiet during Diega's story, with an occasional raising of her eyebrows. "Do you think this Sir Gawain is here in this time?"

"I don't think so. He thought the last time we met that we wouldn't meet again."

"So why do you think you are here now?"

"I think it has something to do with the sword, Excalibur. That's been the impetus of all the other time travels. I think I've been led here because I believe that Governor Alvarado has the sword."

"What can he accomplish with this sword?"

"Probably nothing with the sword that he couldn't do otherwise. I think I'm to retrieve the sword, and then I will return to my own time. I just don't know what I'm supposed to do with the sword once I have it."

"God will reveal the reason when the time is right. In the meantime, I think you have another purpose here, which is to fight the injustice of Governor Alvarado."

"Do you know what the purpose is for him being here? I mean, there is another governor. Alvarado is just specially appointed for a specific reason. I think it has something to do with gold. There was a shipment being sent to Spain on the Cartagena when it was overtaken by pirates. I think that's why the soldiers who accompanied me were coming here, to tell him that the gold was stolen. He probably has orders to increase the gold shipments being sent to Spain. I know that around 1849, there will be a gold rush in California, but that will be much further north of here. Do you know if they have already found gold somewhere around here?"

"I don't, but that would explain the disappearance of people. They could be being forced to get the gold. I'm not sure why he is heavily taxing people though. Perhaps Friar Felipe could offer a suggestion."

"Can this friar be trusted? We don't know who the governor may have on his side. He could be paying people to act as spies."

"He most certainly can be trusted. We can make a trip to see him. He was originally at the mission of San Juan Capistrano, but he has been here for several years now, but before we talk with him, I will need to educate you about the culture here."

"Please. The more I understand, the less likely I'll do or say something foolish."

"When any empire takes possession of a new land, they generally follow a pattern. One of the first things is to settle the land. That, of course, doesn't make the indigenous peoples very happy. So, the next thing they do is to try to assimilate the indigenous peoples into their culture and religion. In the case of the Spanish in Alta California, they have tried to accomplish that by founding missions. So far, there are nineteen missions in Alta California, with a couple more planned. They run up the coast from Baja California to San Francisco de Asis, connected by El Camino Real. The missions aren't just the church but the immediate area, houses, and buildings surrounding the church. The purpose of the missions is to aid in converting and incorporating the native peoples. The missions also house soldiers to protect the community and to keep the indigenous peoples in line."

"Yes, but the indigenous peoples, even if they are indoctrinated into the culture, aren't generally seen as first-class citizens by the colonizers," interrupted Diega. "That's not right."

"It may not be right, but that's the way it usually is. Back to what I was saying, the missions instruct the indigenous peoples in religion, language, customs, and so forth so that they are slowly incorporated into the empire. You may hear the new converts called neophytes. There will always be some of the indigenous people who will not accept being incorporated into the empire. After the missions are established, presidios are established as military forts to protect larger areas. Finally, pueblos, such as Reina de Los Angeles, are established as agricultural communities."

"Somewhere along the way, I heard the term, *peon.* What is a peon?"

Rosa sighed. "Peons are the laborers. Mostly they are the indigenous peoples who are assimilated, or they are of mixed heritage. Often, they are forced to work to pay off a debt. Some of the ranches will house peons, and in return, the peons do the work on the ranch."

"So, they are basically slaves," scowled Diega.

"Not technically, but what you say contains much truth. Don Carlos and Doña Catalina did not agree with this, which is why they returned to Spain and why they probably will not return."

"Do you support peon labor? Is that why you remained here?" Diega's blood was beginning to boil. "I'm of mixed heritage. Will you put me to work? Is that why you're fine with me being here?"

"No. I do not support peon labor. I remained here for another reason."

Diega began to soften. "Why did you remain here then?"

"You are not the only one with a secret that few know. Diega Pulido is actually my daughter. Don Carlos is her father."

"What?" asked Diega astounded.

"Doña Catalina is my sister. She could not have children, but she and Carlos wanted them desperately. So, they asked me if I would have their child for them. I agreed. When I became pregnant and started to show, Catalina and I remained here out of sight for months. We said that Catalina was having a difficult pregnancy, and that I had to take care of her. Once Diega Pulido was born, everyone accepted her as Catalina's daughter. I didn't return to Spain so that they could live as a family."

"That's very noble of you. It must have been hard for you."

"It was. It is." Rosa's voice trembled as she choked back tears.

Diega walked over and hugged her. "I'm so sorry. I don't know what to say."

Rosa cleared her throat and regained control of her emotions. "A mother will sacrifice much so that her child can have a better life." Both Rosa and Diega remained silent. Rosa eventually broke the silence. "You said earlier that *Diega* isn't that common of a name in your time. Do you know why you were named that?"

Diega's eyes turned upward to the ceiling as she searched her memory. "I remember my mother telling me once. I had a great, great, I don't know how many greats, grandmother who was named Diega; I think her last name was De la Vega. She supposedly handed down a story that a descendant of hers would do something remarkable. My mother did some genealogy research. That just means she went back through records to find out about her ancestors. She said that nobody else had been named Diega; so, she chose that name for me."

Rosa became suddenly excited. "See. You are an answer to my prayers!"

"What do you mean?"

"Your ancestor is my Diega!"

"That's sort of a longshot. Don't you think? I mean just because my name is the same as hers doesn't prove anything. The story could also refer to anybody."

"I know in my heart it is you," beamed Rosa.

Diega changed the subject. "I need to find some more clothes. Is there a place in Reina de Los Angeles I can buy some?"

"There is a woman who lives here on the ranch, who can make clothes for you. Her name is Sesasi."

"Is she a peon?"

"No. She is free to leave at any time. She chooses to stay here and help."

"Are there any other people who stay here?"

"There are a total of four. Besides making clothes, Sesasi helps with the upkeep of the interior of the house. There is Bernardo. He is excellent with horses. Ati helps with everyday chores on the ranch. Citlali prepares meals, and I do a little bit of everything. Sesasi and Citlali stay here in the hacienda. Ati and Bernardo live in a separate smaller house. As I said previously, they are free to leave at any time. We share in the profits we make from the harvests. We do have other people who help out at certain times of the year with harvests, but we pay them. Unfortunately, there aren't a lot because most of the people who would do this kind of work are peons." Rosa paused a moment. "So, is the matter of you staying here settled?"

"If you will let me stay, I will. I don't really have anywhere else to go. I'll do my part though to earn my keep."

"Then the matter is settled. Besides, you are a descendant of my daughter."

"I still don't know that for a fact," replied Diega.

"I do. Now let me show you around the house. My brother-in-law, Diega's father, was slightly eccentric. He has quite the collection of various objects, and he even built hidden passageways in the house."

"Really! Where do they go?"

"I'll show you when we get to them."

The two-storied hacienda was rectangular shaped and surrounded a courtyard. They were in the grand room and walked into several rooms on the first floor: a dining room, a smaller reception room, a room where business was conducted, an entertainment room, and armament and trophy room, a small library, a patio, and a small chapel. There was a small outbuilding adjacent to the grand room for bathing. The kitchen and pantry were in a separate building with a covered walk a short distance from the dining room. Rosa said that this was to prevent heat from entering the house and to minimize the risk of fire in the main house. The second floor consisted of mostly bedrooms with each bedroom having a terrace that encircled the entire second floor.

Rosa pointed out a room that Diega could use for her bedroom. There was also a small wine cellar underground.

"This is such an extraordinary and beautiful house," exclaimed Diega. The family must have been very rich."

"Don Carlos was the richest caballero in Alta California."

"What exactly is a caballero?" questioned Diega.

"Caballeros own the ranches, and some are Spanish nobles."

"Ok, now where are these hidden passageways you mentioned?"

"What does this word *ok* mean?

"I'm sorry. I try not to use that word in other times, but it is a very common word in my time. It originated in the United States. Describing what it means is difficult because it is used in many different ways. It generally means something like *all right* or as a word for acceptance of something."

"Ok," repeated Rosa slowly as if trying to match the way Diega had used it.

Diega laughed. "You've got it. Now for the hidden passageways."

"There are two that merge into each other. One is in the library." They walked into the library and Rosa went to one of the shelves. She reached under the shelf, and Diega heard a clicking noise. With her hand under the shelf, Rosa pushed, and one section of a bookcase opened inward into darkness. "I haven't been in here in years. I do not like to go in. You can explore it yourself later. Rosa pulled the bookcase back until another clicking sound indicated that it was closed. "The other hidden passageway is in the armament and trophy room."

They had been in this room earlier when Rosa was providing a tour of the hacienda, but they had just walked through the door, and Diega had not paid a lot of attention to what all was inside. Once she examined the room more carefully, she was amazed at what Don Carlos had in this room. Various types of swords hung on the wall and in stands. There were rapiers, sabres, broadswords, longswords, cutlasses, and even a katana. Sir Gawain would love this, she thought. There were several flintlocks, both pistols and long guns. On the wall hung a coiled bullwhip with a gold-laced handle. Diega noticed a French rapier hanging on the wall and felt drawn to it. She walked over, looked at Rosa as if to ask if she could take it down. Rosa nodded, and Diega removed the rapier. It was a beautiful sword whose metal was untarnished.

"Carlos took extra care of that sword, polishing it regularly," stated Rosa.

Diega examined the sword carefully. On the hilt, she saw something scratched into it. She looked closer. Weak-kneed, her legs almost gave out from under her. What was scratched into the hilt was the name *D'Artagnan.* This was D'Artagnan's sword; she could hardly believe it.

"Is something wrong?" asked Rosa.

"This rapier has the name D'Artagnan on it."

"The other person who traveled through time?" asked Rosa.

"Yes."

"This can't be a coincidence," posited Rosa. "I was right. You are the answer to my prayer. Feel free to use the sword and anything else in here. In fact, you can have the sword."

Diega was still marveling at the sword while Rosa was talking about the hidden passageway. "I'm sorry. What did you say? I was still admiring the rapier."

"I was just going to show you the second hidden passageway." Rosa moved a rug that uncovered a trap door. The floor in this room was wooden, and the trap door blended in so well, she would not have noticed it even without the rug covering it, if she had not looked closely.

Rosa opened the door in the floor, and Diega looked down. There were iron handles in the wall going down to the ground about seven feet below.

"This passageway runs into the one from the library. This part of the hacienda was built over rock that leads to a cave below. We can go outside, and I'll show you the cave entrance." The mouth of the cave wasn't as close to the hacienda as Diega expected. It was perhaps one hundred yards away. Vines grew down covering the entrance to the cave. In fact, there were a lot of vines growing down, and one would have to know precisely where the entrance to the cave was. Otherwise, solid rock was behind the vines. Rosa walked immediately to the right spot and parted the vines, and they walked in. The mouth of the cave was quite spacious with a high ceiling.

"Where are the passageways that lead up to the house?"

Rosa pointed, and Diega walked behind a gap between two rocks. There was a narrow path that led about twenty feet to more vines. Behind the vines, Diega could see a wooden door. She turned around and walked back through the gap to the mouth of the cave. Rosa was gone. "Rosa?" called out Diega.

"Over here."

Diega followed the sound of the voice, which was difficult to pinpoint due to the acoustics inside the cave. She found Rosa hidden behind more rocks. "What's over here?"

"Move that rock," ordered Rosa pointing to one of several rocks. The rock was heavy, but Diega was able to move it. Underneath was a chest.

"Is this a treasure chest?"

"In a manner of speaking. When Carlos, Catalina, and Diega left, Carlos left a good portion of his wealth behind so that I could use it to take care of the ranch. The money from the harvests usually earns us enough to live on, but some years, I've had to use some of the money to get by. I've used it sparingly, and a good bit remains."

"I can't believe that you're trusting me with this information," exclaimed Diega.

"I trust very few with this knowledge, but what would my faith mean if I could not trust the answer to my prayer?"

"You are a remarkable woman, Aunt Rosa."

The two women went back to the hacienda. Diega was looking at the alcohol that was available and thought how good a margarita would taste. There was no ice and no triple sec, but she tried to make a reasonable facsimile of one. She took some tequila mixed in a little cognac, added lime juice and some mint. In place of sugar, she used some agave syrup. She made one for Rosa and one for herself.

"What are you doing over there, child?" asked Rosa, "besides making a mess."

"There is a drink in my time called a margarita. It's a mixed drink or also called a cocktail. Unfortunately, I don't have the right ingredients; so, I've made a substitution. I'm going to call it a margarosa, in your honor."

"I've never seen people mix alcohols together. Everyone just drinks it straight."

Diega handed her one, and Rosa waited for Diega to try her margarosa first. Diega was no mixologist, and the drink wasn't quite what she was expecting. About that time, Sesasi walked into the room.

"Here, Sesasi," said Rosa, handing her the drink. "Try this and tell me what you think."

Sesasi took the glass and took a sip. The look on Sesasi's face told Diega that Sesasi felt the same way about it as she did.

Rosa laughed and took the glass back from Sesasi. "I might as well try it myself, but by the looks on both of your faces, I probably shouldn't." Rosa took more than a sip, and her face contorted. Both Diega and Sesasi began laughing.

"I guess I'll have to experiment some more."

"Don't waste good alcohol by trying to perfect this."

"Ok. I mean, alright. Point taken."

"Wait here, Sesasi," said Rosa. Diega was curious as Rosa walked out, leaving the two women alone in the room. Both were quiet, not knowing what to say. Soon, Diega heard a bell ringing. She started to go see what was going on, but Rosa had said to wait here. Rosa walked back into the room and a few minutes later, two men and another woman joined Rosa, Sesasi, and Diega in the room. Diega hoped that she wasn't going to make them try the margarosa; she didn't think she could handle the embarrassment.

"This is Bernardo, Ati, Citlali, and you know Sesasi. Everyone, I would like to introduce to you my niece, Diega, who has come from Spain. She will be our guest for a while." Ati, Citlali, and Sesasi slightly bowed to Diega, but Diega noticed that Bernardo had a strange look on his face. "I wanted you to meet her. Please treat her as one of our family. Sesasi, would you be willing to take Diega's measurements and make some clothes for her. She didn't bring much on the long journey from Spain."

"It will be my pleasure." Sesasi smiled at Diega and left the room. Diega supposed she was going to get something to measure her for clothes.

"Don't let her help with the cooking," kidded Rosa. Citlali had a puzzled look on her face; so, Rosa handed her the glass with the margarosa and told her to take a sip. Citlali did and made the same grimace as Sesasi.

"I understand now," coughed Citlali.

Citlali and Ati left the room, but Rosa put a hand on Bernardo, indicating for him to stay behind. Once the others left, Bernardo, Rosa, and Diega were the only ones left in the room.

"Ati, Citlali, and Sesasi joined us shortly after the family left over twelve years ago, and they wouldn't know you. Bernardo has been with the family for over twenty-five years. He can also tell who anyone is by the way they ride a horse. He would know that you are not the real Diega Pulido as soon as you mounted a horse. I'm not saying that the real Diega Pulido was a better or worse rider than you, but Bernardo would know. He is truly gifted."

Bernardo still had a puzzled look on his face.

Rosa continued. "Bernardo, this is Diega Scott, but she is to be known as my niece, Diega Pulido. She is the answer to my prayer. I don't know how, yet, but I know it in my heart."

A look of understanding slowly began to show on Bernardo's face. He smiled and hugged Diega tightly. "Welcome home Señorita Diega." With that he turned and left.

Sesasi entered the room with a long, narrow ribbon. "Let's go to your room, Señorita Diega, and I will make the necessary measurements to make clothes for you." They went upstairs to Diega's bedroom, and Diega undressed. Sesasi put the ribbon around Diega at various places and marked the ribbon.

Diega noticed that the ribbon Sesasi used wasn't like the traditional tape measure she was used to seeing. "Aren't you going to write down the measurements on paper?"

"I am making the marks on the ribbon. Don't worry. I've made clothes for many people." Sesasi continued measuring. "You are very tall, Señorita Diega."

"Please, you can just call me Diega."

"You are a very beautiful woman, Señorita Diega. With the clothes I make you, all of the men will flock to you!" Sesasi smiled and left the room so that Diega could dress.

After dressing, Diega put away the few things she had. She kept the small bag with her, she supposed, to comfort her more than anything. She walked back downstairs but didn't see Rosa anywhere. She walked to the door and started to go outside, but before she opened the door, she heard raised voices. She opened the door very slightly and peeked out to see Rosa surrounded by eight soldiers. One had a sword pointed at Rosa. Diega knew Rosa was in trouble. Diega calmed herself and quickly ran to the armament room. She grabbed four unloaded hand-held muskets. She found the paper cartridges containing the black powder and musket ball and hoped they were not too old. There were paper cartridges for the long guns and for the pistols. She bit the end off the paper cartridge and spit it out. Next, she poured a little powder into the pan. The remainder, she poured down the barrel and put the paper and ball in and jammed it down with the ramrod. She quickly repeated the process with the remaining pistols. She left the pistols on a table while she grabbed two rapiers off the wall. One of them was D'Artagnan's rapier. From her bag, she pulled out a black hood. This was the same black hood she had been forced to wear in the Bastille. She always carried it with her and even slept with it, which is how it had made the time travel journey with her. The black hood she had been forced to wear in the Bastille had shamed her. She never wanted to feel that way again, and keeping it with her was a reminder to never feel helpless and scared again. She had never worn it since the Bastille, but she would don the hood today, not for shame but for justice and courage. She put it over her head and tightened the rope to keep it on. A black hat was in the corner of the room, and she retrieved it and put it on her head. She put a cloth in her mouth so that the swords would not cut her mouth and put the swords, tip to hilt, centered in her mouth so that the hilts extended outward. Tying the scabbard for D'Artagnan's rapier tightly around her waist, she inserted two of the pistols through the belt holding the scabbard. Before leaving the armament room, she picked up the remaining two loaded pistols from the table.

An image of how she looked flashed through her mind. The soldiers would see a black-hooded figure with a black hat burst through the door wearing a dress with two swords held in her mouth, two pistols by her side, and a pistol in each hand. As she opened the door, she saw Bernardo lying on the ground with blood pouring profusely from his forehead. One of the soldiers must have hit him hard in the head with the butt of a flintlock. The soldiers were laughing and shoving Rosa from one to the other. They stopped and stared at the sight of the hooded figure standing in the doorway. One started to raise his gun, and Diega charged toward them. Before the soldier had raised the gun halfway, Diega fired her pistol, the musket ball hitting him in the forehead. The powder was still effective. She shot another in the chest. Throwing both emptied pistols to the ground, she pulled out the two pistols held by her belt and fired both, dropping two more soldiers. Four soldiers lay dead while the remaining four readied their swords. Diega grabbed the swords and charged with a rapier in each hand. Two soldiers advanced toward her, and she unarmed them so quickly that even they appeared astonished but not as astonished as when a rapier plunged into each's torso. Diega pulled out D'Artagnan's rapier from one of the soldiers just in time to parry the thrust of the sword from one of the remaining soldiers. Knocking the sword out of his hand, she slit his throat with her rapier. Only one soldier remained, and he quickly held his hands in the air and closed his eyes. A thought entered Diega's mind and with quick flicks of her sword, she carved the letter *H* into the side of his neck. The soldier put his hand to the wound, and Diega put the tip of her rapier at this throat.

"I'm going to let you live as a warning to what will happen if any soldier tries to do this to anyone else in this pueblo. You are going to tie the bodies of the soldiers to their horses and lead them back to where you came. You will always carry the scar with the letter *H* to remind you."

The soldier was so scared, he could hardly speak. All he could manage to utter was, *H*?

"Like a bird of prey, I will be watching. If you do any injustice, I will swoop down and snatch you. El Halcón will be watching!"

The soldier nervously and quickly put his seven comrades, belly to saddle on their horses and tied their arms to their legs to keep them from falling off. He tied the reins to a single rope and led the horses away from the hacienda.

Rosa was still shaking. By this time, Ati, Citlali, and Sesasi had arrived after hearing the sound of musket fire. Citlali had a wet cloth and held it to Bernardo's forehead.

"Let's get him out of the hot sun," ordered Rosa. "Bring him inside."

Ati and Diega helped Bernardo inside. Citlali and Sesasi gave Bernardo some water to sip, and they put some herbs on his head and wrapped a bandage around it.

Diega had taken her hood off. She and Rosa were sitting beside Bernardo. "I'm sorry Aunt Rosa, I'm afraid I made matters worse."

"How can they be worse than Bernardo and I being killed, which would have surely happened if you hadn't saved us. I told you that you were the answer to my prayer, but I would have never guessed that God would send an avenging angel of justice."

Bernardo looked up at Diega and smiled. He weakly squeezed her hand.

"He will be fine," said Sesasi. "He has a hard head." She hadn't meant it as a joke, but Rosa and Diega chuckled.

"I'm serious Aunt Rosa. What do I do? I was wearing a dress. The soldier knows I'm a woman. When he gets back, he'll tell everyone. They'll know that I'm the only new person to arrive here. I should leave, but I don't want to leave you in danger."

Rosa put her finger to Diega's lips to hush her. "Listen to me Diega. First of all, you killed seven soldiers and sent the eighth one back. Believe me when I say that the last thing he will tell anyone is that a woman did this. By the time he describes you, they will think Death itself descended. But you can't let our hacienda be the only place you are seen, or they will put it together. You are going to have to be seen at other places, but you are going to have to be careful. I don't want to see anything happen to you. Maybe after a few times, you can stop. You cannot be seen in a dress though. The first thing Sesasi makes for you needs to be pants. They will need to be black, along with a black shirt that can match your hood. I'm sorry child to make you wear pants."

"I'm not," interrupted Diega. "I prefer pants."

Rosa's eyebrows rose, adding more wrinkles to her forehead than she already had, producing a horrified look on her face.

"It's ok. I mean alright, Aunt Rosa. Women in my time wear both."

Rosa just shook her head. She called Sesasi over and told her to make the black shirt and pants for Diega. Ati said that he could find her some black boots. Bernardo was now sitting up.

Rosa looked at Diega. "Another thing is that you will need to act as ladylike as possible around others. We want people to think of you as exactly opposite of your avenging persona."

"That may be hard to do. I accompanied the soldiers for several weeks. They know I'm not exactly the ladylike type."

"That may be so," answered Rosa, "but you must do your best now that you're here."

"What did the soldiers want?" asked Diega. "Tell me what happened."

Rosa began. "The soldiers knew I lived here alone. They said that my taxes were too high to pay, and they were going to confiscate the ranch and hacienda. I told them to get off my property and that if I owed taxes, I would pay it at tax collecting time. They didn't like that; so, one of them shoved me. That's when Bernardo came up telling them that if I told them to go, they needed to go. One of the soldiers took the butt of his gun and hit Bernardo on the head. They were shoving me around saying that all they needed to do was kill me, and they would take the land anyway. One of the other soldiers said it would be much easier with me dead. They could kill everyone here and dispose of the bodies. They would then blame my death on one of the native people."

"That's awful!" fumed Diega.

"This Governor Alvarado is a bad man."

At the military headquarters in Reina de Los Angeles, Governor Alvarado was talking with Captain Juan Ramon when a soldier knocked on the door. "Enter," commanded Captain Ramon.

The soldier entered, saluted, and closed the door. "We have a situation," said the soldier. One of our men has returned with seven dead soldiers, and he has quite a story."

"What?" gasped Governor Alvarado.

"Send him in," ordered Captain Ramon.

The soldier exited and sent in the other soldier. The man entered and saluted.

"What is going on?" demanded Captain Ramon.

"We went to the ranch like you ordered us. We had everything in order when a demon descended on us. He wore a black hood, and his eyes were cold as death. I imagine if anyone were to look upon his face, the person would die immediately."

"What is this nonsense?" bellowed the captain.

"It is not nonsense. The man killed by gun and sword. He left me alive to tell the story, and he carved this into my neck so that I would carry it with me forever." The soldier pulled down his bandana, uncovering a fresh wound that had only recently stopped bleeding.

Alvarado rose from his chair and walked over. The captain was already looking at the wound. "It looks like a letter," gasped Alvarado.

"Is this supposed to mean something?" demanded the captain.

"The man called himself Halcón. That is what the *H* is for. Like a hawk, he will swoop down and kill us if we harm the people."

"Where did this happen?" asked the captain.

"At the Pulido ranch," replied the soldier.

"Where?" sputtered Alvarado.

"At the Pulido ranch," repeated the soldier.

Governor Alvarado turned to the captain. "Why wasn't I informed of this? I just had Señorita Diega Pulido escorted there earlier today. Don Carlos Pulido, who owns the ranch, and his wife Doña Catalina are coming back from Spain. Don Carlos is the richest caballero in Alta California."

"That is all, Private. You are dismissed," ordered the captain. The private saluted and headed for the door. The captain walked behind him. "Oh, Private?" said the captain as the private had his hand on the door. The private turned around. A gasp escaped his open mouth and his eyebrows shot upward. The captain's sabre had impaled him, the point pricking the wooden door. "Sorry about this, Private, but your death is going to absolve us of any wrongdoing."

"Why did you kill him?" gasped Alvarado.

"We are going to claim that this group of soldiers went rogue and that they certainly weren't acting on any orders from us. We have the utmost respect for the Pulido family and will see that no future harm comes to them."

"Quick thinking," replied Alvarado. "It's getting a little late to call on them now, but we'll pay them a visit first thing in the morning. It will also give them some time to calm down."

No one at the Pulido ranch slept well that night. Diega tossed and turned, expecting soldiers to arrive at any moment to arrest her. She hoped that harm to innocents wouldn't continue to follow her. She finally went to sleep near dawn. She hadn't been asleep long when Sesasi woke her. "Can't I sleep in?" mumbled Diega sluggishly.

"No," exclaimed Sesasi. "Your Aunt Rosa said that soldiers may come here this morning, and you must be ready. I have a dress ready for you, and we need to fix your hair."

"Where did that dress come from?" questioned Diega.

"I haven't had time to make a new one for you yet. This is a dress that was here. Because you are so tall, I had to add length to it with another fabric. It may look a little strange, but it will do."

"Actually, it looks quite nice."

"As soon as the soldiers leave, you are taking a bath."

Diega didn't know if Sesasi seemed so direct because Spanish wasn't Sesasi's native language or if Sesasi was always just that direct. You mean I'll take a bath if the soldiers haven't arrested me."

"Your Aunt Rosa says they won't."

Diega put on the dress, which fit nicely, and Sesasi helped Diega with her hair. No sooner had they finished than they heard horses ride up. Diega peered through the window and saw Governor Alvarado with several solders. She hurried down the stairs and when outside to find Rosa already there.

"Ladies," began Governor Alvarado. "I heard what happened, and I came to express my outrage over what happened to you yesterday. Captain Ramon will explain how this happened."

"I arrived a few months ago and found the troops here in a sorry shape. The previous captain ran things rather loosely."

Captain Ramon locked eyes on Diega and stopped speaking for a few seconds. Diega knew the look. The captain was attracted to her. "As I was saying, the men didn't like being in a strict regiment. I've had to really work with them. This group of eight soldiers who accosted you yesterday were rogue. They weren't acting on my orders. I would never order such a thing be done to civilians. I'm surprised that the remaining soldier even returned, but he won't be bothering you ... or anyone ... ever again. We'll see to it that you are protected."

"No harm will come to the Pulido family as long as I'm governor. Once your nerves are settled, I'd like to invite you to my house for a party."

The sound of a galloping horse caused everyone's attention to be drawn away from the governor and the captain. Miguel rode up and quickly dismounted. He went over to Diega. "I came as soon as I heard. Are you alright?"

"Yes," replied Diega. She started to say more but was cut short by Captain Ramon.

"Corporal!" shouted the captain. "What are you doing here, and on whose orders did you leave your post."

Miguel saluted. "Sir, I just came to see if Señorita Pulido and her family were alright."

"And you don't think we can do that?" berated the captain. "This is the very thing I was talking about, soldiers running off on their own. Corporal, you will immediately return to your post. Do you understand?"

"Yes sir."

"I have a mind to put you on a ship to Spain or lock you in the stockade. You will never leave your post again unless ordered to do so."

"Yes sir." Miguel looked deflated and embarrassed as he mounted his horse and rode off.

"Don't worry. I'll have these men whipped into shape."

"I'm sure you will whip them well, into shape I mean," interjected Diega. The captain gave somewhat of a scowl, and Diega remembered that she was supposed to be ladylike. "What about this Halcón? He was positively dreadful. I didn't know who to fear more, him or the soldiers."

"So, he really was here," said Alvarado. "We thought it might have been something the returning soldier made up."

"No, he was here and quite dreadful looking," informed Diega.

"We'll take care of him," asserted Alvarado. "Now, how about you come next week to the party at my place. Perhaps you'll allow the captain to escort you ... to make sure of your safety."

The captain took Diega's hand, slid up the white glove, and kissed her hand. "I would consider it an honor," beamed Captain Ramon.

"We'll be there," interjected Rosa, "and my niece would be honored as well if Captain Ramon would escort her."

Captain Ramon mounted his horse. The others had never dismounted. Captain Ramon waved his hand, and everyone rode off.

"You are going to have to try to be more ladylike," demanded Rosa.

"Was having Captain Ramon escort me punishment for not acting more ladylike?"

"Of course not," retorted Rosa. "I can't stand him anymore than you can. He's pompous and arrogant, but we have to play along. Sometimes you have to play the fox rather than the hawk."

"Time for your bath," ordered Sesasi.

"I give up," ceded Diega.

Diega felt much better after her bath. She had just finished putting on her dress when Rosa came in. "Please come with me, Diega. We are going to see Bernardo."

"How is he doing today? Is he feeling better?"

"He's back at work," replied Rosa.

"Already!"

"I told you he had a hard head," announced Sesasi as she entered the room. "I'll have your black shirt and pants ready tomorrow. By the time of the governor's party, I'll have two new dresses for you."

"Beggars can't be choosers, but I hope one will be a plain dress."

"If you insist, I'll have one for you tomorrow, but I don't know why such a beautiful woman would want a plain dress. I would think the pants would be enough."

"I can only wear the pants as Halcón."

Diega walked with Rosa to the pasture where horses were grazing. Bernardo wore a sombrero, but Diega could still see a bandana wrapped over his head wound.

"Aw, Señorita Diega," beamed Bernardo.

"I wish you all would just call me Diega."

"Of course, Señorita Diega."

"These are beautiful horses!"

"Do you ride well?" asked Bernardo.

"I ride. I'll let you be the judge of how well."

"Just as a musician can play even better with a finer instrument, a good rider can ride even better with a fine horse. And I have a fine horse for Señor Halcón." Bernardo whistled, and a beautiful black stallion galloped over to them. Since you will wear black, you need a black horse, and Tornado is one of the finest horses I have ever trained." Bernardo made a motion with his hand and said, "Bow to the lovely lady, Tornado." On cue,

Tornado extended his right leg, bent his left knee so that it touched the ground, and bent down his head.

"Wow! I'm impressed."

Bernardo saddled Tornado and asked Diega to mount the horse. Next, he asked her to ride around so that he could see how she rode. Diega rode the horse around the pasture at various paces. When she rode back to Bernardo, he said, "Not bad." He gave her a few pointers, which Diega quickly mastered. She was glad she had taken the equestrian lessons. "I want to work with you every day that you are able. You may have to ride faster than you've ever ridden, and Halcón needs to be able to do a few tricks."

"What kind of tricks?" asked Diega excitedly.

"Like running from behind the horse and leaping into the saddle or running from the side of the horse and jumping on. With a regular saddle, there is a limit to the tricks that can be done, and the tricks I will teach are more to save your life than to use to show off.

"Why not use a special trick saddle when riding all the time?"

"Because it will limit your and the horse's maneuverability. You don't want a trick saddle when you have to ride the horse fast for long distances."

Diega spent the rest of the day with Bernardo. She was glad when it finally ended. Sore, tired, and sweaty, she went back to the hacienda and took another bath.

"Glad to see you're listening to me about being more ladylike, two baths in one day," jested Rosa. "You'll get a brief reprieve from riding tomorrow. We're going to pay a visit to Friar Felipe, but don't worry, we'll back by noon so you will still have plenty of riding time."

Diega slept well that night. The sound that awoke her was Sesasi's voice asking, "Bath for you Señorita Diega?"

"You're kidding, right?" yawned Diega.

"Yes, Señorita Diega."

"Sesasi, please call me Diega."

"Yes, Señorita Diega."

Diega shook her head and dressed quickly. Rosa was waiting for her downstairs, and they ate a light breakfast. When they went outside, Bernardo had a carriage waiting for them. "We're taking a carriage?" muttered Diega.

"To keep up your appearance of a Spanish lady," rebutted Rosa.

"Don't worry, Señorita Diega. You will get plenty of riding when you return," jested Bernardo as the two women got into the carriage.

"Bernardo, please call me Diega."

"Yes, Señorita Diega."

Rosa chuckled under her breath as she headed the carriage toward Reina de Los Angeles. They arrived at the Church of Our Lady Queen of the Angels, which Rosa said was an extension of the Mission San Gabriel Arcángel that was about ten miles east. Friar Felipe, who Rosa said was of the Franciscan order, greeted them inside. "This is my niece, Señorita Diega Pulido," announced Rosa.

"It is a pleasure to meet you," smiled the friar.

"Likewise," demurred Diega. Friar Felipe was one of those men whose age was difficult to determine. He had thin white hair and was slim but sturdy looking. Perhaps he was in his fifties, but Diega thought she could be a decade off either way.

"I knew your parents, Don Carlos and Doña Catalina, but that was a long time ago. I've moved from mission to mission quite a bit in Alta California."

"Friar Felipe is truly a servant of God," asserted Rosa. "I have seen friars who have converted the native peoples but not really care about their welfare. These friars are tools of the government who keep the indigenous peoples in forced servitude and treat them like second-class citizens, but Friar Felipe tries to help them and allow them to return to their own people. He sees everyone as a child of a loving Father."

"You put me on a pedestal; I am but a follower of Christ doing the best that I can. Señorita Diega, you must think this a beastly land. I heard what happened to everyone at the ranch with the soldiers. You're fortunate to be alive. I hope that everyone's nerves have calmed. Is it true that this Halcón arrived on the scene to save you?"

"Yes," interjected Rosa. "It is true. Thank you for your concern, but tell me what you have heard lately."

Friar Felipe smiled and turned to Diega. "Your aunt knows that I hear a lot as a friar. Sometimes I think she visits just to learn the latest." Felipe turned, looked around to see that they were alone, and then turned to face both women. There has not been much talk of Halcón. The soldiers, led by Captain Ramon, have tried to keep it quiet. I have heard that tomorrow during siesta, two soldiers will post a notice that taxes are to be collected on a certain date. The notice will also say that wine must be given instead of grapes. They want one bottle of every five. Apparently, making the wine from grapes is too time consuming for them."

"Are you certain of this?" asked Rosa.

"Yes. They will also demand a higher percentage of taxes than in the past from the caballeros."

"Do you think this will cause the caballeros to revolt?" questioned Rosa.

"To protest, definitely. But how can they revolt against so many soldiers? A revolt would be pointless. They would end up imprisoned and their lands confiscated."

Diega had been listening to the exchange but finally had to interject in the conversation. "Do you know how long the specially appointed Governor Alvarado will be in power until Governor de Arrillaga is allowed full control again?"

"No one knows," answered Felipe. "We aren't sure why he was specially appointed over this area in the first place."

"My niece thinks it has something to do with gold. Apparently, a ship with gold from this area was sent from Veracruz to Spain, but it was robbed by pirates before it reached Havana. She overheard that soldiers were to be sent immediately here to inform the governor of something important. She actually made the journey with them but didn't learn any more of their intentions."

"That's quite a theory!" exclaimed Felipe. "But it would explain most of what has been happening with the disappearances of people and why the Spanish would want someone to specifically oversee the operation, but I have not heard of any significant amounts of gold being found in this area."

"Keep listening," advised Rosa, "and let us know if you hear anything else."

Friar Felipe smiled. "I will continue to be your secret spy."

The women bid Friar Felipe good-bye, left the church, and headed back to the ranch. After they were on the road, Rosa said, "I think Halcón needs to be seen tomorrow when the notice is posted. If there are only two soldiers who will post the notice, that won't put you into too much danger. You will have to ride in and out as quickly as you can."

"That's what I was thinking too."

When they got back to the ranch, Sesasi had Halcón's clothes ready and laid out on Diega's bed. Diega tried them on and thought they would work great. The shirt was cut to minimize the appearance of her breasts and hips, but she still had plenty of flexibility. Sesasi had also fashioned a binder to flatten the appearance of breasts. "I need to wear these while riding today. I don't want to wear these on a horse for the first time tomorrow."

Diega met Bernardo and told him the plans for tomorrow. Bernardo told Diega where notices were posted. "I had planned for you to ride another horse today. We'll start out with the other horse and then let you ride Tornado some more. I think you need to ride Tornado tomorrow." The other horse's name was Thunder. He was also a black stallion and looked a lot like Tornado. Diega rode Thunder for a few hours and then rode Tornado for about two hours. During breaks to give time for the horses to rest, Bernardo instructed Diega in the use of the bullwhip. She didn't seem to have a knack for it, but Bernardo kept encouraging her and telling her that she would get the hang of it soon enough.

The next day in Reina de Los Angeles, two soldiers marched down the street during the siesta. One was beating a drum, and the other carried the notice. The neophytes, Mestizos, Castizos, and other castes raised their heads from their naps as the soldiers marched down the street. Once they saw them, they lowered their heads and returned to their naps. When the soldiers reached their destination, the drummer stopped, and they began to post the notice.

A horse raced down the street carrying a rider in black garb with a black hood and black hat. The passing rider caused some to look up, and few barking dogs gave chase. As the two soldiers finished tacking the notice, Halcón rode up and brandished a rapier to one of the men's throats. Diega purposely lowered her voice as much as she could to try to sound like a man. Still, she wanted to speak as briefly as possible. "Take down that notice." The men hesitated, and Halcón pushed the rapier into the skin of the soldier causing blood to trickle down. The other soldier immediately took down the notice. Halcón, with rapier still touching the one's throat, handed another notice to the other soldier. "Put this up. Hurry." The soldier was so nervous that he dropped the notice. As he bent over to pick it up, Halcón slashed the letter *H* into the back seat of his pants. The soldier stood up quickly with the new notice in hand and promptly posted it. Halcón shouted, "Back to the barracks, slapping one soldier on the back with the flat part of the sword. They ran away, stumbling as they hurried. Halcón rode quickly out of town. With all of the excitement, everyone was fully awake from their siestas. A mob of people gathered around the new notice that read: *Let it be known that Guillermo Alvardo is an enemy of the people and will soon face justice.* Underneath the proclamation was the name, *Halcón.*

No further appearances of Halcón occurred that week, but Friar Felipe said that the appearance of Halcón had been the talk of the pueblo. A reward of one thousand pesos had been offered for the capture of Halcón. Diega spent the rest of the week up until the governor's party working with Bernardo and the horses and practicing with the whip. At night, after dinner, Rosa showed her how to dance. In the back of Diega's mind, though, she wondered if all of this was what she was supposed to be doing. She kept thinking of Excalibur and how it played into all of this. She wondered if her gut feelings had been accurate. The sword could be half a world away.

The day of Governor Alvarado's party had arrived. Sesasi had made a beautiful dress, as fine as any Diega had seen. The color was mostly what Diega called a cinnamon rose. It had a high waistline and a low rounded neckline. The top of the dress had black lace that was sewn over the top of the dress, exposing a little of Diega's chest. The sleeves ran down between her shoulders and elbows, and she had long white gloves. Rosa lent her silver jewelry: bracelet, necklace, and earrings.

The party was at the governor's house, which was next to the military compound. It had a large courtyard, which was where the party was held. Guests were announced as they entered. Rosa and Diega each got a glass of wine and stood by themselves for a moment.

"It looks like this is where all the wine is going that they collect as part of taxes," muttered Diega.

"You are receiving the attention of many men tonight. They are looking at you every chance they get. You are very beautiful, Diega."

"Thank you, Aunt Rosa."

Alvarado approached the two women. "I'm so glad you came tonight. I must say Diega, you look absolutely stunning. I believe you will be dancing all night."

"Governor?" interjected Rosa while he seemed in a good mood. "Might some of the women be given a tour of your house. Many of us have never been inside before."

"Er ... yes, of course, but only if I may have the first dance with Señorita Diega before Captain Ramon takes the rest." The governor looked around and saw Miguel standing nearby, and he motioned for Miguel to come over. "Corporal, please lead a tour for some of the ladies, but please don't go into my study. It's quite a mess at the moment." Alvarado led Diega to the dance floor while Miguel gathered some of the ladies who wanted to see the house.

Diega was glad that Rosa showed her how to dance; the governor was right. She was on the dance floor most of the night. Poor Miguel only got to dance with her once. She danced with every single man there, as well as some married ones, to the displeasure of their wives. She even danced with Sergeant Gonzales, whom she hadn't seen after arriving in Reina de Los Angeles.

On the way home, Diega asked, "What did you find out on the tour? By the way, that was very sly the way you contrived the tour."

"His distraction with you gave me the perfect opportunity to ask, but I didn't find out much. The only thing I can tell you is where his study and his bedroom are."

"That might come in handy."

Rosa looked at Diega with raised eyebrows.

"Ew," cringed Diega. "I don't like what's going through your mind, Aunt Rosa. Hopefully, that look is just you joking. The knowledge of where his bedroom is will come in handy for Halcón, not for me."

"Oh, are you a mind reader too, to know what I was thinking?"

"I don't have to be. Your look plainly gave it away."

"I was jesting at your expense," chortled Rosa. "But I bet you could read the captain's mind easily too."

"Ew again, but you're right. He danced so much with me that I think my shoes are worn out. Poor Miguel only got to dance with me once."

"Do you take a fancy to Miguel?"

"I have a boyfriend in my time. Of course, in this time he's not been born yet. But I don't have those kinds of feelings for Miguel. I feel guilty because I know he likes me, but I don't feel the same way."

"Well, you don't need to fall in love with a soldier anyway. Every one of them is after Halcón."

"Miguel is a good man. He is just caught in a corrupt system."

"We'll see," replied Rosa.

Two days later, Diega was planning a daring move. She couldn't help thinking about what was in Alvarado's study, and she was determined to find out even with Rosa and Bernardo trying to talk her out of it. Diega took the carriage into town and went to the governor's house during the day. Miguel had told her at the party that it was his turn to guard the house with a few other soldiers on Mondays. She found Miguel near the gate at the front of the house. She smiled and walked over to him. A couple of the other soldiers smiled at Miguel and left the two alone.

"If the captain sees me talking with you, I'll be in real trouble," he stated.

"Well, if you want me to leave ...?

"No!" he implored her before she could finish the sentence.

"Perhaps one or two of the other soldiers can stand at the gate while you I and talk on the grounds."

That was enough persuasion for Miguel. He went over and talked to two soldiers who walked to the gate still smiling."

"I couldn't get a good look at the grounds the other night because I was dancing so much. I wish you would have asked me to dance more. It's such a chore, dancing with people you don't want to dance with." Diega led Miguel unknowingly around the house so that she could get an idea of its defenses and any vulnerabilities.

"I wanted to dance with you much more, but you were always dancing with someone else."

"Well, you should have cut in."

"I couldn't cut in with the captain or any of the caballeros. The captain would have kicked me out immediately. It's a wonder I was even allowed to attend in the first place."

They passed a few other soldiers, and Diega smiled warmly at them. They returned the smile and gave the two some distance.

"Are there always this many soldiers guarding the house?"

"Yes."

"Even at night?"

"Yes. Plus a few inside in the grand salon. We change shifts at five o'clock when we are relieved by the night shift. Each shift is for twelve hours. May I call on you at your ranch sometime," he suddenly blurted.

"Of course. I would love for you to visit."

"I don't usually have much time off, but I'll come by the next time I can."

"Wonderful. I'll look forward to seeing you. Now, I suppose I'd best not delay much longer. I don't want to get you into trouble with the captain. Then you definitely wouldn't be able to visit me."

"I'm so glad you came by to see me."

Diega felt badly for using Miguel so that she could gather information, but she tried to convince herself it was for the overall good. She got into her carriage and rode back to the ranch. When she arrived, she told Rosa and Bernardo what happened and what she had learned.

Later that day, Diega, in a very plain dress with a scarf over her head, was again in the carriage on her way to Reina de Los Angeles, but this time Bernardo was driving. He dropped her off near the market and took the carriage back to the ranch. Around four o'clock she started making her way to the governor's house, careful not to approach from the side of the military compound. She quickly changed into Halcón, minus the hat that she figured would just be a nuisance on this outing, and hid in some bushes that covered her but that were not too thick to prevent her from moving.

At five o'clock, the day shift began to leave. Fortunately, the change from day shift to night shift was slightly disorganized. Nothing like the changing of the Guard in London. When the soldiers were far enough away, and the night shift had not yet taken position, she ran to the fence that surrounded the governor's house. The fence was covered with vines. When she had walked around the house with Miguel, she had noticed this spot that seemed to have been dug out by an animal. The vines were enough to cover her, and this spot was between where the guards stood. She could tell by the worn spots that the guards pretty much stayed in place rather than walk along the fence, which is probably why whatever animal dug the hole chose that spot. She just hoped that the animal wouldn't come back and find her in its spot.

Diega lay flat on the ground, with the fence inches above her. When it grew completely dark, she crawled out from underneath the fence as she made sure no soldiers were looking her way. She ran to a tree near the house and climbed it. The tree branches had not been cut back, and some of the limbs extended to the roof. Diega chose the sturdiest looking limb that touched the roof, and she slid along it. She had asked Sesasi to make her some softer shoes to wear instead of the black boots so that she could maneuver more easily. The main concern she had at the moment was any noise she might make getting onto the roof. Think soft landing, she said to herself. The soldiers weren't paying much attention, but a noise would certainly alarm them. The worst that could happen, she thought, would be that she would have to fight her way out and make a run for it. Deciding that she couldn't wait any longer, she maneuvered from the limb to the roof. Although she made a slight noise, the sound did not rouse the soldiers. The balcony connecting the governor's study and bedroom was nearby, and she quietly crawled the short distance where she held onto the roof and swung her legs to the balcony. Dropping quietly onto the balcony, she peered into the study; it was empty. She opened the door enough to squeeze through and quickly closed it.

Inside the study, the first thing she did was look for hiding places. Before she could pick one, she heard footsteps approaching. Curtains hung to the side of the door leading onto the balcony. The curtains could be used to cover the glass door to keep the sun from beating into the room. She hid behind the curtains, glad that she didn't bring her hat. As Halcón, she peered around the curtain just as the door opened. Alvarado walked in carrying a cigar box. He went to a portrait hanging on the wall and pressed along the bottom of the portrait. A clicking sound was made, and Alvarado pulled open the portrait revealing a hidden safe. Taking his key ring and finding the correct key, he opened the safe, took the contents out of the cigar box and put them into the safe, closed the safe, and finally closed the portrait. Alvarado blew out the lantern and left, taking the keys with him. Halcón heard the bedroom door open and then close. She moved from behind the curtains and sat down behind a couch, leaning her back against it. She waited about three hours to make sure that Alvarado was asleep and to allow time for boredom to set in for the soldiers.

Halcón rose and walked to the door. She drew out her sword in case she had to cut the throat of a nearby soldier. Opening the door, she quickly peered out, but didn't see any soldiers nearby. Alvarado must not have wished to be guarded that closely in his own home. Next, she opened Alvarado's bedroom door and crouched once inside. The room was dark, and she heard Alvarado snoring. Since she had already been in a dark room for several hours, her eyes adjusted quickly to the bedroom. A thought went through her mind. She could easily kill the governor, but another would just take his place, or Captain Ramon would, which would be worse. There was still too much unknown, and killing Alvarado now would be pointless. Dismissing the thought, she looked around for the keys. Where would he keep them? She thought about the objects she slept with in her own time, but that was because she wanted them with her in case she time traveled. Finding nothing on this side of the bed, she crept to the other side. Lying on a table next to Alvarado's head were his keys. Not knowing which key opened the safe, she had no choice but to take the entire ring of keys. Crawling on her hand and knees, she arrived at the table and reached up, grabbing the entire set so that they didn't jingle. Holding them tightly, she walked around the bed crouching over. As she neared the door, she stood up and quietly opened the door. Seeing no soldier around, she softly closed the bedroom door and opened the door to the study.

Moving her hand along the bottom of the portrait, she found the latch that opened the portrait to the safe. The key ring held many keys, but most were too big for the safe. Only four keys were viable options. The second key that she tried opened the safe. Her eyes grew wide as she stared at the contents. The Governor was keeping some of the gold for himself, but she would have expected as much. There was enough gold to fill at least seven cigar boxes. Alvarado had to be using this as temporary storage. Where was he storing the gold once this safe was filled, and how was he transporting it? Halcón pulled out a bag she had brought and emptied the safe. She closed the safe and put the key ring on the table. There was no point in risking going back into Alvarado's bedroom. Besides, he would know soon enough that he had been robbed. As a final touch, Halcón used her sword to carve the letter *H* into the portrait.

Getting out with this much gold was going to be harder than getting in. She put the bag around her neck and went out to the balcony. Rather than taking the route she used to get in, she put one leg and then the other over the balcony rail onto the tiny bit of space on the other side of the railing. She crouched, grabbed the bottom of the rails, lowered her legs letting them dangle in the air, and dropped to the ground. She rose and ran behind the tree. When she felt it was safe, she ran to the opening in the fence, pushed the gold through, and then crawled through. She remained flat on the ground until she saw that she could safely escape. Running back to the bushes, she grabbed her clothes. One of the soldiers must have heard a noise.

"Who goes there?"

"It's just some nocturnal animal," replied another soldier.

Her heart beat rapidly now that she had completed this adventure. Still, she had to be careful in case other soldiers were around. Getting caught after coming this far would be because of her own carelessness. She ran, lugging the gold, about a mile out of the pueblo until she came to Bernardo who was waiting for her with Tornado. They raced back to the ranch with dawn still several hours away.

The reward for Halcón had been raised to five thousand pesos. A few days later, Rosa and Diega went to see Friar Felipe to see what he had heard.

"Governor Alvarado was livid according to people who heard him shouting at the soldiers guarding his house. No one seems to know what Halcón did at the governor's house though. Surely, he wouldn't risk a simple break-in without some purpose."

While Rosa was talking to Felipe, Diega quietly snuck off and put the bag with the gold along with a note from Halcón in the Friar's study. The note simply said, *This gold was stolen by Alvarado. Give it back to the poor whom he has taxed so heavily.* Diega walked back to the sanctuary. Friar Felipe apparently hadn't even noticed she left. After visiting Felipe, Rosa and Diega went back to the ranch.

Over the course of the next few days, Diega went on three different nights to the tavern in Reina de Los Angeles. Although a proper lady would never go into such a place, she knew from Friar Felipe that Sergeant Gonzales spent about every night there. She wanted to see what information he would give her. Of course, they wouldn't let her in, but when she said she wanted to play chess with Sergeant Gonzales, that seemed to work. She would play chess and try to teach the sergeant more magic tricks. After several drinks, his tongue would loosen; so far, she hadn't really gotten any useful information from him.

On the third night at the tavern, Diega bought wine for everyone in the tavern. She sipped the same cup, but others, including the sergeant had several cups. After a while she commented, "Is this Halcón still on the loose? It's frightful that some masked bandit is riding around. Aunt Rosa warned me not to come out. You don't think this Halcón would harm a lady, do you?"

Sergeant Gonzales choked on the wine that Diega had bought for him. "Halcón is a scoundrel and a coward. Let him cross swords with me, and he'll be finished. He is afraid to fight honorably and in public against a real swordsman. All he can do is carve the letter *H*. I would be more than happy to have the chance to carve him!" The sergeant stood up and brandished his sword as if fighting an imaginary Halcón. "I'll toy with him and embarrass the scoundrel before I run him through with my sword."

"Please, Sergeant Gonzales, such talk in front of a lady," replied Diega coyly. Diega was trying to act as Aunt Rosa had told her, but acting this way was difficult for her; she wasn't really the lady type.

"Please forgive my manners, Señorita Diega."

"Perhaps you'll get your chance. The reward is quite handsome."

"He's too afraid to show himself to a skilled opponent."

"I suppose I must go. I fear there may be a storm tonight, and I should get back."

"You're leaving already? Don't you want a rematch to see if you can beat me this time in chess?"

"The rematch will have to wait until another time, but I'll buy one more round for everyone." Diega bid the sergeant good night and left the tavern.

"Such a fine and perfect lady," remarked the sergeant. "She is a good friend."

Outside, no one was around, and Diega loosened the cinches of the soldiers' horses so that they would slip. This could give

Halcón some additional time to escape if needed. Diega went behind a building, and seeing no one, changed into Halcón. She put Diega's clothes in a bag and hid it so that she could retrieve them later. Halcón slinked around the tavern, peering around the corner to make sure she could enter unseen. Seeing no one, she quickly rounded the corner and opened the door to the tavern. Everyone was looking at the sergeant duel the imaginary Halcón, but they looked over when Halcón slammed the door shut and barred it.

Halcón puffed a slim cigar and blew out a cloud of smoke before flicking the cigar towards the sergeant.

"Who are you?" asked the Sergeant in a quavering voice.

"I'm Señor Halcón, of course" replied Halcón in a voice as deep as she could muster.

"You're foolish enough to come in here with soldiers present?"

"I see only ten."

"Only," emphasized the sergeant, "ten?"

"I thought someone may want to claim the reward on me. It should buy plenty of wine or mezcal."

"Stand back," demanded the sergeant to his troops. "I shall claim this reward. The reward now states dead or alive. I hope you are ready to die, scoundrel ... rogue."

The other men weren't content to let the sergeant claim the reward. With swords drawn they started to charge Halcón, but they stopped when Halcón pulled out a pistol. Halcón waved the pistol, motioning them back. "I believe the sergeant has asked for the honor first."

"I should have known a scoundrel wouldn't fight fairly and honorably," chastised the sergeant.

Halcón holstered the pistol, withdrew the rapier from its scabbard, and held it ready for action. Halcón thought about what she had always been taught, and what she told others. Never underestimate an opponent.

Sergeant Gonzalez attacked Halcón with vigor, but every thrust was easily parried. Sergeant Gonzalez tried to advance, but Halcón beat him back and drove him to the fireplace, which wasn't burning in this heat. Gonzales stumbled and fell with his butt hitting the stone hearth. Halcón laughed and offered a hand to help him up, but the sergeant wouldn't accept. Instead, he charged from the hearth with a harsh thrust. Halcón turned like a matador sidestepping a charging bull. She kicked Gonzalez in the butt as he passed by. The others in the tavern roared with laughter. The sergeant's face grew red, and he doubled the vehemence of his attack. Halcón let Gonzalez back her up to a table where she planted her hand and jumped over the table. Gonzalez backed away and motioned for Halcón to come from behind the table. Halcón again planted her hand on the table and bounded over it, but instead of advancing, she sat on the table with her legs crossed and folded as if in a half-lotus pose. This infuriated the sergeant even more, and he advanced and attacked. However, Halcón still easily parried the sergeant's thrusts and swings. A half-full cup of wine was on the table beside Halcón, and she picked it up with her free hand and threw it, splashing Gonzalez in the face. The room howled with laughter again while the sergeant had to stop and wipe the liquid from his eyes. The irate sergeant charged Halcón, but she did a back somersault off the table, pulling it down. The sergeant's sword stuck into the wood from this thrust. He put one leg on the table and pried the sword loose but lost his balance and fell over. Halcón leapt over the table. Halcón ran and poured some wine into a cup as the Sergeant rose from the floor. Then, she ran, jumped onto a table, and sprang from the table onto the mantle over the fireplace. She turned around and shouted, "to the sergeant's effort." She took a sip of wine as Gonzalez raced to the mantle. He swung his sword at Halcón's legs, but Halcón jumped, and the sword missed. Landing back onto the mantle, she threw down the cup and somersaulted over the Sergeant, landing behind him. Before he could turn around, she swiftly slashed the letter *H* into the Sergeant's pants. Everyone again laughed at the poor sergeant's expense.

The sound of pounding came from the barred door. Gonzalez yelled, "Halcón is in here." Halcón ran to a shuttered window, opened the shutters, and jumped out. The soldiers in the room ran to the door and pulled up the bar. Three more soldiers were standing outside, and the sergeant ordered everyone to capture Halcón.

One of the soldiers who had been in the tavern remarked to the sergeant, "Is Halcón a woman? I thought I could make out the hips and breasts of a woman, and the voice sounded like a woman trying to make herself sound like a man."

"Halcón is not a woman!" rebuked the sergeant.

The soldiers who had their horses tied outside the tavern ran to mount them. Some of the saddles slid off as the soldiers tried to mount. A few others were able to mount, but the saddles slipped as they rode off causing them to fall from their horses.

During this frenzy, Halcón grabbed the bag with her clothes and snuck into the church. She found an empty room and swiftly changed, putting Halcón's clothes into the bag. Next, she went to the nave, sat, and prayed. Sergeant Gonzalez and two other soldiers entered the church.

"Señorita Diega," said the breathless sergeant. "I thought you were leaving."

"Oh, sergeant!" acting surprised. "I decided to come and pray before riding back."

"Have you seen Halcón?" he huffed.

"What? You mean he is here?"

"That devil attacked us in the tavern, but don't worry. We'll find the rogue."

"I haven't seen or heard anything, sergeant."

"You'd better go back to your hacienda. I'll have these two soldiers accompany your carriage to make sure you get home safely."

"Thank you, sergeant. I'll leave immediately."

The sergeant left, and the two soldiers remained. These two soldiers had not been in the tavern; so, Diega felt comfortable taking the bag with Halcón's clothes with her. She hoped they would not question what was in the bag, and they didn't. She put the bag into her carriage, and the soldiers accompanied her back to her hacienda.

A week had passed since Halcón had crossed swords with Sergeant Gonzalez. Diega continued to train. She had gotten fairly good with the whip, and she was able to do some tricks with both Tornado and Thunder. That night, Diega talked with Rosa about her plans for the next day. "Taxes are being collected tomorrow in Reina de los Angeles. I think Halcón should pay a visit."

"Diega, your escapades are getting more and more daring and dangerous. Don't you think you're beginning to take too many risks? There are lots of soldiers and only one of you. Sooner or later, your luck will run out."

"If I don't do something, then nothing will get done. We can't wait around until the Mexican revolution for independence!"

"What is that?" asked Rosa.

"In about two years from now, a revolution will start that will last over ten years that will result in a new nation, called Mexico, breaking away from Spanish rule. Alta California will eventually become a state of the United States."

"Will that really happen?"

"Yes," confirmed Diega. "Maybe you should think about leaving here and going to Spain."

"I told you my reasons for staying here, and you're changing the subject."

"I'm not going to just ride in without a plan." That was a lie. She didn't have a plan, but she wasn't going to tell Rosa that. "Are you going into town to pay taxes?"

"Yes," replied Rosa. "Everyone around here must go pay taxes."

The next morning, Rosa took the carriage into Reina de los Angeles to pay taxes for the ranch, including taxes for Diega, Bernardo, Ati, Sesasi, and Cetlali. She arrived to find the governor himself supervising the tax collection. When he saw Rosa, he walked over.

"I could not possibly take taxes from you this year after what happened with the soldiers at your ranch. You are forgiven for paying any taxes this year."

"That's very kind of you governor, but I must do my part if others are doing theirs."

"If you insist," replied the governor, "but I will negotiate a reduced rate for you this year because of what happened. I insist."

"Why are there so many soldiers around?"

"Please, do not let that sight bother you. We can't be too careful with that scoundrel, Halcón, around."

Halcón was hiding out of sight behind a building on the edge of the pueblo. A barking dog was creating a ruckus, and several teens rushed to investigate. When they saw Halcón, they were about to start cheering. Before they could do so, Halcón held a finger to her lips indicating for them to be quiet.

"Would you like to help me?" urged Halcón.

"Yes!" the teens exclaimed while nodding.

"See if you can get some more of your friends and run to where the taxes are being collected. Tell them you saw Halcón on the west end of town."

"But Señor Halcón, you are not at the west end of town," informed one of the teens.

"Of course, he's not," said another. "He wants the soldiers to go in the wrong direction so that he can ride in."

"Oh," replied the first teen.

"Can I count on you?" appealed Halcón.

"Yes," replied the second teen. "We'll lead as many soldiers the wrong way as possible."

Halcón advanced cautiously toward the center of town where the taxes were being collected while the teens grabbed anyone they could find, including several dogs that were barking excitedly. Halcón was as close as she could get until the teens played their ruse. Suddenly, a group of about twenty teens, children, and a few adults, along with several barking dogs ran to the square.

"What's going on here?" Governor Alvarado tried to shout over the noise.

"Halcón!" shouted several in the crowd.

"Halcón is skulking around at the west side of town," shouted an unknown voice within the crowd. "We'll show you."

"Captain Ramon," ordered Alvarado, "take as many soldiers as you need to find Halcón. I want him captured! Understood?"

"Yes, Governor." Captain Ramon ordered a group of about forty soldiers to follow him to apprehend Halcón.

Halcón quickly estimated that about ten soldiers remained at the tax collection area. She figured she would have at most two minutes before the soldiers rode back, aware that they had been duped. She wouldn't have much time and would have to act quickly. As the soldiers rode around a building, Halcón rode up and dismounted.

Halcón quickly disarmed the soldiers charging toward her with swords. She ran to the governor and pointed a pistol at his head. If anyone makes a move, the governor is dead." Throw all of your weapons as far away as possible. If you don't throw them far enough, I'll cut off one of the governor's ears."

"Do as he says!" ordered the governor nervously.

The soldiers did as he ordered. Halcón grabbed two bags of collected money. Still pointing the pistol at the governor, she whistled for her horse to come over and she put the money into saddle bags. Halcón briefly took her eyes off the governor to secure the saddle bags, and the governor dove under a table. Three soldiers near her charged her. She used a tornado crescent kick, hitting one of the end soldiers. The force of the kick knocked him into the other two soldiers, and all three tumbled to the ground. By this time, two more soldiers were upon her. A roundhouse kick took one out of the action, and a spin hook kick took out another. A punch toward her face came from another soldier. She redirected the punch by pushing his arm. This opened up his body, and she punched his ribs, cleared his arm out of her way and hit him hard in the nose. Then, she grabbed his hair, bent him over and kneed him in the ribs. She punched the back of his neck, kicked him in the face while he was still bent over, and kicked his leg out from under him. Out of the shadows a teen boy tossed a walking staff to her. She caught in on the back of her hand, lifted her arm straight over her head, let it fall and caught it as it fell. The remaining four soldiers had grabbed their flintlocks. Before they could aim, she went to work with the staff. A front strike with the staff broke one soldier's nose, and he dropped his gun. Like a whirlwind the staff whirled side to side, up and down, overhead, and front and back. Three of the four soldiers lay moaning on the ground, out of commission. She performed some spinning tricks with the staff, hand and neck rolls and spins around her body. The fourth solder threw down his flintlock at this showy display and ran in the other direction.

Halcón ran toward Tornado. Before she reached the horse, she performed a butterfly kick in the air just for the heck of it. She whistled for the horse to start moving. She caught up to it, put her hands to its neck, bounced, and mounted the horse. The Governor ran toward her as she was mounting the horse and grabbed at her. When she saw him, she dismounted and whistled for her horse to stop. She saw Captain Ramon leading the returning soldiers back to the square; so, she punched the Governor in the face as hard as she could, knocking him to the ground. She ran and sprinted up and over the horse's rear, landing in the saddle, and galloped off as fast as she could with the soldiers in pursuit.

Halcón rode is a circle around the city. As she rode by the teens, they pushed a wagon onto the road, which temporarily slowed down the pursuers. She sprinted down El Camino Real toward Rosa's ranch, but she knew she couldn't go there with the soldiers that close behind. She wasn't sure what to do. Thunder was the better horse and could go the distance ordinarily. This time, he was carrying two full money bags. The bags were sturdy and secure, but the added weight and the awkwardness could slow him down just enough. She heard musket fire and a few musket balls whizzed past. They couldn't really aim while riding that fast on the road at that distance, but all it would take was one lucky shot, unlucky for her. She nudged Thunder in the sides, and the horse sped faster. Up ahead she saw a figure in the road. He was motioning, but she couldn't understand. It looked like Bernardo. He held his arm level and then ducked under it. Halcón thought she understood now. She leaned down along the side of Thunder just as a musket ball whizzed by. That was the lucky shot that would have gotten her. She spoke into Thunder's ear, telling him to lower his head. Thunder and Halcón rode under a thick rope stretched taut between two trees. She kept riding but took a glance back just in time to see several riders clotheslined off their horses. With the bodies lying on the ground, the soldiers had to temporarily halt. Diega rode around a bend in the road and saw Ati. As she passed him, he pushed a wagon in the road and lit it on fire. He must have poured alcohol over it because the fire caught quickly. He pushed and rolled a second wagon into the road and lit it up as well. A few of the soldiers who had ridden past the first obstacle now faced the second obstacle. By the time the soldiers got past both obstacles, Halcón was nowhere in sight.

With no soldiers behind her, Halcón rode to Rosa's ranch around to the hidden cave. She hid Thunder inside, unsaddled and rubbed him down and fetched him some water to drink and oat mash to eat until she felt it was safe for him to go back to the pasture.

Diega dressed back into regular clothes and took the hidden passageway into the library. After several hours, Rosa, Bernardo, and Ati had still not returned home. She was worried and went to hitch a horse to another carriage. She rode the carriage to El Camino Real when she saw Rosa's carriage with Rosa, Bernardo and Ati. She turned the carriage around and followed Rosa back to the hacienda.

Once inside, Diega nervously asked why they arrived back so late.

"They questioned everyone there to see if they knew anything," replied Rosa.

"Did the teens and children get into trouble for helping Halcón," asked Diega, concerned.

"Fortunately, no," said Rosa. "Everyone talked so much about how quick Halcón was that Captain Ramon simply suspected that the teens and children had indeed seen Halcón but that Halcón changed locations by the time the soldiers arrived."

"What about you two?" questioned Diega eyeing Bernardo and Ati.

"The soldiers knew that Halcón had help; so, they scoured the woods. We had to stay hidden. After they gave up the search, we met at a predetermined location but figured that the soldiers may still be stationed along the road. We had to take a long loop around. We had about made it back to the ranch when we saw Doña Rosa's carriage through the woods. We rode with her the remaining short distance."

"I'm glad neither of you were hurt," confessed Diega. "Thank you so much for the help. If you hadn't done that, I probably wouldn't be sitting here now." Thank your Aunt Rosa. She came up with the plan in case you needed help escaping.

Diega spotted an incredulous look on Rosa's face. "How did you do ... I don't even know what you call it," marveled Rosa. I've never seen such fighting. The soldiers are saying that Halcón is possessed."

"I've had training. I'm an exceptional fighter, if I say so myself."

"Exceptional doesn't even begin to describe it. Bernardo and Ati, you should have seen her. I've never seen anything like it. She decimated ten soldiers as easy as breathing."

"I wish I could have seen that," remarked Bernardo.

"I'm sure you need to rest after all of that," exclaimed Rosa, "and a bath."

"Yes, Aunt Rosa."

"By the way," called Rosa. The reward for Halcón is now ten thousand pesos.

Governor Alvarado put a wet cloth to his jaw. Through a barely opened mouth, he hissed when he spoke. "I think that outlaw broke my jaw."

"If he broke your jaw, you wouldn't be talking as much as you are," jabbed Captain Ramon. "Here, let me take a look." Captain Ramon grabbed his jaw in the palm of his hand causing the governor to let out a shriek of pain. "It's not broken; it just feels that way to you, but I imagine you'll be slurping soup for a while."

"That's twice that bandit robbed from me," seethed Alvarado.

"What do you mean twice?" interrogated the captain. "Have you been stashing away extra gold?"

"Only the amount we agreed upon. Don't criticize me. You're appropriating gold yourself."

"I just want to make sure you're not taking more than your share."

"If you don't catch this meddlesome bandit, neither of us are going to have a share."

"What he's taken is just the tip of the iceberg. Don't worry. I'll catch him," fumed the captain.

"He's a devil."

"I don't care what he is! If he's a bird, I'll shoot him out of the sky. If he's a fox, I'll rouse him from his den. If he's a bull, I'll mount his horns on my wall. A hawk may catch a few rodents; a fox may catch a few chickens, but the hunter always catches them. He may have won a few battles, but I'll win the war.

The next day, Rosa and Diega paid Friar Felipe a visit. Rosa kept him occupied while Diega took the bags of money into the friar's study with a note from Halcón to use the money for the poor.

Several days passed with no more sightings of Halcón. Diega continued training with Bernardo. One day, around noon, Ati came to where Diega was training to tell her that Miguel had arrived. "Tell Aunt Rosa to stall him. I'll come out from the library shortly." Diega ran to the hidden cave entrance and made her way to the library. She kept some clothes in both the library and the armament room for occasions such as this. She had explored the hidden passageway system many times but had not used it in an emergency situation until the day of the tax collection. This was her second emergency. She arrived at the doorway to the bookcase in the library and pressed the latch to open it. Once in the library, she found her clothes and dressed.

"There she is," exclaimed Rosa. I didn't know you were in the library. I thought you were outside. I sent Ati to find you, but he said he didn't see you."

"Sorry, Aunt Rosa. I was engrossed in a book when I thought I heard talking. Hello, Miguel. I'm so glad you finally came to see me."

Miguel rose from his chair and fumbled with his hat. "I would have loved to have come sooner, but with Halcón breaking into the governor's house, no one has been given any freedom until today. They are now calling him Halcón del diablo. I thought that I had better come and see you before Halcón strikes again, and we are never allowed to leave."

"Let's hope that doesn't happen," replied Diega. "Do you want to come outside with me?"

Outside, Diega leaned against a wooden gate. She was wearing a white dress that showed off her bare shoulders. Diega bent her leg to put her foot against a post to brace herself. There was a slit in the dress that ordinarily wouldn't show her legs, but with her knee bent, the slit exposed her legs from knee down. Her boot-heeled sandals looked like a cross between sandals and boots, almost as if a pair of short boots were cut in places to expose parts of her feet. Leaning back, she held onto her wide-brimmed tan hat with one hand to keep the breeze from blowing it off. Part of her dark hair hung over one shoulder in the front, with the other side falling in back. Diega noticed Miguel staring at her as if he were mesmerized. She stood up straight and let her dress fall to cover her legs. She wanted to neither tempt nor tease Miguel. That seemed to break the spell that was cast over Miguel, and he roused as if he had been brought back from a vivid daydream.

Not knowing what to say, she said the first thing that came into her mind. "Does Captain Ramon treat the soldiers well?"

"Hardly, but I'd rather talk about something else."

"Of course."

"I was talking with your Aunt Rosa. I'd like to see you sometime." He looked down as if expecting the worst.

Here it was, thought Diega. How do I not hurt him? "You're seeing me now," she teased.

"I mean more than that."

"If you're talking marriage, I know I'm old enough, but I don't want to marry without my parents being here." Chicken, she said to herself.

"I know I'm not in the class of people you would marry, but I like you and think about you all the time."

"First of all, I will marry for love, not because a person is in a certain class. Let's just take things a step at a time." Chicken shit, she told herself again, but the thought of hurting him was more than she could bare.

"I'd like that, but it may be a while."

"Why is that?"

"A group of us are being ordered to the Mission San Juan Capistrano to collect taxes. We leave in ten days. Another group left yesterday morning for the Mission San Buenaventura."

"Why did you want to be a soldier?"

"To defend my country. To fight for my country, of course."

"Who are you fighting for?" pressed Diega.

"I told you. I'm fighting for my country."

"Are you fighting for the land, for Napoleon's brother, who now rules Spain, for the Spanish resistance? Tell me exactly what you're fighting for?"

Miguel was beginning to become enraged at Diega's goading. "I fight for the people."

"And are you fighting for them, or are you just a tax collector?" Diega could tell that her words suddenly clarified something for Miguel. She could almost see that understanding snap him back into awareness.

Rather than being angry, Miguel looked defeated. "What am I supposed to do? I'm not a caballero. I'm not a farmer or a businessman. I'm a soldier, and first and foremost, a soldier obeys orders."

"Even if those orders hurt the people you want to protect."

"Those with higher ranks have those ranks for a reason. They are privy to more information than I have. How do I know their orders are not for the greater good?"

"I can't answer that for you, Miguel. You're the only one who can know if what you're doing is for the right reason."

"I suppose I need to head back now."

When she saw Miguel today, he was excited; he was leaving defeated. Diega went inside with tears in her eyes.

"What's wrong, child?" asked a concerned Rosa.

Diega told Rosa about the events that had transpired, how Miguel had looked at her, how she didn't tell him that she led him on earlier, how she didn't tell him that she didn't have the same feelings for him as he did for her, and how she tried to get him to see he was being used but ended up making him doubt himself. "He loves me, but all I do is use him and hurt him."

"Do you think perhaps you really do love him but are not letting yourself believe it?"

"I don't think so," wept Diega.

"Time will tell. If you don't like what you're doing to Miguel, then do something different."

"How? I have to be Halcón, and Halcón needs information."

"You can only be you. If you try to be someone else, you'll fail. I've heard you talk about this Sir Gawain. Even though he took on different personas, deep down he was still himself. Now, stop crying. It will do you no good."

"Isn't there a time for everything, as the Bible says ... a time to cry and a time to laugh?"

"But who says those times have to be equal in length?"

The next day, Diega told Rosa and Bernardo that she was going to spy on the soldiers who had left for San Buenaventura. Rosa and Bernardo implored her to stay. "You said, I had to be myself, Aunt Rosa."

"Don't use my words against me", chastised Rosa. "You also don't need to be reckless."

"I'm not going to fight an entire army. I just want to get to the bottom of what's going on here."

San Buenaventura was about seventy miles away from Reina de Los Angeles, and it marked the northernmost point of Avarado's governance. Beyond that, de Arrillaga governed as the legitimate governor. She didn't intend to go all the way to San Buenaventura. Going all the way there and then following them back would only increase her chances of being detected. Besides, she had a hunch she wanted to follow. She would wait at a point about two-thirds of the way there for their return and would see where they went from there. The soldiers would take wagons since they were collecting taxes. The journey there would probably take them at least three days, and they would spend at least one day collecting taxes. Diega waited for three days after the soldiers left Reina de Los Angeles before she left. She took the garb of Halcón with her, hidden away, in case she needed it, but she couldn't ride a long distance dressed as Halcón.

Diega found a wooded area off El Camino Real. Two days later, she finally saw the soldiers returning from San Buenaventura. They pulled three wagons of produce and goods received as taxes. Money was probably in one of the wagons as well. As she expected, she also saw three smaller wagons carrying peons. The wagons had bars so that no one could escape, and the peons had to stand. Approximately fifteen peons were in each wagon, or forty-five total. No doubt, these peons were people who could not afford to pay the high tax rate. Diega let the wagons pass, and she followed from a safe distance in order not to be spotted. From what she had seen previously, the soldiers were unorganized. She had seen no sign of advance scouts, but they could have someone holding back a ways to see if they were being followed.

The soldiers made camp in the woods that night, and Diega rode ahead and found a spot for the night. The night was cool, but she didn't dare build a fire. Some of the food she brought with her still remained, but she would have to ration it; the only thing she had that she could hunt with was a musket, and that would make too much noise. The next day, she allowed the soldiers to pass before once again trailing them. After noon, she came to a spot in the road where she saw tracks continuing toward Reina de Los Angeles, but another set of tracks broke off to the east. The soldiers must have split up with part taking the collected taxes back to Reina de Los Angeles. This appeared to be the main group because there were more tracks. The other group had taken a slightly worn path that wasn't really a road and certainly wasn't wide enough for wagons. She expected that the peons had been unloaded and were on foot to wherever they were going. What she was unsure of was how many soldiers were accompanying them.

Diega followed the group that went eastward into the forests and mountains northeast of Reina de Los Angles. At one point, she came within sight of them and had to ride into the woods to keep from being seen. About fifteen soldiers on horseback accompanied the peons, who were forced to walk. At the end of the second night of following them, she ate the remainder of the food she had brought. Finally, on the fourth day, they had reached their destination. Diega rode back a ways and tied Tornado to a tree. She put on her Halcón outfit and snuck though the woods to a spot where she could see what was happening. She saw about forty peons, not counting the new arrivals, panning for gold in a river. About twenty soldiers, not counting the soldiers who brought the new peons, guarded the group panning for gold. As night approached, the soldiers herded the peons and led them about a mile to a cave where they fed them and locked them in for the night. Four soldiers were stationed there as guards, and the rest walked back to the military camp.

Diega waited until darkness had completely set in before slinking near the campfire where all of the soldiers were gathered. Fortunately, they did not have sentries posted around the area. She could not make out some of the conversations, but she could hear a few.

"How many soldiers are you going to leave with us?" bellowed one of the soldiers already stationed at the camp.

"Probably ten," said the corporal in charge of the group coming from San Buenaventura.

"Is that all?"

"There are only fifteen of us. Besides, enough of these peons will die off soon enough. The last time we were here there were about sixty. There are only forty now."

"Well, tell Captain Ramon that when the next batch arrives, we need more soldiers. We were promised to rotate back to Reina de Los Angeles, but nobody has left yet! How are you going to transport the gold from here?"

"In about a month, an escort will come to transport it."

Diega's stomach growled from hunger, and she left before any more sounds could give her position away. Finding her way back to Tornado was difficult in the dark. Although she wanted to leave immediately, leaving at this hour would not be safe. She would also have to be careful not to leave in the morning at the same time as the departing soldiers. Her blood boiled at the thought of the forced labor and poor living conditions of the peons, who were neophytes and mestizos who couldn't afford the high taxes. Although, this was what her hunch had told her, seeing it was far worse. To make matters worse, Alvarado was taking a share for himself; no doubt, Captain Ramon was as well.

The next morning, she left early and rode hard now that she didn't have to follow behind the slow-moving soldiers and peons. Tornado seemed to like the change of pace too. Having served in the Marines, she was a good judge of directions. She had brought a compass from the ranch with her. It probably wasn't as accurate as a compass from her own time, but it worked well enough. She rode south out of the mountains, and then west. When she reached Rosa's hacienda, everyone gathered around her. Rosa was crying, and even Bernardo fought tears. Rosa hugged her so hard that she couldn't breathe. Her stomach growled again.

"When was the last time you ate?" asked Rosa.

"I don't know. It's been three days or more. I can't remember."

"I'll take care of Tornado," said Bernardo as he patted the horse. "You go eat."

And eat, she did. She gorged herself with enough food to satisfy three people. Next, she took a bath at the insistence of

Rosa. After her bath, she told Rosa what she had seen and about where the gold was. Rosa became indignant.

"I'm going to tell Friar Felipe," ranted Rosa.

"What can he do? He'll also want to know how you know this?"

"You're right. Anger is making me not think rationally."

"There's something else I need to tell you, Aunt Rosa?"

"Oh, what's that?"

"I'm going to leave the day after tomorrow to head down toward San Juan Capistrano."

"You just arrived. We were worried sick the whole time you were gone. Friar Felipe told me when the soldiers returned, and when you didn't arrive, we thought something had surely happened to you. You can't put us through that again."

"But Aunt Rosa, you were the one who said I was the answer to your prayer. You have to let me do what I must."

"I didn't know the answer would be so personal to me. You are a daughter to me. I've lost one; I can't lose another."

Diega felt truly loved, and she loved Rosa like a mother. "Thank you. You don't know how much that means to hear you say that. I think answers to prayers are personal. They have to be, or they wouldn't mean anything. I'll be careful. I think the reason I'm here is for Excalibur, and I feel like I will find it. I don't think anything will happen until I do. I don't know why I feel this way, but it is a feeling I deeply believe. If I can help others along the way to finding it, then that's an added benefit."

"I don't want to lose you when you find the sword."

"I know. I don't want that either, but I have no control of when I travel through time. This ability sometimes feels more like a curse than a blessing, but then I think of the remarkable people I've met and treasured along the way."

Rosa and Diega hugged for minutes, comforting each other as they cried.

Diega rested most of the next day and repacked what she'd need for the journey to San Juan Capistrano. Bernardo suggested she take Thunder this time in order to provide some rest for Tornado. Diega had ridden Thunder a lot, and he was a good horse. She felt more comfortable with Tornado though, and he adapted to situations easily, but even a horse as good as Tornado wouldn't be one hundred percent without some recuperation time.

Diega left the day she planned, early in the morning. As before, she didn't don the Halcón garb but carried it with her. As was the case in San Buenaventura, she suspected that those of lower status who couldn't pay the high tax rate would be taken prisoner to find gold. She thought a second location of gold may exist, but she would have to find that out first-hand. She made the journey two-thirds the way there as she had with San Buenaventura and found a suitable spot to wait out of sight. She waited a day, but a feeling kept nagging at her. Mountains were to her east, and she wondered if this group might split off farther south of her. Although she hesitated to go farther, she thought she probably should. She rode south most of the day. Suddenly, she saw a dust cloud ahead of her. Fearing that this might be the soldiers, she went off the road into some nearby woods. Soldiers soon passed her location, and she hoped she had not been spotted. Like before, three wagons carried the collected taxes and three smaller wagons held about forty-five peons. How could Miguel take part in this? The group passed her and only went about two miles farther before stopping to make camp. This group made camp beside of the road, and Diega dared not go past them. The next morning, the smaller group immediately set off in a northeast direction, and the larger group with the wagons headed home.

Diega followed a safe distance behind. The soldiers and peons went about twenty miles before reaching their destination, which they covered that day. Approximately fifty peons, not counting the new arrivals, were at this location. However, this operation was different. Rather than panning for gold, this group was mining. Most had pickaxes, but there were also explosives, lots of explosives. This required more soldiers to be present, and the soldiers were the ones handling the explosives. About sixty soldiers were stationed here. Because explosives would be heard from miles away, they must not have used those that day.

The soldiers and new peons arrived just as the operation was shutting down for the day. Like before, Diega rode back a ways and tied Thunder to a tree. She dressed as Halcón but left her hat there so that she could move around without it brushing against tree limbs. She arrived back at the site in time to see the peons being led to a cave for the night. She hoped they had been fed while she was taking care of Thunder and dressing as Halcón. The fact that more soldiers were here than at the other camp caused Diega to worry that she might be seen. The soldiers ate before the sun set; so, Halcón had to stay far enough away that she couldn't even hear voices let alone conversations.

Night arrived, and the soldiers gathered around a fire. The soldiers who had arrived pulled out several bottles of alcohol, probably mezcal taken from San Juan Capistrano. With darkness set in, Halcón dared to get closer. Once she got closer, she saw Miguel sitting apart from the main group. Halcón found herself taking a hidden position near him, and questioned herself for doing so since she would hear more from a different location. Something about Miguel drew her to him. He looked depressed. The sergeant in charge, not Gonzalez, must have thought something was wrong with him too because he took a seat beside Miguel.

"What's wrong, Corporal Navarro? Why are you by yourself and not drinking with the others?

"Sergeant, I just feel that asking more in taxes than these people have and then forcing them to do labor isn't right."

"What's that? Am I hearing you right? Are you a solider or a priest? I take that back. Even some of the priests I've known have displayed more soldiery behavior than you're displaying now. We don't question orders, Corporal, we obey them. The only redeeming value these peons have is that they are promoting the welfare of New Spain, which is more that I can say for you. You're not their mother, and your responsibility is not to them. I'm disgusted with you, Corporal." The sergeant stood up and walked away.

Halcón's blood boiled. She felt bad for the way the sergeant treated Miguel, but she was disgusted at the attitude of the sergeant toward these people, whom they basically kidnapped. She was proud of Miguel for speaking his mind. Maybe there was hope for him.

Leaves rustled and twigs snapped near her. From her crouched position, she tried to turn around as much as possible to see what was making the noise. A soldier urinated about twelve feet from her. Most of the men were urinating into the fire bragging that they could extinguish it. This man apparently had more modesty than the others. Halcón closed her eyelids almost shut, afraid the soldier might see the whites of her eyes. He finished and began to walk straight toward her, seemingly unaware of her presence. Closer and closer he came until he almost tripped over her. He startled and grew wide-eyed. At first, he was too startled to speak. Unfortunately for Halcón, that didn't last. He yelled, "Halcón. Halcón is here. Halcón unsheathed her sword and pierced his heart. Also, unfortunate for Halcón was that the man's voice was loud and carried over the merrymaking of the other soldiers.

Halcón was ready to run when she heard a click and Miguel's voice ordering her to stop. She turned around and Miguel had his flintlock aimed directly at her. The next few moments happened seemingly in slow motion. Halcón loosened her hood and pulled it off her head. Miguel gasped. "Diega?" he said in both a questioning and astonished tone. Diega brazenly walked to him, around the flintlock, and kissed him passionately on the lips. She stared into his eyes and knew then that she cared more for him than she let herself believe. With Miguel standing there in shock, she put the hood over her head, tightened it, and ran.

A few moments later, shouts came of "there he is" along with musket fire. Halcón knew that the best course of action was to keep moving and keep the soldiers spread out as much as possible.

Over the commotion, the sergeant bellowed, "Use your swords. You'll shoot each other if you keep firing. Besides, too much gunpowder is here to be shooting wildly."

Two soldiers ran out of nearby cover toward Halcón with swords ready. Halcón jumped upwards and grasped a low-hanging tree limb. She swung her legs up, kicking them in their faces and breaking both soldiers' noses. She had her whip and used it as a soldier, ignoring the sergeant's order, raised his musket to fire. The whip lashed around the gun, and she pulled it out of his hands. She took the musket, whip still wrapped around it, and shot the soldier. Quickly, she untangled the musket from the whip and dropped the musket to the ground. That was foolish, she thought. The sound will only draw others here. Another soldier appeared, and Halcón cracked the whip, splitting the soldier's cheek and lip. As he fell to his knees, holding his face, she ran before other soldiers could arrive.

Halcón had a thought to lead as many soldiers as possible in a direction away from camp. Hopefully they would think she was fleeing and would pursue. She just had to make sure she led them away from Thunder. Then she would double back and try to free the peons locked in the cave. Soldiers pursued her shouting. She would occasionally let one or two catch up to her to keep the others heading in that direction. As one soldier ran up, she snapped the whip around his legs and pulled them from under him. As he started to get up, she plunged her rapier into his heart. Letting two more soldiers catch up, she came from behind them and smashed their heads together. She ran a little farther before letting another soldier catch up. As he thrust his sword to her abdomen, she sidestepped it and cut his throat.

She broke a few branches to create the impression that Halcón was still fleeing in the direction she had been heading. Then, she carefully went about fifty yards in a perpendicular direction and began to double back to the camp. She heard soldiers giving chase in the direction she had planned as she made her way back.

Fortunately, no one stayed behind at the camp; they were all chasing Halcón in hopes of claiming the reward. Halcón would have to act quickly. The lock was made of iron and no keys were left behind that she could see. There was plenty of gunpowder and fuses. She could put a little gunpowder in the keyhole and light a fuse to it. Hopefully, that would blow open the lock. The peons started to make a commotion, asking to be freed. She told them that she would free them, but they would have to be quiet and move back. Halcón opened a nearby barrel of gunpowder and took some to pour into the keyhole. She stuck in a fuse and ran back to the fire from which she pulled out a stick with one end on fire. She ran back and lit the fuse. Although there wasn't a lot of gunpowder in the keyhole, the explosion would probably make enough noise to bring the soldiers back. How much time that would take, she didn't know. Fire sizzled and snaked up the fuse toward the keyhole. The pop of the exploded gunpowder rattled the lock, and the smell of the small explosion filled the air. The peons ran to the gate, and Halcón tore off a small piece of clothing from one of them in case the lock was hot. She put the cloth around the lock and pulled hard. It came loose. As peons poured out, she told them to go in different directions to have a greater chance of escaping.

"Diega," called a voice behind her.

She whirled around and saw Miguel walking toward her. The peons scattered when they saw him, afraid that he might shoot.

"I figured you would come back to free the peons." Miguel's voice had a sense of urgency. Soldiers will be here sooner than later. You need to hurry. I brought you a uniform. If you blend in as a soldier, it might increase your chances of escaping. You can put your hair inside the hat."

"Halcón," came a voice from inside the cave.

Halcón spun around again. All of the peons, except two, had left the cave.

"We cannot go," lamented the peon. "My wife was stabbed by a soldier earlier today. She has lost much blood and is dying, and I will not leave her. Thank you for saving all you could and for being a champion for the oppressed. Let me wear your clothes, and you take the uniform to escape. With all the soldiers, it is your best chance of escaping alive. I will put on your clothes and use the gunpowder to blow up the cave with my wife and I inside. With me wearing your clothes, they may think that you have been killed and won't search for you. Please, do as I ask. You don't have much time, and I will not leave my wife. Blowing up the cave and much of the gunpowder will slow their operation."

Halcón hated what she was about to do, but what the peon said made sense. It was his chance to get some revenge on the government that had ruined his life. Diega quickly undressed. The man was either not surprised to learn that Halcón was a woman, or he hid his surprise well. The peon dressed as Halcón, while she dressed as a soldier. "I won't give you the hood. I can't explain it, but I must keep it." Halcón was taller than the man; so, she cut off part of the bottom of the pants legs and cut two holes for eyes. Although what she fashioned was a mask rather than a hood, hopefully the soldiers wouldn't notice.

While Halcón and the peon were exchanging clothes, Miguel pushed a barrel of gunpowder to the cave. He led a gunpowder trail to several other gunpowder storage locations. All it would take for them all to explode was to set one off.

"I hear voices," warned Miguel. "Go, now!"

Dressed as a soldier, Diega ran into the woods. She kept D'Artagnan's rapier, the bullwhip, and the black hood, but the peon had the rest of Halcón's garb. She couldn't bear to look back. She heard soldiers shouting in threatening tones. Then the tone changed to excitement and fear. Finally, there was nothing to hear but a thundering explosion like she had never heard before, then several more in rapid succession. The whole sky lit up in an eerie orange glow and smoke plumes rose to the sky. Soon, she could smell the exploded powder. She ran past several peons. If they thought she were a soldier they might try to harm her, but they ignored her. No doubt the explosion urged them on with only one thought in mind, escape! Diega reached Thunder who was whinnying and rearing up on his back legs. The explosion had rattled him. Either that or some of the peons had gotten to him first and tried to take him. Diega spoke some comforting words to him to calm him, but the horse didn't settle completely until they left the area.

Two things entered Diega's mind that she had not thought about previously. The first was that she hoped Miguel was ok. An explosion such as the one she heard could have taken the lives of several soldiers. The second thing was that she was wearing the uniform of a soldier. If she encountered any soldiers on the road, every scenario she could think of ended in her being chased. She removed as much of the uniform as she could to try to make it look less like a uniform.

The going was slow, as it was dark and Diega needed to be careful that Thunder didn't injure himself. In all the excitement, Diega had no clue what the time was when she left. She traveled a few hours before the sun rose, but she had not yet made it to El Camino Real. She kept on until she reached the road; then she and Thunder found a secluded place well off the road to rest for several hours. She rubbed mud on the uniform she wore to try to hide the fact that it was a uniform. After resting, she rode a few more hours before deciding to stop that day. She spent a rather uneventful night, and then headed out the next day. She rode most of the day, going off road when she thought she saw more than a few horses at one time coming her way. Eventually, she reached the sanctuary of the ranch and her new-found family.

With Halcón presumed dead, Diega could take some time to regroup, but Halcón would need a new outfit. Diega desperately wanted to determine what had happened to Miguel. Miguel would probably never want to see her again. Rosa went into Reina de Los Angeles to ask Friar Felipe if he had heard any news; he said he hadn't. That told Diega that Governor Alvarado and Captain Ramon wanted to keep things quiet. She didn't have to wait long to find out about Miguel. Two days after she arrived back at the ranch, Miguel came to see her. They went outside to have some privacy and sat next to each other.

"I didn't know if you would ever want to see me again," admitted Diega. "I thought you might expose me as being Halcón."

"No one in their right mind would believe me if I said you were Halcón. They would think I was crazy. People expect Halcón to be a man. Even if they did know Halcón was a woman, they would never suspect you; you're the daughter of a wealthy caballero. Besides, I love you."

"I know."

"You know?"

"It was sort of obvious, but still, I thought you might hate me now that you found out."

"You used me," he said with directness.

Diega replied with the same directness. "I did use you. I'm sorry for taking advantage of your feelings, but I'm not sorry for the information I discovered."

"Did you ever care for me?"

"Of course, I cared for you. I didn't want to admit to you that I didn't have the same feelings for you as you had for me. But the friendship I had for you is starting to develop into more. A week ago, I wouldn't have said this, but I think I'm falling in love with you."

"You're just saying that to get more information from me."

"No. I'm not."

"How can you possibly love me? You're more self-assured than I am. You're more convicted to your principles than I am. You're braver than I am."

Diega interrupted him. "The man I saw the other night was brave. He was able to tell his commanding officer what he felt even though he was rebuked for it. He was willing to sacrifice his life for others. That sounds like a brave, principled, self-assured man to me."

Miguel leaned in and kissed her. He started to pull back, but Diega held tightly so that they could kiss longer. She grabbed his hand and held it.

Finally, she let loose. "Tell me what happened when I fled."

"I ran toward the edge of the woods and when several soldiers were just about to come out, I turned to face the fake Halcón as if I had just come out of the woods an instant ahead of them. One of the soldiers raised his flintlock, but I put my hand on it and lowered it. I said the whole place could blow up if he shot. Then the sergeant came out of the woods and berated us for not attacking Halcón. The sergeant charged with his sword toward Halcón, but Halcón shouted for him to stop, or he would drop the torch he was holding igniting the gunpowder. Since I knew he planned to ignite the gunpowder anyway, I casually walked into the woods. No one noticed; everyone's eyes were glued to Halcón. The sergeant chastised the fake Halcón and told Halcón to be honorable and duel him with swords. The fake Halcón acted his part well. He said that if did duel the sergeant and won that the soldiers would just shoot him. The sergeant raised his musket, and the fake Halcón dropped the torch, which ignited the gunpowder. I, as well as several others, ran. Aside from the soldiers you killed, the explosion killed about twenty more, including the sergeant." But everyone believes Halcón is dead."

"Do you know what Governor Alvarado or Captain Ramon said?"

"I didn't hear directly. I heard that both were furious at the escape of the peons and the destruction of the mining operation, but I heard they were very relieved that Halcón had been killed in the explosion. What do you plan to do next?"

"Lie low until I can find out more. Alvarado has a second site with peons panning for gold in the mountains northeast of Reina de Los Angeles. At some point, he will need to ship the gold to Spain. Even if I continue to free peons, he'll just get new peons to mine or pan for gold; I need to think of a way to stop him permanently."

"Please take care of yourself, Diega. I'm worried for you."

"Diega will take care of herself. You need to be concerned about Halcón taking care of herself!"

The next day, two pieces of mail arrived for Rosa, which was quite the occasion since she rarely received mail. Everyone gathered around to see what news they contained. She opened one of the letters. "Wonderful."

"What's wonderful?" appealed Diega.

"I heard that a famous painter from Mexico City has been visiting the Mission San Diego de Acalá. His name is Rafael Ximeno y Planes. He'll be here tomorrow. I commissioned him to do a painting of you."

"You what?" sputtered Diega. "Why? Why would you do that?"

"You are like a daughter to me. When you leave, I want something to remember you by."

"I don't know what to say," exclaimed Diega.

"You don't have to say anything except what dress you are going to wear. And take a bath tonight. And you're not dressing as Halcón!"

"What is the second letter?" squealed Sesasi.

Rosa opened the second letter and began reading. A numbness seized her face as she read. Finally, she put the letter down, and tears streamed from her eyes.

Sesasi showed worry on her face. "What has happened?" she asked anxiously.

Rosa was speechless for minutes, but everyone coaxed her into finally divulging the contents of the letter. Her voice was weak, barely above a whisper. "The letter is from the real Diega Pulido. She is getting married and moving to Puerto Rico. Her soon-to-be husband is being sent there as an alcalde to govern one of the local towns. My sister and brother-in-law are remaining in Spain."

"Is that good news or bad?" questioned Diega.

"I don't know. I'm just in shock to have received the letter from her."

"With the Mexican Revolution coming soon, perhaps you could go stay with her.

"I've told you," snapped Rosa, "That part of my life is behind me."

Diega thought back about her ancestor named Diega who lived in Puerto Rico. For the first time, she felt like she understood the nature of time. It had all seemed so confusing before when Sir Gawain explained it to her. Now she realized that one couldn't go back and change history. She understood that everything was happening all at once. She could almost imagine herself looking at time stacked upon itself like sheets of paper where everything that had or would ever happen in time was being played out all at once like millions of simultaneous stage plays where one could cross from one stage to the other.

The next day, Rafael arrived. Diega wore the dress she wore for the governor's party. He worked the entire day, taking only a few breaks. Normally, a portrait could take weeks or months, but Rafael had to get back to Mexico City within a few months' time, and he only had a week, or two at the most before he had to leave. He worked on the portrait an additional three days with Diega sitting for most of the time. She was getting stir crazy and yearned to get back into action as Halcón. Fortunately, for Diega, he told her he could finish the painting without her having to pose any longer. He would finish the portrait in a couple of days.

Rosa went to pay Friar Felipe a visit the next day but returned sooner than expected with Miguel accompanying her. Diega was outside when they arrived, eager for the outdoors after spending so many days inside sitting for the portrait. She ran and kissed Miguel and hugged him tightly. When she let him go finally and stood back, she noticed an air of uneasiness. By the looks on Rosa's and Miguel's faces, she knew something was wrong. Before she could ask what, Rosa spoke, "Friar Felipe has been arrested. He was discovered passing money to a poor family. When they searched the church, soldiers found what was left of the money that had been passed to him by Halcón."

"What's going to happen to him?" worried Diega.

"No one is saying," replied Miguel.

"I think I need to pay a visit to Sergeant Gonzalez tonight and see if he'll tell me even if I have to fill him with a cask of wine."

"And I think it's time that I invite the caballeros over for dinner," added Rosa.

Rosa went to the tavern that night, and Sergeant Gonzalez was there as expected.

"Señorita Diega, it has been a while since you've been here."

"And it's been a while since I've beaten you in chess. Last, as I recall, you won, but I'm feeling lucky tonight. Wine for everyone, on me." The tavern dwellers cheered, and Sergeant Gonzalez pulled out the chess board and began setting up the pieces. Diega quickly won the first match but then let him win the next one. She wanted him gregarious, not angry, but she also wanted to challenge him so that he wouldn't get bored. They had been playing for three hours, and Diega kept buying wine for everyone. Even with the sergeant's tolerance to alcohol, he was pretty inebriated by this time. Diega was feeling drunk herself; so, she slowed her drinking. It would be a pity for Sergeant Gonzalez to tell everything that Diega wanted to know but she not remember it in the morning due to a hangover.

"What's going to happen to Friar Felipe? He was always a likeable fellow for a friar."

"Yes. It's a pity," slurred Gonzalez, as he took another gulp of wine. The friar should have known better than to cavort with an outlaw such as Halcón. Captain Ramon wanted him executed immediately, but the governor said the people would revolt if Friar Felipe weren't given a trial. He'll be found guilty of course and then executed by a firing squad."

"When is the trial?" probed Diega.

"Well, I really shouldn't say."

"But it is a public trial, is it not? You said yourself that the governor wanted the public to see what happens to those who go against the law."

"Did I?" Sergeant Gonzalez looked shocked, as if he had given away too much information, but then the last gulp of wine seemed to erase any convictions he may have had. "I suppose I did." Gonzalez struggled against the wine, forcing himself to think.

"Stay with me Sergeant," coaxed Diega.

"What"? Yes ... Yes, of course. Let's see. Today is Tuesday. The trial won't be tomorrow. It won't be the day after. It will be the day after that, the same day the ship arrives to take the gold."

Diega grew excited but tried to contain herself as much as possible. "You say a ship is coming here, on Friday?"

"Yes. The ship should arrive that morning to transport the gold to the resistance government in Spain to use to fight against Joseph Bonaparte so that the ousted King and the real Spanish government can be reinstalled. If we can weaken that bloody Napoleon, maybe Europe can be rid of him for good. I hate the French. A good Spaniard always hates the French. We were foolish to align with them in the first place. Spain has always tried to shore up foreign governments, but it hurts us in the end. Spain sent Katherine of Aragon to marry into the English House of Tudor. We sent Anne to marry King Louis XIII of France. And look what has happened. We lost twice to the English, first under the English House of Tudor and just a few years ago at the Battle of Trafalgar. And France now controls Spain."

The rantings of Sergeant Gonzalez were starting to attract attention.

"Here," interjected Diega. "Have some more wine."

The sergeant took another gulp and seemed to forget what he had been saying.

"I think we'd better call it a night, sergeant. Look, you've won another match," lied Diega, as she pushed the chess pieces off the board. She looked to find the highest ranking soldier in the tavern, after Sergeant Gonzalez. "Corporal, perhaps you should escort the sergeant back to his quarters. He's had a lot to drink tonight."

"Yes, Señorita Diega," he replied.

The sergeant was nearly passed out, and the corporal struggled to get him out of the tavern. Diega left the tavern and took her carriage back to the hacienda.

Sesasi woke Diega early the next morning. "Hurry and get dressed. Rosa wants to see you."

Diega's head hurt from the wine she had drunk the night before. She hoped some breakfast would help. She dressed and went downstairs where she saw the artist Rafael already working on the portrait. He works nonstop, she thought. The dining area was empty; so, she went into the courtyard where she saw Rosa and Bernardo eating breakfast.

"Are we eating outside this morning so that Rafael won't overhear our conversation? I doubt he hears anything but the brushstroke on the canvas."

"We have to be careful," stated Bernardo.

"You look like you have a headache," ventured Rosa. "You must have drunk too much last night."

"Just a hazard of the job. To find out information from the sergeant, I had to drink some."

"I think you drank more than some," bantered Rosa. "Did you find out anything."

"Yes. A lot! Friar Felipe is going to have a trial on Friday morning, but he will be found guilty and sentenced to execution by firing squad."

Rosa cursed under her breath and shook her head.

"But that's not all. A ship will be anchored offshore to transport the gold they have collected to Spain. We must stop that from happening. If the gold doesn't reach Spain, perhaps he will be forced to give up his governorship."

"We need a plan this time," asserted Rosa, "a real plan, and a good one."

"I've had plans," said Diega feeling slighted.

"But most of yours come together as the event is happening." Rosa hesitated. "I know you have plans, Diega. Some people are planners and some take action. You are more of a person who takes action. We just want to help make sure your actions succeed."

"Bernardo and I," Rosa looked at Diega, "and you, are still working on it. "I'm hoping that the caballeros will help."

"Are they coming for dinner?" asked Diega.

"Yes. Tonight."

"What about Rafael?" continued Diega. "If you don't want him overhearing this conversation, how will you manage tonight?"

"One of the caballero's wives, Doña Inez Torres, met Señor Rafael previously. She will be entertaining him tonight. He is supposed to finish the painting on Thursday and head to the Mission San Diego de Acalá on Friday."

"When do we start planning?" asked Diega.

"I hope Miguel will come today," added Rosa. "He said that he would come if he could. Talking with him may give us some additional insight."

Miguel arrived at noon. The first thing he did was hold and kiss Diega. "I can only stay an hour at most. Did you find out anything?"

Diega told Miguel about the plans to hold Friar Felipe's trial, followed by his execution, on Friday. She also told him about the arrival of the ship to take the gold that had been panned and mined to Spain. "We somehow need to stop the ship from going to Spain. I wonder where the gold is being kept? Would they transport it from Reina de Los Angeles to the ocean? How far is that?

"About thirty kilometers away." Miguel thought deeply. There is a structure on the coast near where the ships anchor. A select group of troops always man the station, supposedly for the purpose of guarding the coast. That must be where the gold is kept. I can tell you it is not in the military compound in Reina de los Angeles."

"We need a way of scattering all of the soldiers as much as possible," pondered Rosa. "How many soldiers are in the pueblo and how many are at the location on the coast?"

"About eighty soldiers remain in the pueblo," answered Miguel. "There were more but Captain Ramon sent at least twenty to help clear the debris and to get the gold mining operation reestablished after Halcón stopped it and freed the peons. I'm not sure how many are along the coast. Diega and I were both there when we landed. I estimate about twenty soldiers there, but I can't be entirely certain. I think that would have to be about right though given the size of the building and the accommodations. The governor would want only people he could trust, the fewer the better. This is a crazy idea, but there are a few cannons on the coast pointing out to sea. We could use those to sink the ship. Do you know how to load and fire a cannon?"

"Yes, but loading it and getting the elevation and direction just right will take some time. Plus, if it misses, I'll have to reload and adjust."

"I'll help you," decided Miguel.

"How will you be able to do that? They'll shoot us both."

"Let's think about this," conjectured Rosa. "The governor will want to see for himself that the gold is safely transported to the ship, and he will be accompanied by additional soldiers. First, he'll want to oversee the trial of Friar Felipe. So, there will be time between the trial and the transporting of the gold. The question is, how do we rescue Friar Felipe from the firing squad and then have enough time to get to the ship to sink it? We need a way of diverting as many soldiers as possible or a way to delay the governor from heading to the coast."

"Unfortunately, Halcón cannot be in two different places at the same time," lamented Diega.

"If the caballeros are on our side, I may have a way of diverting a portion of the soldiers, but we can't count on that until we find out where they stand tonight. We need to think of a contingency plan."

"We need at least two Halcones," puzzled Diega.

Bernardo had been listening quietly but spoke up at the mention of two Halcones. "Sesasi made another Halcón outfit for me."

"I can't let you do that," exclaimed Diega.

"I can ride a horse better than you can," he said proudly. "I have trained you in riding. I need to do more than train. I need to do my part."

"I've not let any of you stop me," admitted Diega. "I won't try to stop you from doing what you feel you must. Everyone thinks Halcón to be dead. Having Halcón back in action is one thing they won't count on."

"We need to create a disturbance at the trial. If we can get a mob of people protesting, that will slow the Governor from going to the coast," speculated Rosa.

"This is a plan, Aunt Rosa, but it still doesn't seem to be a full plan."

"As you've said, Diega. That's where you are at your best."

That afternoon, Sesasi and Ati went into town and spoke with as many people as they could, urging them to attend Friar Felipa's trial on Friday morning. Not that they had to do much convincing. Most of the town folk planned to be there anyway. They were just uncertain of the day of the trial. Sesasi and Ati urged them to reach out to all they could so that there would be as many people as possible at the trial on Friday.

Later that day, the caballeros arrived at Rosa's hacienda. Citlali had made a grand dinner. After dinner, Don Torres was the first to speak, "Thank you for your hospitality, Doña Rosa. Dinner was excellent, but I don't think you asked us here to feed our bellies. What is your purpose for us being here?"

"You are correct, of course, Don Torres. We have been under the yoke of Governor Alvarado for a relatively short time, but it has been a troubling time nonetheless. From the start, there were disappearances that have only grown increasingly common. So far, the peons you have on your ranches have been safe, but for how long? The taxes have grown increasingly higher. Some of you are aware of the taxes in the area governed by Governor Arrillaga, and you know the tax rate there is much lower. Of course, it would be futile for us to have tried anything. What could a few caballeros do against an army? But Alvarado grows stronger while we grow weaker. Sooner or later, the tipping point will occur, and then what chance do we have? Even a man of God, like Friar Felipe, is not safe. His trial is already decided, his fate already determined. Do you know why Alvarado was a special appointed governor? It is because there is gold in this area. Alvarado won't admit this for fear of a gold rush. This is part of the reason for the arrest of Friar Felipe. He knows of this scheme, and Alvarado wants to silence him for it. He takes the neophytes and peons who cannot pay his high taxes and forces them to pan and mine for gold. These men, women and children do not survive long due to the harsh working conditions and lack of food, which is why he continues to take them away for forced labor. What happens when he runs out of laborers? Will he not then turn to your workers? And this gold he collects, he sends to the resistance in Spain. What happens when a grateful, restored Spanish King gives his thanks to Alvarado? Whose land will the King give to Alvarado? I wager that it will be all of our lands. First, we should stand against the abuse to the people, but if that reason is not enough, we should stand against Alvarado before we can no longer do so."

How do you know this story of gold to be true, aside from the testimony of Friar Felipe, who deals in gossip as much as religion?" shouted one of the caballeros.

"A ship will be off the coast to transport the gold to Spain. If you want to verify that what I say is true, then be there to witness it."

"What do you want us to do?" asked Torres.

"I ask that all but two of you attend the trial to show support for Friar Felipe and to protest the sham of a trial that will occur and the sentence of execution by firing squad."

The caballeros excitedly conversed among themselves with an occasional audible statement of, "he wouldn't dare," or "an execution is uncalled for."

Don Torres' voice rose above the crowd. "I pledge my support against Governor Alvarado and the injustices he has perpetrated. Who stands with me?"

One by one, each caballero pledged support.

"I'm glad we are all of one accord," declared Rosa. "If anyone alerted Alvarado, they would receive a pledge of thanks, a firm handshake, and a knife in the back."

Torres emphasized Rosa's point. "If we don't all stand together here and now, we will stand together in line on the wrong end of a firing squad."

Don Ramirez interjected, "Doña Rosa, you asked that all but two of us attend the trial. What do you propose for those two?

Rosa smiled, "I propose that two of you be exceptionally brave, that you be foxes on the chase. Are there any takers?"

Mid-afternoon on Thursday, the artist Rafael had finished the portrait and signed his name at the bottom.

"Come take a look, Diega," called Rosa.

Diega came beside Rosa and marveled at the portrait. She had never had one done of herself.

"It captures your likeness well, don't you think?" smiled Rosa. "It looks just like you."

"It does," admitted Diega.

"Well, I should hope so," scoffed Rafael.

Rosa and Diega ignored him and admired the portrait. Diega thought he captured not only her physical likeness but something more. If she had not known the woman in the portrait as herself, she would have said that the woman had a fierce independence and fighting spirit about her that the clothes couldn't camouflage.

"I want you to label the painting," stated Rosa.

"Surely you jest," gasped the artist. "Why would you distract from this image with a title. You know of whom the painting is."

"Years from now, people won't know though."

"At least let me put it on the back," he protested.

"No. On the front. It doesn't have to be big. You can put it in the lower corner opposite your signature.

The artist capitulated. "What do you want me to write, *Portrait of Diega Pulido*?"

"Yes," answered Rosa.

"And put the name *Scott* in parentheses after Pulido," added Diega. She looked over to Rosa, who nodded approval.

Rafael looked thoroughly perplexed but shrugged his shoulders and painted in the title.

Mid-afternoon on Thursday, Sergeant Gonzalez entered the governor's study where he found the governor and Captain Ramon.

"What is it, Sergeant?" commanded Captain Ramon.

"I have urgent news from multiple sources that you should hear."

"Go on," commanded the captain.

"Don José Ramirez is riding to Monterey to see Governor Arrillaga to tell him he has no confidence in your leadership ability. These sources say he will ask the governor to send troops or at least word to Joseph Bonaparte in Spain that you are supporting the Spanish resistance. Also, Don Salvador Ortiz is riding to the Mission San Diego de Acalá to deliver that message via ship to Spain."

"Are you questioning my leadership?" snapped the governor.

"No, of course not, Your Excellency. This comes from several sources."

"Who are these sources, Sergeant?" probed the captain.

"Three dons reported this information. They do not agree with what Don Ramirez and Don Ortiz have done, but they are concerned by the charges against Friar Felipe. I sent soldiers to the ranches of Ramirez and Ortiz, and the peons confirmed that they left yesterday morning on horseback with food and water for their journeys."

"Thank you, Sergeant. You're dismissed," ordered Ramon.

The sergeant left and Captain Ramon turned to Governor Alvarado. "I say we go ahead and kill this friar, now. The trial tomorrow will only cause trouble."

"No," replied Alvarado. "The people need to see what happens if they conspire or turn against me. I want to put fear into their hearts. The more urgent matter is to stop these dons before they get to their destinations."

"I don't want us to spread our troops too thin."

"How many do we have, captain?"

"We have eighty in the pueblo and twenty along the coast."

"We have plenty to spare. I want you to send fifteen soldiers in each direction to capture the dons and bring them back to me. I'll make them pay for their insolence and treason."

"That will leave fifty for the pueblo."

"I can count, captain!"

Don José Ramirez and Don Salvador Ortiz sat at the table in Rosa's hacienda as Citlali brought out dinner.

"Do you think our ruse worked?" asked Don Salvador.

"Yes," replied Rosa. "Fifteen solders were sent in each direction to apprehend you. I dare say you are having better meals tonight than those soldiers."

"I'm glad you didn't mean for us to really go," responded Don Salvador. "I'm too old to make such a brazen journey."

"You are no older than I am," replied Rosa.

"I didn't mean to offend."

"No offense taken. Such a journey is best made by a person in their twenties."

"The hidden passageway is a clever idea," commented Don José. "If by chance any soldiers come here, we can easily hide out in the cave below."

"My brother-in-law was a bit of an eccentric," stated Rosa.

"I apologize in advance for saying this, but I almost hope soldiers do come here so that we have the chance to use the passageway," exclaimed Ramirez.

"Please don't wish that on us," pleaded Rosa. "If you are that anxious to use the passageway, please feel free to do so. You can even spend the night in the cave if you like."

"Well, I would like to venture through it, but I don't want to spend the night in a cave."

"That's a very ingenious plan, Doña Rosa. I look forward to seeing what other yet-to-be known plans you have to unfold," said Don Salvador.

"You'll have to wait until tomorrow," smiled Rosa.

Early Friday morning, Halcón and Miguel watched the building on the beach as they waited for the sun to rise. They, along with Rosa, decided that trying to sink the ship before the trial might be a better idea.

"There are three sentries," said Halcón. What time will the rest of the soldiers awake?"

"A bugler will sound the call at sunrise."

"That means we have a small window of time in which to operate. Does the bugler wait until the sun shows on the horizon or sound the bugle at twilight?"

"Generally, at the first sign of sunrise, but I don't know if that happens here for certain."

"Let's pray it does."

"In case I don't have chance to say it later, I love you, Diega."

"I love you, too." Diega kissed Miguel softly on the lips. "Wish me luck. I'm going to sneak over and take out the sentries. You know what to do next."

"Yes. I sneak over and put a ring of gunpowder around the building along with brush around the windows and doors so that it will cause a fire to keep the soldiers from escaping. Then I join you and we fire the cannons. If all goes well, we'll sink the ship before the fire dies down enough for the soldiers to come out."

Diega kissed Miguel once more and skulked away toward the building. The sentries were posted around the perimeter of the building, one on each side, except for the side facing the ocean. Halcón belly crawled on the sand, on the north side of the building. She would start there and then move to the east side and finally to the south side. At first, she thought about going to the west side facing the ocean and making a noise at the corner of the building, but she didn't want one sentry to alert the others. As she approached the sentry along the north side, she pulled out a knife. Although she had been good at knife throwing, she hadn't done it in a while; so, she had practiced the day before. Each throw would have to be perfect, or everyone would be alerted, and she would have twenty soldiers to combat.

The first throw hit the sentry in his heart, and he fell to the ground. Fortunately, sand surrounded the building. Still, he made enough of a noise to alert the sentry posted on the east side. Halcón ran to the fallen sentry and pulled out the knife. She hugged the side of the building as she approached the corner where the sentry on the east side was approaching. As he rounded the corner, Halcón slit his throat with the knife and covered his mouth. Only one sentry remained. It was still dark, but twilight would make its presence in about ten minutes. She moved to the corner between the east side and the south side of the building and peered around the corner. The last sentry had his back toward her. She couldn't tell if he was alert or only half paying attention. She snuck to within about ten feet of the soldier when he started to turn around. She threw the knife, hitting him in the side as she ran toward him. He was just about to scream out in pain when she pulled out another knife and slit his throat. Halcón grabbed him as he fell to make sure he made no further noise.

Halcón motioned for Miguel, who ran out with a small keg of gunpowder. He had managed to bring two kegs. She was amazed that he was able to sneak two small kegs out of the military installation without being detected. As he poured gunpowder around the building, she went to a shed covering kegs of gunpowder to be used for the cannons. Fortunately, the powder was in small kegs that she could carry. Pulling off the covers of the cannons, she discovered that the cannons were twenty-four pounders. First, she poured gunpowder down the barrel of each of the three cannons, stuffed wadding in each, and rammed it down. By this time, Miguel had started the fire, and she could hear yelling from inside the building. Miguel rushed over and together they loaded the cannon balls and rammed in more wadding. They had to hurry. By now the fire was visible from the ship, and it would pull up the anchor and sail off. The brush would also burn off quickly, allowing the soldiers inside to escape. The cannons were on a carriage so that they could be turned. Halcón adjusted the elevation of the cannon by turning the wheel under the cannon at the back. Miguel poured some gunpowder into the touch hole and stuck in a quick match and lit it. The flame quickly traveled down, igniting the gunpowder. The cannon thundered, releasing smoke as it recoiled. The smell of gunpowder filled the air. Halcón had aimed low to try to sink the ship, and the cannonball fell slightly short of the ship. The fire along the building behind them housing the soldiers was starting to burn out. Halcon and Miguel raced to the next cannon and repeated the process of aiming and firing. This time the cannonball struck the ship along the waterline. They had succeeded; the ship would sink. To make certain, they raced to the last canon to repeat the process once more.

"Look out," cried Miguel. Halcon looked up and saw smoke from the ship just as the sound of the ship's cannon fire reached them. The cannonball overshot them but struck the building housing the gold and the soldiers. They fired their last cannon at the ship. They wouldn't have time to clean and reload a cannon. The shot hit the ship midway up from the water.

The building behind them was destroyed. The thatched roof had caved in and had caught fire. Halcón doubted that any soldiers remained alive. If any were, they wouldn't be in any shape to fight them. Miguel unhobbled the soldier's horses and chased them off.

Halcón mounted Thunder. "Let's head back to Reina de los Angeles. We can probably make it back in about three hours."

At eight o'clock that morning, Friar Felipe was led to the church where he was to stand trial. Already a crowd had gathered, and they grew more incensed when they saw the friar in chains."

"I told you we should have killed him yesterday," growled Captain Ramon.

"Order all of the soldiers out here to control this mob," shouted Alvarado over the noisy crowd.

When they reached the inside of the church, they found the caballeros waiting inside.

"What are all of you doing here," demanded Alvarado.

"We've come to make sure the friar gets a fair trial."

"I've been light-handed on you bunch so far, but if you obstruct justice, I'll have you all arrested," growled Alvarado.

Suddenly, there were shouts from the crowd, "Halcón. Halcón is here."

The governor's eyes grew wide. "He's supposed to be dead!"

Captain Ramon raced to the door and opened it. "It is Halcón!"

"He's returned from the dead! He really is a devil. Send soldiers to arrest him."

"I don't have enough soldiers to control the crowd and try to capture Halcón," sneered Ramon.

"I want that bandit captured. Send as many as it takes."

Bernardo, dressed as Halcón, sat atop Tornado. A soldier on horseback came riding up behind Halcón Bernardo. The soldier was quickly spotted, and Tornado galloped away. Halcón Bernardo took out his whip and whipped it around a tree limb as he rode underneath, pulling himself out of the saddle as the horse continued running. The soldier riding behind didn't have time to cut around the man suspended in air by the whip, and Halcón Bernardo kicked the soldier off the horse. Halcón Bernardo whistled and Tornado came trotting back to retrieve his rider. He saw a group of fifteen or so soldiers trying to make their way through the crowd to come after him. He would have a slight lead by the time the soldiers could get through the crowd of people but not much of one. His primary objective was to get them as far away from town as possible, leaving only about thirty-five soldiers there. Between the crowd and the hopeful arrival of the real Halcón, they may stand a chance of ousting Alvarado.

Halcón Bernardo raced Tornado down the road. Tornado could have probably left the soldiers behind, and still could if need be, but he wanted to keep the soldiers on his trail. Bernardo knew the land well, and he veered off the main road with the soldiers following. Not far down the road, he came to a foot bridge over a gully. The sure-footed Tornado raced onto the bridge. None of the soldiers dared follow, going down, across, and up the sides of the gully instead. The side road eventually merged into the main road. All of the soldiers still remained in pursuit. Halcón Bernardo turned off into a wooded area where a horse trail snaked through the woods. About midway along the trail, around a bend, the trail forked. Halcón Bernardo turned off the trail completely and into the woods. He led Tornado behind some thick growth for cover. About ten seconds later, the soldiers came to the fork, and they split off with about half going in each direction. After a minute, Halcón Bernardo took Tornado back to the path and they went in the direction opposite the soldiers. At this point, the soldiers were several miles away from Reina de los Angeles. The horses would be exhausted after the chase, and they couldn't return to town quickly if they had to.

Back in town, the soldiers who remained were struggling to contain the raucous mob. Inside the church, Captain Ramon leaned in and whispered to Alvarado. "It's over for us here. I suggest we leave Friar Felipe to the crowd and have the remaining soldiers escort us back so that we can take what gold we can and leave."

The governor's face was pale. "I'll proclaim that Friar Felipe is free of all charges. You order your men to escort us back."

Once Governor Alvarado made the proclamation, the mob cheered, and they all tried to enter the church, which provided the distraction Alvarado and Ramon needed.

"Half of you soldiers go with the governor. The other half come with me. We'll meet in fifteen minutes outside of the governor's house."

Ramon raced to his office, ordering his soldiers to remain outside. He went to where he secretly hid his gold and stuffed as much as he could carry into a duffle bag. He walked out and ordered the soldiers to accompany him to the governor's house.

The governor packed hurriedly. He had packed almost more gold than he could carry. He tied a sword around himself, took a pistol, and dragged the bag into the hallway and down the stairs. He reached the bottom of the stairs, gasping for breath.

"Going somewhere, Governor?"

Alvarado spun around face to face with Halcón. "You ... you ... how can you be here? Soldiers are chasing you."

"Perhaps they will be, but first ..." Halcón stopped in mid-sentence as she noticed Excalibur hanging by the governor's side. It had been in the house all along, but how had she not seen it, either at the party or when she had snuck into his office and bedroom? "I'll take that sword," she said, untying it from the governor's waist, "and that pistol as well so that you're not tempted to use it."

"And I'll take your life," came a calm voice.

Halcón spun around to see Captain Ramon in front of about thirty soldiers crowded into the entry way of the house.

"Thank God you're here, captain," mewled the governor.

"Shut up," snapped Captain Ramon.

Suddenly, Miguel leapt in front of Halcón as a shot rang out from one of the soldiers. Miguel fell hard to the floor, and Halcón shouted, "Miguel."

Captain Ramon turned to the soldiers and yelled. "I don't want any of you interfering. I will take care of Halcón myself. Out into the courtyard, Halcón, where we have some room to fight."

Halcón looked down at Miguel, and Sergeant Gonzalez ran over to him.

"I think he's dead, but some of you help me get him to a doctor," shouted Gonzalez.

Four soldiers approached and lifted Miguel as best they could. Halcón saw them going out the door carrying his body as she went into the courtyard.

Governor Alvarado ran into the courtyard as well, almost gleeful. "You are done for now, Halcón. Captain Ramon was a master fencing instructor in Spain. He was probably the best swordsman in Europe, and he has never lost a dueling match."

The sound of the gunshot brought the townspeople to the governor's house. Rosa, the caballeros, and the artist Rafael fought their way through the crowd and into the courtyard.

"En garde," snapped the captain as he raised his sword.

Halcón unsheathed her sword and the two approached. The opponent's swords touched, almost as if in a handshake and an acknowledgement that one of them would end the life of the other's owner. The battle had begun! Almost from the start, Halcón knew that she had never faced an opponent with a sword such as this one. There was no testing his skill before seriously engaging. This was a fight for her life from the start. Monsieur Blanchet, her former fencing instructor, may have been an Olympic Medalist, but he would have been no match for Captain Ramon. She feared that she might not be either. Ramon was the finest swordsman she had ever faced. Perhaps better than Sir Gawain, although they only sparred and never really fought in a real battle. Halcón's hood was stifling and did not give her good vision. She would have to shed it if she had any hope of winning this duel, but Ramon was relentless in attack and pursuit. Finally, she was able to back away far enough, and she held up a hand signaling to stop.

Rafael was busy sketching the action as fast as he could, eyes glued to the combatants.

"I give no quarter; I accept no surrender," replied Ramon calmly but sternly.

Halcón undid the rope holding on her hood, and she pulled the hood off, throwing it into some nearby bushes in the courtyard. The crowd gasped at seeing that Halcón was a woman. She thought she detected a moment of surprise on the captain's face, but if he had shown shock, it had quickly faded back to the emotionless face she had seen through the hood. She knew that

Captain Ramon regarded her as an adversary, and it mattered none to him whether she was a man or a woman. At least she could breathe and see better now.

Captain Ramon advanced and the fight renewed. Every thrust, parry, riposte, counter-parry, or counter-riposte Diega made was for nought. Diega tried the Lancelot move that Sir Gawain had taught her. Sir Gawain had told her that with that move she could defeat ninety percent of those she fought. Captain Ramone countered the exact way Sir Gawain said it could be countered. She then followed the sequence he showed her if that happened, which he said would defeat another five percent of swordsman, but Captain Ramon countered that as well. She had asked Sir Gawain about the remaining five percent of swordsman who could successfully fend off *the Lancelot* and its additional strokes. Pray that you are better was his response. The captain spoke not a word at this move. In fact, he had not spoken at all. No praise at any of her moves, no taunts, no bragging, just silence and a stone-cold face. It seemed that the best she could do was to temporarily bind the captain's sword. The captain's strokes were at a blinding speed. She turned at an unexpected thrust, but not fast enough. The point of his sword barely entered the bicep of the arm not holding her sword. She leapt backward as a slash grazed her abdomen. Captain Ramon pursued relentlessly as she retreated. She tried to use obstacles such as tables, chairs, rails, or posts to slow him down, but nothing held him back for long. She sprang from a rail and somersaulted over the captain. She turned before her feet hit the floor, barely landing in time to parry Captain Ramon's thrust. Thrust after thrust drove her back against a wall. She turned in time to avoid being skewered. They had to have been fighting at least thirty minutes. The captain showed no sign of diminished stamina. The captain's feint drew her off balance, and he swung his sword to her neck. She ducked, avoiding decapitation, and then rolled to avoid a downward thrust. She was on the ground, a definite disadvantage, fending off the onslaught. Somehow, she was able to fight her way back to a standing position. Both double feinted at the same time. Diega thrusted. As Captain Ramon, parried her sword downward, she went downward with it and then thrusted it upward and into the upper abdomen of Captain Ramon. His eyes barely widened, almost imperceptible, and he made no sound. She thrust the sword deeper until the point punctured through his back. She yanked out the sword, and the life of the captain, as he fell to the ground.

The courtyard was crowded but completely silent. Diega walked over and picked up her hood. The governor had retaken possession of Excalibur, and Diega yanked it out of his hand. "How did you get this sword?" she demanded.

The governor appeared to be in complete shock and could barely get words out. After a minute, she was able to piece the story together. Napoleon had given the sword to King Charles IV of Spain, who had given it to Alvarado when he appointed him as a special Governor over this area. Shortly afterwards, Napoleon controlled Spain and appointed his brother, Joseph Bonaparte, as King of Spain.

As Diega held the sword, she could feel its power coursing through her.

"Shoot her," cried out Alvarado.

One soldier took aim and shot. Although Diega held the sword, it took over her movement and raised her arm, blocking her from the musket ball. The remaining soldiers started firing, but Excalibur swung her arm with lighting speed blocking and shattering the musket balls. Debris from some of the shattered balls ricocheted back hitting some of the soldiers.

"She's a devil!" cried some of the soldiers.

"She's an avenging angel," cried some of the peons.

All of the soldiers fled but one. Sergeant Gonzalez walked up to Diega. "So, you are really Halcón?" he asked.

"Yes," she replied. "I truly like you. I'm sorry to have taken advantage of you."

"You cannot be sorry. You fought against injustice. You made a fool of me in the swordfight we had, but I understand why. You were trying to establish your Halcón persona as a defender of the people. I'm just glad you didn't take my life."

"I would not take your life, Sergeant. Please forgive my actions against you."

"A true friend does not have to be forgiven."

"Sergeant, I think you need to be put in charge here, if the caballeros are in favor."

"Yes," replied those standing near.

"There is nothing to be in charge of," joked Gonzalez.

"There will be." Diega grew somber, and her voice quivered. "Is Miguel dead?"

"He is with someone who passes as a doctor, but it doesn't look good for Miguel."

"Will you take me to him?"

Gonzalez nodded.

The caballeros grabbed Alvarado to lead him to the jail. As he was being led out, he shouted, "at least the gold will make it to Spain."

Diega walked over to him. "No. It won't. Miguel and I sank the ship this morning before the gold could be transported." She turned and left with the sergeant.

The doctor was not really a doctor, but he had extracted the musket ball. Diega had noticed that her own wounds had disappeared by holding Excalibur and its scabbard. She put one of Miguel's hands on the sword, and she laid the scabbard over the wound. Within minutes, no apparent sign of a wound was visible, but Miguel did not awaken. Perhaps he was too far gone for the sword and scabbard to work. She kissed Miguel softly on the lips. "I love you," she whispered.

Rosa waited outside of the room. Along with her were a few caballeros, Friar Felipe, Sergeant Gonzalez, and a few peons. The peons wanted to know if she might know the whereabouts of some of their family members who had disappeared. Diega told all present about the gold operation that was overseen by Governor

Alvarado and the locations of each one. She also told them about the building along the coast that held gold that was supposed to have been transported to Spain. Sergeant Gonzales was surprised that he did not know about this operation and scheme, but he said that Captain Ramon had put him in charge of the pueblo, and he was to be stationed there. Diega asked that the gold be used to help the peons and their families and not to go only to the caballeros. Those caballeros present said that they would see to it that the gold made its way to those who had been forced to bear the burden. Friar Felipe thanked Diega for helping the people and for helping to save his life.

Back at Rosa's hacienda, Bernardo greeted her and talked about his thrilling ride as Halcón. He grew somber when Diega told him about Miguel, and he left her to be consoled by Rosa. Diega began crying. Everything hit her all at once, fear of Miguel dying, relief that justice had been done, sorrow over the loss of the peons' lives who panned and mined for gold, realization of just how close she came to dying at the hands of Captain Ramon, and the thought of waking up tomorrow in her own time.

Rosa came over and put her arms around her. "Tell me what you're thinking daughter."

Hearing the word *daughter* caused Diega to cry even harder. "Do you really consider me as a daughter?"

"Yes, and no one could be prouder of their child than I am of you. God answers prayers with gifts beyond our asking."

"If what happens that I think will happen, then I will wake up tomorrow in my own time. I don't want to leave here." For the first time, Diega thought she understood how Gawain must have felt.

"Diega, I will pray that you remain, but ultimately, that is not our decision. If you are over two hundred years away tomorrow, know that I am here loving you. I don't know how yet, but I will get word to you in the future. As you know, I'm a pretty good planner when I put my mind to it."

Diega laughed through her tears. "Yes, you are."

"If it makes you feel better, I will sit outside of your room tonight."

"There's no need. You've been my aunt, my friend, and I'm now glad to call you, my mother. I'm going to go talk with Ati, Citlali, Sesasi, and Bernardo. I want to see Tornado and Thunder too." Diega walked to the door, stopped, and turned. "If Miguel does live, will you explain why I'm not here?"

Rosa nodded solemnly.

That night Diega gathered the belongings she would take with her in case she traveled through time. She gave what was left of the magic tricks to Rosa to give to Sergeant Gonzalez. She kept the black hood and held onto Excalibur. Although she was exhausted from the events of the past few days, her mind was restless, and she lay awake. At one point, she felt determined to make herself stay awake, but sleep eventually won the battle that many of her other foes had not.

2027 AD

The next morning the effects of time travel told her that she was no longer in the same time as when she fell asleep. Through the nausea and confusion, she felt Excalibur and was relieved that it had traveled with her. She felt the black hood and was comforted that it made it back with her. She also found some gold in her pocket that Rosa had no doubt put there. When the confusion and nausea finally passed, she realized that she wasn't at her home in Jacksonville. Instead, she was in the bed in the room she slept in at her parents' house. She found some of her clothes in the room and combed her hair before walking out of the bedroom. She had the black hood in a pocket and held onto Excalibur, as if daring it to disappear. She walked into the dining room, and her mother turned around, immediately dropping the plate of scrambled eggs she was holding. Her father looked up as the plate shattered on the floor.

Diega's mother ran to her crying and squeezing her tightly. Her father put his arms around both of them. The happy reunion was short-lived.

"Diega", began her father, "I thought you weren't going to run off anymore without telling us. You had been doing so good."

"Where have you been?" sobbed her mother. "You've been gone six months. You don't know what you have put us through."

"Young lady, it's time for you to tell us the truth," demanded her father. What have you been into and why are you carrying that sword? Do you have a drug addiction? Are you suicidal?"

"Sit down, and I'll tell you."

"No lies this time," warned her father.

"You won't believe me, but I travel through time ... because of this ... sword, Excalibur."

"Stop the bullshit, Diega," shouted her father while her mother cried hysterically. "Are you insane?"

"How can someone I didn't know believe what I said, but my own parents won't."

"Probably because you imagined it," replied her father. "If you really believe what you're saying, we need to get you to a doctor."

"Dad, this really is Excalibur."

"You can buy swords like that anywhere."

"I'll show you! Come outside."

Outside of the house was a large boulder. Diega stuck the sword into the rock. "Try pulling it out." Her father tried but could not. Diega lifted it out with one finger.

"This is just one of your magic tricks."

"It's not. What will it take for you to believe me."

"You're not going to get me to believe in magic and time travel, no matter what tricks you can do. Let us take you do a doctor."

"So that I can be locked up in a psych ward."

"If that's what it takes to break this delusion you're under."

Diega was furious, but she understood her parents' reaction. Who could believe such a thing? She felt as cornered as she had in the sword fight with Captain Ramon. If she went to a psychologist or psychiatrist, she would be hospitalized or given medication. Her parents wouldn't listen to her explanations. If she left, she would alienate them for good. What was even worse was that the comfort she wanted from her parents, they were unable to give. She had an idea.

"Mom, just listen to me a minute. You had an ancestor named Diega whom you named me after. Her name was Diega Pulido. I met her aunt, who was really her mother, in Mexico, and I pretended to be her." Suddenly, her idea didn't sound so good after actually hearing what came out of her mouth, and her mother continued crying. "Look, let's go inside, maybe you'll believe the internet." That sounded crazy to her to. She felt she was just digging a deeper hole for herself. Yet that was all she had at the moment. She ran inside to the computer and searched for Rafael Ximeno y Planes. She found that he was indeed a famous artist. She searched some more and found the portrait he had painted of her, which was in an art museum in Los Angeles. She was able to find a picture and showed it to her parents. The caption read, 'Portrait of Diega Pulido (Scott).' "See," cried Diega. "It's me."

"Yes, it does look like you, but anyone can put stuff on the internet and make it look like a genuine website," answered her mother.

She searched for *Halcón* and found an old article from the Los Angeles Times dated 1970, which read:

'On the one hundred and twentieth anniversary of California becoming a state, we continue this series of tales from California's past. There may have actually been a real-life hooded figure in what was known as Alta California in the early 1800s. Regional folktales have been passed down for several generations of a hooded figure known as Halcón (Spanish for hawk), who was a Robin Hood-like person who gave money to the poor. The story is that years before the California gold rush of 1849, gold was discovered in Los Angeles and Orange counties. A governor by the name of Alvarado forced the indigenous people to pan for or mine the gold, which he planned to send back to the Spanish resistance in Spain. At the time, Joseph Bonaparte, brother of Napoleon Bonaparte had been appointed as the ruler in Spain, and the Spanish resistance would use this gold in the fight to oust Joseph Bonaparte and reestablish the monarchy of King Ferdinand VII of Spain. Halcón overthrew Governor Alvarado and freed the indigenous people from their forced labor. Some historians have suggested that Halcón may have inspired Miguel Hidalgo y Costilla, who is considered the Father of Mexican Independence. Although there is no written record of Hidalgo's speech that began the revolution leading to Mexico's independence, some historical references quote Hidalgo as saying, *just as Halcón fought against injustice in Alta California, so must we fight for injustice as a nation.* Moreover, Halcón may have been a woman according to folklore. Support for this also comes from the famous artist, Rafael Ximeno y Planes, who painted a portrait of Diega Pulido (Scott). Some of his sketches of Halcón show a woman who resembles his portrait of Diega Pulido (Scott). It must be stated that Rafael Ximeno y Planes also provided drawings for editions of Robinson Crusoe and Don Quixote; so, his drawings of Halcón may have been drawings for another fictional book. Interestingly, there is another portrait of a Diega Pulido De la Vega, who lived in Puerto Rico, painted by the American painter, John Singleton Copley. The two Diega Pulidos do not resemble each other. Overall, there is little historical evidence to suggest the existence of Halcón, but this was during a time and place where such documentation was not made, and if it was, it didn't survive to today. No doubt, the tales of Halcón have been embellished with each generation as some tales tell of incredible feats. Whether Halcón is folklore or a conspiracy theory, it certainly makes for an entertaining story.'

"See," said Diega. "Halcón was me."

"This article proves nothing," declared Diega's father.

Diega's parents made an appointment for her with a psychologist for later in the week. It was the first appointment they could get. Diega was despondent, and her parents would not let her leave their sight. Her father locked up the sword, and her mother slept in the room with Diega at night. Her parents wanted to call Spencer to let him know that she was safe at their home, but she begged them not to call him. They protested, but in the end, agreed not to call him.

Two days after her arrival in her own time, a package was hand-delivered and addressed to Diega Scott. Her parents wouldn't let her open it by herself; so, she had to open it in front of them. Diega tore open the plain brown wrapping to unveil an old box. She opened it, and it was filled with letters and photographs. She started at the bottom where there was a letter from Rosa, which she read aloud, translating from Spanish:

'I told you I was a planner. I don't know if this letter will ever be seen by your eyes, but I trust that God will deliver it to you. First of all, Miguel lived. I know the answer to that question provides you comfort. Diega Pulido married a man named De la Vega. She invited me to Puerto Rico to the wedding, and I now live there with them. Miguel came with me. I won't say any more about Miguel as it is my hope that you will be reunited with him, whether it is in your time or mine. Shortly after you left, I received a letter from my sister and brother-in-law. Once Diega sailed from Spain, Catalina said that she realized the emptiness of a daughter leaving and didn't know how I had lived losing her. She asked for my forgiveness and pleaded for me to go to Puerto Rico. Catalina said that I had lived long enough without my daughter, and it was time for me to spend the rest of my life with my daughter since she had already had so many years with her. I gave the ranch to Bernado in exchange for his promise to let Ati, Citlali, and Sesasi remain, which I knew he would even without me asking. I left him the remaining gold hidden in the cave. Just as you said, the Mexican revolution started shortly after I left. I told Diega about you, and she has promised to perpetuate your remembrance down through her lineage and that somehow this box would get to you. I told her everything I knew about you, including where you and your parents lived and when. I told her the exact date that this was to be delivered. I also commissioned a portrait of her by the American painter, John Singleton Copley. My hope is that you will be able to see Diega Pulido. I don't know how Miguel could have mistaken you for her, as I hope you will see, but I suspect, as the saying goes, that love is blind. I will end this letter by simply saying, I love you, daughter.'

Diega looked at the other objects placed in the box. There were details of births, and each generation placed something in the box. Eventually, there were photographs leading up to the present. The last piece in the box was another letter:

'Diega, this memorial has been years in the making. I hope to meet the famous Diega Scott (alias, Halcón). My ancestor, Diega Pulido De la Vega, in memoriam to Rosa, set aside some land for you, and it awaits your arrival in Puerto Rico. The deed is included.

Love,

Your cousin, Alejandra Maldonado.'

Diega finished the letter and was pulled out of her trance-like state by the heaving sobs of her mother. "Mom. What's wrong?"

"I remember putting the silver hawk into this very box when I was a girl in Puerto Rico. My mother told me it was for Diega. I thought she meant my ancestor. The name stuck with me so much that I gave you that name when you were born."

"What?" exclaimed Diega's father. "Not you too? Tell me that you aren't drawn into Diega's delusion!"

"Enough, James," snapped her mother. "I believe everything she has said to be true."

James shook his head. "Well, I'm still incredulous."

The following day, her parents canceled her appointment with the psychologist, and they headed for Diega's apartment in Jacksonville. Diega insisted that she take Excalibur; she been through too much with the fabled sword to simply leave it locked away at her parents' house.

2027 AD

Diega didn't know what to expect when she arrived at her apartment building in Jacksonville, Florida. She had been gone for six months, and she obviously couldn't pay the rent from a different time. Her mom suggested that they at least go to the apartment to see if a notice was on the door in case her belongings had been taken somewhere. The car pulled up to the apartment building and parked. As the family got out of the car, the nagging feeling returned once again that someone was watching her. Looking around, she saw a figure dart around the corner of the building. Diega thought to herself that a person running behind a building proved nothing. The person could have run for any number of reasons.

When she reached her apartment door, no notices were posted. Diega turned the doorknob and the door opened. This startled her, especially after feeling she was being watched and seeing someone run around her apartment building. The person could have been looking for something in her apartment or even living in it. Those fears fled away, and she felt relieved when she saw Spencer eating cereal. He was just about to put a spoonful into his mouth when he saw her. Milk and cereal completely missed his mouth and fell from the spoon, hitting the floor. Her statement, "What are you doing here?" collided with his statement, "Where have you been?"

They both laughed and then hugged each other. Diega thought about Miguel and wanted to avoid kissing Spencer until she had decided what to do. Of course, she couldn't have Miguel, but having feelings for him suggested to her that perhaps she didn't need to be with Spencer. On the other hand, she didn't want to throw away an otherwise good relationship because of a ghost.

"Diega, you've got to quit doing this. I've been worried sick about you. Why haven't you called me?"

Diega interrupted Spencer before he could continue. "I'll tell you, but now is not the time. What are you doing here?"

"We need to talk soon. If you don't love me anymore, then tell me." Diega started to speak. "I know. You'll tell me later. The reason I'm here is that I've been waiting for you. I figured you hadn't paid your rent; so, I paid it ahead for a full year."

"I don't need your money for the rent!"

"Well, pay me back in installments if you like. Or, if you don't want to be here anymore, I'll sublease it. I just didn't want you to lose your apartment and have your things sold off."

"Thank you. I didn't mean to sound ungrateful for ..."

Suddenly, Diega's father opened the door. Standing at the door was the person Diega had seen run around the building, the person she thought had been spying on her for over a year, not counting the time she had been away.

Her father grabbed the man. "I thought I heard someone outside the door. "What are you doing spying on my daughter?"

"I'm here to protect Diega."

"How do you know my daughter's name?" asked Diega's father.

At the same instant that James Scott was asking his question, Spencer shouted, "He's lying. He's not here to protect you; he's here to harm you."

"Don't believe him, Diega," urged the stranger. "He's the one who will hurt you if he has to."

"Why would I hurt her? I'm the one who's been watching out for her."

"Stop it!" screamed Diega. "Both of you seem to know something I don't, and I want to know what it is right now."

"My name is Gingalain," said the stranger, "the son of Sir Gawain. The man you call Spencer is Lovell, who is also the son of Sir Gawain."

"Please don't believe him," pleaded Spencer. "I'm Gingalain, and that man is Lovell. He wants to take Excalibur away from you. That's why he's suddenly shown up here."

Diega had a horrified look on her face. "I don't know who to believe."

"Diega, how can you say that? How can you doubt me after the time we've been together?"

She looked directly at Spencer. "This whole time you've been saying that your name is Spencer. Then I find out you're someone else?"

"I'm sorry, Diega; I had to protect you," declared Spencer.

"I think everyone's crazy!" exclaimed James looking to Sofia.

"No," said Sofia. "It means that Diega has been telling the truth this whole time."

The stranger who called himself Gingalain addressed Diega. "If you don't trust either of us, trust Excalibur."

That made sense to Diega. She didn't know whom to believe. She couldn't tell who was lying. But she felt she could trust the sword. The question in her mind was how to ask the sword who to trust and who was the enemy. The only thing she knew to do was ask directly, as stupid as it would look. She closed her eyes. "Excalibur, point your tip to my enemy."

"Enough!" shouted Lovell.

Diega opened her eyes. "Spencer? You're Lovell. How could you? You've been playing me this whole time?"

"Don't you dare judge me. You have such admiration for Sir Gawain. He was my father, Diega. He abandoned me. If you want to blame someone for the way I am, blame Sir Gawain. The only thing that comforted me was magic. I found Morgan le Fay's spell books and transformed myself from a human, with two human parents, into a powerful sorcerer. I should have died fifteen hundred years ago, but magic has kept me youthful. It's given me wealth. The only thing I'm missing is more power, which is now finally in my grasp."

"How is Excalibur going to give you more power?" questioned Diega.

"You see it as King Arthur's sword, as a pretty relic," sneered Lovell. "The writings of Morgan le Fay describe a book known as the Book of Thoth. A person who reads the book from cover to cover will have all the magical power ever known. The problem is that some genies put traps in the book to prevent a person from ever finishing the book. Morgan le Fay read part of the book but fell into one of its traps, but she could see the traps as magical ropes. She knew that Excalibur was a magical sword that could cut through all the snares, allowing her to finish the book. She never got the chance to use Excalibur, but I'll do what she couldn't. I'll use Excalibur to cut through those snares, and I'll read the book, which will give me more power than any magical being has ever known."

"First, you have to find the Book of Thoth," taunted Gingalain.

"Ah, I had almost forgotten you were here, brother. Do you think Archer was able to keep me from the book? I let his group of knights hold on to the book. That way I didn't have to be tempted to read the book and fall into a trap before I got Excalibur. The book stayed in England for a few hundred years. In

1534, King Henry VIII declared himself as the Supreme Head of the Church in England, and Thomas Cromwell oversaw the dissolution of monasteries and convents. Fearing the discovery and capture of the book, the knights moved it to Scotland. Then in 1650, when another Cromwell, Oliver Cromwell, became Lord Protector of the Commonwealth, the book was moved again. This time, the knights took it to Oak Island, off the Coast of Nova Scotia, or New Scotland. There, they constructed an elaborate design of traps to protect the book. During your most recent travel through time, Diega, I went to Oak Island and retrieved the book. I have waited centuries for this. Give me the sword, Diega."

"No, I won't."

Lovell waved his hand, and Diega heard muffled choking noises behind her. She turned and saw her parents' faces turning red as they struggled for air.

"What are you doing to them?" she cried. "Stop it!"

"Then give me Excalibur," demanded Lovell. "If not, I kill them and then kill you, and I can take it anyway."

"Don't harm her parents!" ordered Gingalain.

"What can you do to stop me?"

Gingalain held up the Club of Dagda. Out flew the arrow that Archer had shot into it over fifteen hundred years earlier. It struck Lovell between his eyes, killing him instantly. With his death, the spell over Diega's parents was broken. They fell to their knees coughing and gasping for breath. Diega knelt beside them but could do nothing but watch until they improved enough to stand. She was afraid to hug them until she knew they were breathing normally.

"Are you both alright?"

"Yes," replied James. "I'm sorry I doubted you."

"I can't fault you," Diega replied. "What I've been through is just too unbelievable." Diega turned to Gingalain. "Thank you for saving me and my parents' lives."

"I was sent to watch over you. I arrived a few years ago. It has taken me awhile to learn this language that you call English, which is not at all like the English I spoke."

"What do you know of my heritage?" asked Diega.

"Sir Gawain had four children. You are a descendant from each of those children."

"Wait a minute! Do you mean that Spencer, I mean Lovell, was my ancestor? Ew! Ew! Ew! He was my boyfriend!"

"He was a very distant ancestor."

"That doesn't make it any better," gagged Diega.

"Try not to think about it," encouraged Gingalain. If he had recently retrieved the Book of Thoth, then hopefully it is here."

They searched Diega's apartment and found the Book of Thoth in her bedroom.

"What now?" inquired Diega.

"I don't know," responded Gingalain. "I thought maybe you would know what to do next."

"Perhaps I can help," came an unknown voice.

They startled and turned to see a beautiful blonde-haired woman dressed in a tunic.

Diega held up Excalibur, ready to fight. "Stay back."

"I'm not here to hurt you," she giggled.

"Are you Gersemi?" inquired Diega.

"Yes. My father, who you knew as Sir Gawain, loved you tremendously," replied Gersemi.

"Do you know this person?" asked Sofia.

"Yes. She is the daughter of Sir Gawain and the Norse goddess Freya. And apparently another of my ancestors. How did you know how to find me?" asked Diega, turning to Gersemi.

"My father told me much about you, including the time to which you were born." Gersemi told Diega that once King Lot II returned from his adventure in France with Diega that his wife Marian had arrived, and they happily spent the rest of their lives together.

"I'm glad I was able to transport Marian to the right time and place," stated a relieved Gingalain.

"Do you know what to do with this book," implored Diega, holding up the Book of Thoth.

"Yes," replied Gersemi. "Throw it away."

"What?" gasped Diega and Gingalain simultaneously.

"That's the first thing I've heard today that makes sense," deadpanned James.

"Why would we throw it away?" exclaimed Diega.

"Because it is a fake," stated Gersemi calmly. From Marian, I knew the exact year and place this book would be when Loki captured Blanchemal. I hid in the forest where Gingalain, Blanchemal, and Loki were. When Gingalain transported here, Archer was left alone. Without him knowing, I magically exchanged the real Book of Thoth in his possession with a fake one. Neither he, nor the knights dedicated to protecting the book, knew they were protecting a fake book all of that time. I have kept the real Book of Thoth safe with me, but don't think they dedicated their lives for nought. If I hadn't magically swapped the books, then Lovell would have had the real Book of Thoth. I didn't want to take the chance that he might try using it before you were born."

"Ok. I have several questions," declared Diega. So, Gingalain and Gersemi, you are brother and sister. Did you ever meet before the incident in the forest?"

"No," replied both. "We didn't really meet then."

"How do you speak English, Gersemi?"

"You must remember that I've been alive for thousands of years. From Sir Gawain, I knew the languages you would speak. So, I eventually learned English."

"How did Lovell know I would be the one to ultimately have Excalibur in my possession?" asked Diega.

"That's a good question and a mystery," answered Gersemi. I don't know the answer. I can only speculate how he could have known. Perhaps he was in the forest as well. He knew Blanchemal and Gingalain and could have been following them. He could have also learned about you through magic. He was a powerful sorcerer and could have used magic to determine when the bloodlines of Sir Gawain would come together. Or perhaps he magically tracked you somehow using something you had from Sir Gawain. He also had in his possession an amulet from Morgan le Fay. That amulet would let him assume the body and memories of a person he killed; you could have met him in one of your travels to the past where he had assumed the body of someone else. Or he may have found you another way. As I said, I can only speculate."

"I guess we'll never know now how he found me. So, do you have an idea of what we do next?"

"I have a hunch," posited Gersemi. "Do you remember what the prophecy said that you saw?"

"Absolutely. I have it memorized. *The trickster rids the land of magic, but himself becomes entrapped. After many centuries, the progeny of the wielder of the sword shall free the imprisoned, but not without much peril.* I think I know! The trickster who rid the land of magic was Loki when he used the Book of Thoth to capture magical beings. He himself became trapped within the book. I'm the progeny of Sir Gawin who was born many centuries later. Even though Excalibur was the sword of King Arthur, the true wielder of the sword was Sir Gawain; he had the sword created for King Arthur. We've all gone through lots of perils. I'm supposed to free those who have been captured in the book!" The answer to the prophecy excited Diega. "What do I do though?"

"I think you'll have to figure it out," replied Gersemi.

Diega sat quietly and thought for a few minutes. "Are some of the captured magical creatures aquatic?"

"Most definitely," answered Gingalain.

"And how many magical creatures are imprisoned within the book?"

"I don't know, but I would say thousands judging by the brief period I was at the edge of the portal.

"Is there an out of the way place we can release the beings that is close to water?"

Gersemi responded, "Probably along the Caspian Sea. It has a low saline content that would temporarily accommodate fresh-water and sea creatures. The Caspian Sea is also landlocked."

"How do we get there?" asked Diega. "I don't want to take a flight there and take the book and Excalibur through Customs. I doubt the two of you have passports either."

"I can transport myself there. Maybe with Gingalain's help, we can all three transport there."

"Diega, you can't leave again," interjected her mother.

"Yeah," added James. "We could drive to Disney World and go in at night. There are lakes there, and people may think what you're doing is just a magic show."

"Mom, dad, I'll be back. You'll be safer here. Please trust me."

James and Sofia both nodded.

"What do we do with Spencer's, or Lovell's, body," remembered Diega.

"I'll take care of him," snorted James.

Diega walked over and hugged her parents. "Let's try this then."

Gersemi and Diega held one hand and put the other on the Club of Dagda. Gingalain put one of his hands on the Club of Dagda and covered both Gersemi's and Diega's hands with his other hand. Gersemi and Gingalain closed their eyes, and the three vanished from Diega's apartment. They arrived at a remote location along the Caspian Sea with the Book of Thoth and Excalibur. Diega held the book and concentrated. It began to glow, and she opened it. Immediately, a vortex started pulling Gersemi and Gingalain, and the two struggled against it. Diega laid the book on the ground. She held Excalibur with both hands and sliced through the glow that emanated from the book. The pull on Gersemi and Gingalain released, but then they began being pushed backward. They braced themselves against a tree. Diega didn't notice a wind blowing. The trees, limbs, and plants didn't move, but from the appearance of Gersemi and Gingalain, a full-fledged hurricane had arrived. Diega then noticed the appearance of a figure at the edge of the glow. The figure was violently expelled from the book, followed by another. Soon, more beings were being expelled faster than Diega could count. The aquatic creatures went immediately into the sea, while the land beings gathered in huddles or awaited others. After several minutes, no more beings exited the book. It stopped glowing and lay still.

Diega feared that the magical beings would immediately flee, but they gathered in various groups. A group of blue genies was hugging each other. Some beings appeared to be gods, others fairies, elves, leprechauns, giants, and so forth. Diega didn't even know who many of these beings were. As she looked through the crowd, she saw Gingalain clutching a woman who she supposed was his mother, Blanchemal. After a few minutes, Gingalain, along with Blanchemal, walked over to Diega, and Gingalain introduced them as best he could. The language difference prevented Blanchemal and Diega from having much of a conversation.

"What's going on?" asked Diega, motioning her head toward the crowd.

"From the languages I understand, I think they are trying to decide what to do," replied Gingalain.

Gersemi joined them, and soon, Loki walked over. Gingalain shuddered, and Blanchemal threw herself between Gingalain and Loki ready to save Gingalain from any attack by Loki.

"I just want to apologize," stated Loki. Being imprisoned has changed by perspective. I don't expect you to forgive me, but I want to say I'm sorry for all the pain I've caused." Loki turned to Gersemi. "I don't suppose you will forgive me."

"I don't know," she replied. "I loved you. I still do, but you hurt me deeply."

"I know it's no excuse, but I had the best of intentions to keep the Book of Thoth out of the wrong hands. I felt confident that our love for each other had made me a new person, but the Book of Thoth was too tempting. I felt as though I were possessed by it and couldn't control myself. As I said, I know it doesn't excuse the bad things I did." Loki hung his head and walked away.

"I haven't seen Merlin anywhere," said Gingalain. "I suppose he must have been killed after all."

"Do try to find him," begged Gersemi. "Can you summon him like you did before?"

"I can try," Gingalain replied. He closed his eyes and concentrated as he held the Club of Dagda. After a few minutes, he opened his eyes. "I guess he didn't ..."

"Looking for me?"

"Merlin," startled Gingalain. "Where did you come from?"

"From where you just deposited me. It seems like it has only been a few seconds since last I saw you."

Gersemi hugged Merlin, and Diega thought she saw astonishment on Gingalain's face. Next, Gersemi called Loki. When Loki arrived, Gersemi announced in English, "Loki, this is our son, Merlin."

"What?" exclaimed Gingalain and Diega in unison.

Merlin and Loki hugged, as Gersemi looked on, smiling.

"Merlin is your son?" marveled Diega. "That means that Merlin is Sir Gawain's grandson."

"Hard to fathom isn't it, Diega? I'm glad to finally meet you, by the way," replied Merlin.

"Surprised," replied Diega, "but I can fathom it." Understanding the nature of time was very confusing for me, but at one point during my travels through time, I finally understood!"

"Even I'm surprised by that. You are only one of a handful of people who do understand its nature."

"Is Sir Gawain here? I haven't seen him," inquired Diega.

"Alas, no," lamented Merlin. "Sir Gawain is fully human, and all humans eventually die. God's purpose for humankind is different than that for magical beings."

"So, I'll never see him again," she grieved.

"Maybe you will or maybe you won't. You never know if there is another adventure in store for the both of you."

"If there were another adventure, about what time period would it occur?"

Merlin laughed heartily. "You may be a descendant of the trickster, but I am his son; so, you can't outtrick me. Nice try though!"

Diega smiled. "It couldn't hurt to try."

"If you'll pardon me, I need to help translate among the various groups."

Diega stood in amazement at the diversity of magical beings who stood before her. A couple of hours had passed by the time Merlin walked back to her.

"Everyone is in agreement, which is quite remarkable," informed Merlin, "that all of us should go to another realm."

"But they just got out of one," puzzled Diega.

"They were confined in a type of prison, unable to move freely as they wished. Where we're going is some place completely different."

"You mean like a parallel world?"

"Something like that but unpopulated."

"I'm curious. How did you travel in time back to the past and why? And just how far back did you go?

"That's an interesting story, one that will take longer to tell than we plan on staying," smiled Merlin.

"Well, maybe you have time to tell me something else. I wondered why Excalibur went to certain times and why Sir Gawan and I traveled through time at seemingly random points in our lives. Excalibur seemed almost sentient, or else it was following some preordained plan."

"That also is a question that you will have to live without the answer to. But we'll give you a gift so that you won't go away completely empty handed." Merlin left Diega and found Gingalain. Diega could see Merlin talking but couldn't make out anything he was saying. She saw Gingalain close his eyes in concentration. Next, Merlin climbed a rock so that he was a little above everyone but the giants. He raised his arms to quiet everyone and prepared to speak.

When Merlin spoke, Diega heard English, but others seemed to be hearing what he had to say in their own languages. He was asking everyone to come together to destroy the Book of Thoth. They didn't need to take this forbidden fruit with them. Everyone gathered around the book and focused all of their magical powers on it. The book began to glow and shake violently. Diega was afraid that it would somehow retaliate against those trying to destroy it, but it didn't. It glowed brighter and brighter, and Diega had to turn away from the brightness. Even with her back turned, she could still see the glow, until suddenly, the glow was gone. She turned around, and the Book of Thoth was gone.

Merlin motioned for Diega to join them. "We are ready to go, Diega, but we'll need your help."

"What can I do?" queried Diega.

"Take Excalibur and slice vertically through the air. It will open the portal to the world to which we are going."

Diega did as Merlin instructed, and a rift appeared. She could see a beautiful world on the other side. Gingalain used the Club of Dagda to hold the rift open. The aquatic creatures were the first to go through, then the others, until only Merlin and Gingalain remained.

As Merlin started through, Diega called out, "I didn't think the Book of Thoth could be destroyed."

Merlin halfway through, replied, "It couldn't be destroyed by humans or even by a few magical beings, but all of us together were able to destroy it."

"Is there something you're not telling me? There are still so many unanswered questions."

Merlin simply smiled and went through the rift. Gingalain also smiled at Diega, jumped through, and the rift closed.

"Wait," cried Diega. "You forgot Excalibur." But no one was there to answer. Before she could say anything else, she blinked and was back in her apartment with her parents, still holding Excalibur. Merlin had said she wouldn't go away empty handed.

Epilogue I: 2027 AD

Diega and her parents arrived in Puerto Rico and drove to where Sofia had grown up. They arrived at the house of Alejandra Maldonado, a cousin of Sofia that she had only seen a few times in her life. Before James could cut off the car's engine, Alejandra ran out of the house. Diega guessed that Alejandra was somewhere between her age and her mother's age. Sofia quickly exited the car and hugged her cousin. Diega got out of the back seat with the box that had been sent to her, and Alejandra turned her attention to Diega.

"So, this is Diega! The young woman that our family has waited to see for over two hundred years! You look just like the painting I saw of you. The painter did you justice; I can see the fiery independence in you."

Diega blushed, not knowing what to say.

"I've heard so many stories of you and Halcón. I won't ask you to talk about them today, but soon you must tell me."

"I remember putting the silver hawk into the box," interjected Sofia, "and I remember that a descendant was to be named Diega who would do something remarkable. I did much of the genealogical research on my own. How do you know so much of this story of Diega, and I don't?"

"The story was handed down for generations," replied Alejandra. "From what my mother said, there were three people, including you, Sofia, who were at about the right age to give birth to a girl who would be a young woman in her twenties now. The family didn't say much to the three potential mothers for fear that they may say something that might jeopardize Diega's birth even though Rosa had claimed that could not happen."

Tears welled in Diega's eyes at the mention of Rosa's name.

"What's wrong child?" exclaimed Alejandra.

"I just wish I could see Aunt Rosa again," grieved Diega. "I miss her, terribly."

Alejandra was shorter than Diega, but she pulled Diega's head into her bosom and stroked her hair. "Oh, child. You were loved tremendously. Just think about it. How could such a thing be passed down for over two hundred years with all of this detail? There had to be a lot of love to sustain it for all this time. Now, let me show you where the land is that has been set aside for you. The house is still there that Diega Pulido De la Vega lived in. It's been a couple of years since anyone lived there. You may have to restore it or build another, but the land is beautiful and overlooks the ocean."

They drove a short way, with Alejandra guiding them, and arrived at the location. The house did look old, but it also looked sturdy. It would have had to have been sturdy to have withstood the hurricanes that had come through Puerto Rico in the last two hundred years. She had a good vantage point of the ocean from this location. A lot of trees were near the house but nothing close enough to damage the structure if it fell. As Diega was in the midst of walking around the house and looking at the flora, she heard a noise coming from inside the house. She ran to the car and grabbed Excalibur, which she had brought with her.

"Who's there?" shouted Diega. "Come out."

A figure walked out of the otherwise deserted house.

Diega dropped her sword. "It can't be!" She ran toward the figure who also ran toward her. They caught each other midway in a bear hug. "Miguel! Is it really you? How are you here?"

"It's me, and I'm just as shocked to see you."

They hugged for what seemed like minutes, and then they kissed, which was soon interrupted by sounds of throat clearing. Diega's mind had emptied of anything else at the sight of Miguel. She clasped his hand and led him over to her family.

"Miguel, this is my dad, mom, and cousin. Family, meet Miguel Navarro."

Alejandra's mouth dropped at the declaration. "You are the ghost, the one who vanished into thin air?"

Now, it was Diega's parents turn to be astonished. "What is all this?" asked James.

Miguel, seemingly just as shocked, began an explanation. When Rosa left Alta California to come to Puerto Rico, I came with her. I lived and worked here for two years. One night, I was talking with Rosa, Diega, and Diega's husband. The next thing I remember, I was standing in the same spot, but the house was deserted. That was about three days ago. I didn't know what to do. I left to go find food and water, and then I saw giant birds flying in the sky and these horseless carriages. I was scared; so, I returned to the house. I was able to get some water from the rain, but I haven't eaten. I had just decided to try venturing out again when I saw and heard your horseless carriage pull up. I don't know how I got here!"

"That's ok, I mean alright. I do know. I saw Merlin speaking to Gingalain. Then Gingalain closed his eyes while he was holding the Club of Dagda. He had to have used that to bring you here to this time."

"I still can't get used to all of this," swore James.

"I need to show you something," shared Miguel, "if we can see. The house is dark inside."

"I brought a flashlight in my bag," responded Alejandra.

Miguel was startled when she turned it on, but Diega reassured him that the artificial light would do no harm. Everyone followed Miguel, who went into a room that must have been used as a library. He put his hand underneath one of the shelves, and Diega heard a click. Miguel pulled a section of the bookcase open, revealing a hidden stairway going below the house. Miguel turned around smiling. Your Aunt Rosa had Diega's husband add this in when he had the house built. They descended the narrow stairway, which creaked with each step they took. When they reached the bottom, Miguel asked for the light to be shown at a particular spot. There was a box that was nailed shut. Miguel pried open the box, displaying a cloth covering. Unwrapping the covering, he motioned for Diega to look. Diega's hand covered her mouth in shock as she stared down at D'Artagnan's rapier. "I brought it here with us," beamed Miguel, "along with your whip."

"What is this covering?" puzzled Diega.

Miguel smiled broadly. "Sergeant Gonzalez thought that if I ever saw you, you would get a laugh out of this. These are his pants that you carved the letter *H* into."

Diega laughed until tears streamed down her cheeks.

Epilogue II: 2031 AD

Diega walked onto the deck that Miguel had added to the house. Miguel came out behind her, and she turned and kissed him.

"I love you, my husband."

"And I love hearing you say that. I used to think I would never hear you say those words. I love you, too!

"Did you really mistake me for Diega Pulido all those years ago."

"I've told you. Yes, I really did."

"Did you recognize her when you saw her in person?"

"Yes, and I don't know how I mistook her for you. We've been through this numerous times. Why are you asking again?"

"This online article started me thinking about it again."

"Is that the article that the reporter did about you?"

"It is!"

"Well, let's hear what it says."

Diega read from the article from her tablet:

'Diega Scott-Navarro was recently named Puerto Rico's Teacher of the Year. This vivacious young woman is full of energy and makes history come alive for her students. Diega doesn't hesitate to tell people that she used to hate history. So, what changed to make her now teach history for a living? Diega credits her change of attitude with a realization that history is not about dates or events but about real people who had interesting stories to tell. Her students love her teaching style of getting into the minds and lives of the people who lived during the history she teaches. She has converted more than her share of people who used to hate history who now love it. Whether it's Latin American, European, or World History, her students say that she teaches as if she had lived in that time period herself. Who knows? Perhaps they are right. A few years ago, evidence was found in the home in which Diega now lives pointing to a previously little-known figure called Halcón. Evidence to support this historical figure was also uncovered in two separate places in Los Angeles. One was a dilapidated building that was torn down, revealing a hidden passageway where a hacienda once stood. The passageway led to a treasure trove of documentation revealing the existence of Halcón. The second place that evidence was found was in a museum containing records from a Friar Felipe describing the escapades of Halcón and identifying her as Diega Pulido. Previous evidence supporting the existence of Halcón comes from the famous artist, Rafael Ximeno y Planes who sketched Halcón in action. This same artist painted a portrait of Diega Pulido, which was labeled as Diega Pulido (Scott). Interestingly, the portrait looks almost identical to Diega Scott-Navarro. Another portrait of supposedly the same Diega Pulido doesn't resemble the portrait by Planes.

Diega Pulido was also an ancestor of history teacher Diega Scott-Navarro. All of the coincidences have caused some people to conjecture that Diega Scott-Navarro actually lived through some of the history she teaches. That would certainly explain how she makes history come alive for her students!'

"Is your secret out?"

"No. The reporter doesn't believe it. Who would, except for conspiracy theorists? But it does help sell subscriptions."

"The article didn't say that you also teach fencing and martial arts. Mentioning that would have made the assertion even more believable."

Diega laid the tablet on the table and smiled beguilingly. "I'm going to change clothes. Wait here." When she returned, she wore a dress that was identical to the style she had worn in Miguel's presence over two hundred years earlier. In the white dress that showed off her bare shoulders, she leaned against the wall of the house and propped her foot against it so that the slit in her dress showed her legs. The boot-heeled sandals exposed parts of her feet, and she held up an arm to keep her wide-brimmed tan hat from blowing off. Part of her dark hair hung over one shoulder. "Do you remember this pose?"

"Do I ever! You are so beautiful, and you're deliberately tempting me. You tempted me the first time you wore the original outfit, and I couldn't do anything to relieve it."

"So, what's stopping you now?"

About the Author

Dewey Dellinger is an educator and administrator. He was born, raised, and lives in North Carolina and has degrees from North Carolina State University, the University of North Carolina at Charlotte, and East Carolina University. His highest degree is a Ph.D. from North Carolina State University. His novel genres include fantasy, action-adventure, romance and romantic comedy, and drama.

Books by Dewey

Once Upon a Knight's Time Series
Once Upon a Knight's Time
Once Upon a Knight's Time: Seeker of the Sword

Romance
Love's Trail in Kenya

Action Heroine
Captain Tomorrow